the Avalon
Ninth

The highly acclaimed Book 1 in the Wessex Trilogy

The Angel of Wessex

ISBN 978-1-874337-08-9

First published in 2003/4 as ISBN 1-874337-08-X
and first reprinted in 2005.

The West Country in the late Victorian era is seen through the life of Christabel Mere, a girl born into splendour but sent away as a baby to be raised in the poverty of the Wessex farming countryside.

She knew nothing of the circumstances of her birth and cared even less for wealth, but it was a time when women had to live by society's strict codes. To join the fight against a government wanting to introduce new laws that further discriminated against women seemed a cause worthy of support. But this innocent act would, itself, reintroduce her to her true ancestry and threaten to destroy not only her happy childhood memories but the Elvingtons, one of the greatest families in all Wessex.

'A beautifully written, gentle and moving read,
with an unexpected twist'

Jacket Price £6-99

Postal Price £5-99 including postage and packing

Cheques made payable to 'Michael Taylor offer'

F4M Publishing, Farringdon House, Nr Langport TA10 9HT, England

the Avalon
Ninth

MICHAEL J. H. TAYLOR

the Avalon Ninth

AN F4M BOOK

Published in 2007 by F4M Publishing
Farringdon House, Nr Langport, TA10 9HT, England

A CIP catalogue record for this book is available
from the British Library

ISBN 978-1-874337-09-6

Main cover photograph: copyright Isobel Taylor
Cover design Kevin Oatley
Arthur's Cross reproduced by kind permission of
Glastonbury Abbey Trust
Pages designed by M Rules, London, England
Printed by BOOKMARQUE, Croydon, Surrey, England

F4M is a fiction imprint division, associated with
The Great Encyclopedia Company

Dedication

To the countless worldwide readers of *The Angel of Wessex*, for hounding me endlessly to complete *The Avalon Ninth* before we were all too old to enjoy it!

Acknowledgements

I give my sincere thanks to the many individuals and organisations that offered their time, information and support during the preparation of this book, in particular Annabel Trodd and those at the Glastonbury Abbey Trust.

THE WESSEX TRILOGY

Book 1: The Angel of Wessex
ISBN 978-1-874337-08-9, first published in 2003/4
as ISBN 1-874337-08-X
and first reprinted in 2005

Book 2: The Avalon Ninth
ISBN 978-1-874337-09-6, first published 2007

Book 3:
Anticipated to be published 2008/9
as ISBN 978-1-874337-10-2

FACTS

This book sources many real events to portray the atmosphere of the period, interwoven within a storyline centred on the year 1883. Most of the locations are genuine, although some place names have been altered. Politicians and statesmen have, on occasions, been placed out of context for the benefit of the plot, but those mentioned were the genuine people of the period.

The Abbey, Chalice Well, the stained glass window depicting Joseph of Arimathea, and the site of Arthur's grave can all be found at Glastonbury, where Arthur's cross was also discovered. Joseph of Arimathea *was* the Virgin Mary's uncle and he *did* journey to England with the young Jesus and returned to establish the Wattle Church. Examples of the Crataegus oxyacanthoides, the Holy Thorn tree, can be found at Glastonbury. The Healing Cup of 'Nanteos' does exist and has been deposited at a bank for safe keeping. The existence of the Holy Lance of Antioch is recorded.

References to Arthur date from AD540, recorded within living memory of this period of British history. The first such reference appeared in the work *De Excidio et Conquestu Britanniae*, by the monk Gildas, who founded the Abbey at Brittany. Actual mention of Arthur's death appeared in

Annales Cambriae, the Welsh Annals of AD960. In *De Principis Instructione*, the ancient work of Giraldus Cambrensis, Glaston (now Glastonbury) was revealed as the ancient Isle of Avalon, covered with marshes and known as *Inis Avallon*, the apple-bearing isle. Also in this work was written that a ship crewed by women, led by Morganis, kin to Arthur, carried Arthur to Glaston after the Battle of Camlann 'that his wounds might be healed'. The much fictionalised version of Arthur's times, by the hand of Geoffrey of Monmouth in AD1136, was said, nevertheless, to have been based in part on facts drawn from 'an ancient book'.

One enigma of history often quoted to decry ancient accounts is the discrepancy between supposedly factual dates. This is certainly true of Arthur's period. Accounts put his death at wildly different times, even in different centuries. One of several explanations can be traced to the year 457, when Victorius of Aquitaine completed calculations to provide the date of Easter in any year. Not surprisingly, given the context, calculations began from the death of Christ, not his birth. Then, in the year 525, the anno domini (AD) system was devised, based on Christ's birth for the Christian calendar. Early writers merely, but mistakenly, added AD to the old system, so hugely distorting dates.

"But the tomb of Arthur is nowhere seen,
whence ancient dirges still fable his coming"

William of Malmesbury, AD1125

CHAPTER 1

A reason for living — 1883

Russell Thackeray paid for the short hansom cab ride with a sovereign. The driver stared down at the gold coin with concern, for the change due was beyond the two silver florins, five silver sixpences and assorted bronze pennies, half-pennies and farthings he held in his waistcoat pocket.

Springing from the confine of the cab, Thackeray was altogether too hurried to be concerned with the change. Instead, he bounded up the steps to the hospital entrance without a backward glance, leaving the driver dazed at his good fortune as he closed the little trap door in the roof. A subordinate waited with the hospital door open.

"Please follow me quickly, Sir. This woman has either completely lost her mind or is blessed with an insight that will prove the existence of the supernatural."

"Who is she?"

"A nobody, I can assure you."

"Will she blab?"

"Don't concern yourself. She hardly knows what she

knows. Her ordeal was so shocking, the significance of her salvation completely escapes her. Fortunately, she doesn't mind talking about it to those she trusts."

"That won't include us, for goodness sake!"

"Of course not. She's never met us. I've set-up a way to eavesdrop, but we must hurry."

Their steps quickened.

"And you say hers was virtually the same experience as this Nancy Adams all those years ago?"

"No, not virtually the same, identical. Were you aware of the Adams' file?"

"I knew vaguely of its existence. I read some of it for the first time while coming here."

They stopped and turned to stare through a small rectangular window in the door.

"I had her moved to this private room as soon as I heard about her."

"Who's that in there with her?"

"A solicitor."

"What!"

"Don't panic. He's an acquaintance, or so I'm led to believe. He must also have read about her survival in the newspapers. He suspects nothing. Nevertheless, I'm having him checked out."

"How long have they been talking?"

"He arrived just a moment ago. I asked the nurse to keep him away until I saw you coming. That way we can hear everything said between them. I've arranged for the door to the adjoining room to be left slightly ajar. We can listen from there without being noticed."

He tapped the door. Immediately, the nurse left the woman's bedside. Once the door was pulled shut, the visitor sat forward on his chair.

"You received my letter?" he asked in quiet tone.

"I did. Thank you for explaining so much that I didn't know."

"Do you blame me in any way?"

"Of course not. We might have only just met, but I'm sure you are entirely honest and honourable. As a close acquaintance of people I know well, I feel I can trust you."

"Thank you."

"You look so kind too."

He smiled. "I've been called fat and bald many times, but never kind-looking. I really appreciate the compliment."

"I speak as I feel."

"Tell me, my dear, what on earth happened to you? The papers were full of your tragedy. I can't imagine what it must have been like. That storm, the death and destruction. The humanity lost, including your husband, Peter, I understand. I'm at a total loss to . . ."

She put her hand on his. He stopped. Her face showed the first signs of sweat and torment. He could sense hesitation in her voice, a slight shake in her hand.

"The shabby ship had creaked and groaned its way across the sea, letting in water whenever the weather worsened, its engine breaking down on numerous occasions. Finally, we neared the African coast. At last Peter and I felt safe. Then came the real storm. It was huge, greater than any words can tell, lashing against the deck. The hull was forced to pound its way up and down through the tempest. We were all doomed, enacting a fearful nightmare from which there was no blissful awakening. Oh, God, I prayed to be anywhere but there. All about was chaos without end. I imagined I had entered Hades itself, an inferno of frightening waves taller than the ship and exploding on every side as they struck the metal plates.

There was no let-up. I couldn't imagine how the ship could survive the battering. It heaved one way and then the other, the bow one moment high up and then plunging under water, causing the crew and passengers to slip and slide around on the rolling deck. I called out for Peter, my wonderful husband of just three weeks. He was nowhere to be seen. Some of the crew tied themselves to anything solid to stop them sliding overboard, while the rest of us clung to ropes hastily strung across the deck.

But, then, without warning, I heard a violent, tearing groan as a rock sliced through the hull. Nobody saw it until it was too late. Exposed one moment and then hidden by the next crashing wave, it penetrated the sea swell as a jagged pyramid. Our great ship was physically lifted, the rusty, broken bow forced upward and clear of the water by the thrust of the unstoppable screws.

I grabbed the rope on the side of the only life-raft, wet and terrified, yet still sufficiently in control to scream out as the wooden crates holding the bibles and medicines broke from their moorings and tumbled overboard. Some half floated in the fury before crashing onto rocks, spilling the precious cargo to the sea floor.

Suddenly, as a final judgement on the vessel, there was a terrible crack as the stern fell back on itself, turning onto its side and rolling into the depths of the boiling sea with a kind of bubbling moan. I think I saw Peter calling out to me while hanging onto a railing. In seconds he was gone with the rest."

"And then what? How did you save yourself?"

"It all happened so quickly, I can hardly remember. Only half the ship remained and this part only seconds from tumbling over. Some of the crew, bleeding and fierce to survive, ripped the raft from my grasp and tossed it into the sea. But, as they jumped, a wave took it away and it hit the side of the hull. That was the last I saw of those men, that is until they were recovered, dead, their broken bodies draped in sheets. Peter wasn't among them. I hope to God he lies at rest at the bottom of the sea. But, I have a dreadful fear that he might have become food for sea creatures."

It took a few seconds for Sir Schofield to recover from the mental picture. "But, Miss Ayres, still you don't say how you, alone, survived."

"I can remember saying the Lord's Prayer and being washed away. I knew I would drown. For the first few seconds of panic I took deep breaths, ready for the moment of being engulfed. Then I was hit by the first big wave that took me deep under. Strangely, in all the chaos, when I clawed back to the surface I remember thinking that the water was warm as I spat it out. Yes, warm and salty."

"What happened to the ship and crew?"

"Gone, all gone. I could see nothing beyond the rocks and crashing waves. Maybe the ship's boiler had exploded, for a fountain appeared, like a volcano erupting underwater. Just the once and then gone again as quickly. I think that is when I gave up struggling. I felt . . . at ease, resigned to my fate to

join Peter. With the ship finally disappeared, my rescue hope
had sunk with it."

"Regretful."

"Perhaps strangely when I look back, I mostly felt regret
for Charlotte Elvington's wasted expense, even more than my
own danger from the fateful voyage. I knew Peter to be a
good, God-fearing man and that he would join Christ in
Heaven. I had no such deep religion to rely on, but a past life
that I would have to atone for."

"Balderdash, Miss Ayres! I believe it was *she* who put you in
danger's path," interrupted Schofield, his neck red and fully
bursting from his shirt collar. "I told that woman the ship was
unfit. She wouldn't listen to my advice as the family solicitor.
I thought she had given up the idea of sponsoring your
mission to Africa. She certainly gave me that impression,
particularly after refusing even to look at the list of alternative
vessels I had drawn up. And now this tragic result."

Sally was lost in her own thoughts and paid no attention.

"I did drown. I know I did. I saw the depth of the water
growing above my head, just like falling down a well, with the
sky's brightness gradually fading from the surface. It became
a dull green, not blue, like the fields of Wessex before the
Spring rain ripens the grass. And calm, so calm, as I floated
downwards. Yes, I died."

"My dear, clearly you survived and we are all much pleased
you did."

"We?"

"James Elvington has been asking after you. Do you want
to see him?"

"Anyone else?"

"Edmond's here too."

"No, I shall see neither." She suddenly paused. Her eyes widened. "There *was* one other."

"One other?"

"In the sea with me. I remember now. She was beautiful, with long hair that looked untouched by the water that engulfed us. Yet, I recall I could see her weeping. Surely, that makes no sense at all. She said something that was lost to me. She pointed behind and then abandoned me, as if she had made a mistake in coming. If only I could remember. I looked and, there, a rope dangled, weighed down by a small box of sodden books. A nail from the broken lid had caught in the rope. A million to one chance. But, I didn't reach it before I drowned. I'm sure I didn't. I can't remember even moving towards it. I was so weak. I had no will to try."

"That makes some sense. You were found on the upturned raft, a rope around your waist. Is it possible . . ."

"Did she survive?"

"As far as I know, no woman was listed as alive or missing, other than yourself."

"The voice of the dead was a living voice to me" whispered Sally. Schofield looked puzzled.

"Tennyson. I was a school teacher . . . once . . . a lifetime ago."

"I've heard enough," came a whispered voice from the next room. "I agree with your findings. I'll tell you what to do in a day or two. Meantime, don't let her be discharged. Oh, and stop all further visitors other than our people for heaven's sake, for fear of your life."

"There's more!"

He turned back.

"I've done some private digging in the archives. Up to now we've taken it on trust that there had been eight other cases before her, as you told me."

"No, Fairbourne, I didn't say that. I asked you *if* you could come up with eight earlier cases of women saying they had drowned and yet survived to tell the tale. There's an important difference. I didn't say she was the ninth. For all I know, she could be the sixth, seventh or eighth. Now you've told me about this Adams woman, I can move Ayres up the list."

"I see. I misunderstood you. Anyway, that's no longer of any importance, because I think I've actually discovered all the others against genuine historical records."

"How many others?"

"Eight."

"Are you serious?"

"Why would I joke about it? You gave me a task and I've completed it." He opened a notebook. "You see, I have it all here. The best documented before Adams is someone named Mary Lawrence. Her confessed drowning dates from 1773. The least certain of my finds and the oldest, which took place in 1443, is mentioned only on a stone tablet. I wouldn't want to totally rely on her being the same as the others, although on balance I think she probably is. What made my research simple was a breathtaking realisation, a remarkable 55 year gap between each woman, starting from Ayres, Adams and Lawrence. Once I found that by chance, finding the link and lineage was fairly easy, 1718, 1663 and so on. What are we getting ourselves into, Sir?"

"1663! Fascinating in a terrifying sort of way."

"Why?"

"I'll tell you later. This Adams woman, she died in 1828?"

"No, she self-confessed to drowning that year. She lived until 1868, just as Lawrence survived another twelve years before being administered powdered foxglove leaves to cure dropsy and died vomiting. There's a lot to read in this file."

"And so, by adding fifty-five years to the date for Mary Lawrence, we get?"

"1828, as I said."

"Plus another fifty-five for Ayres?"

"1883. This year, Sir."

"Good grief, man. If Sally Ayres *is* the Predicted Ninth, then we have had the final warning! If you're right . . . our nation could be heading for imminent catastrophe."

CHAPTER 2

The vicar of Cudwick

For the next few days of her detention, Sally thought of nothing but her encounter with the woman in the water. In truth, she had tried to dismiss all recollections for the sake of sanity, but every such attempt had been well and truly frustrated by the seemingly pointless interest of certain high-minded gentlemen who daily sat by her bed for three or four hours at a time. As she kept saying, she could add nothing more to that she had already told them. If there was more to know, it had left her brain forever or "had been washed away with the tide," as she had once joked.

After a week of endless probing and suggestion, and listening to her murmuring while asleep, the men gave up coming, their mission no further advanced. This allowed her to relax the best she could for the first time. For, while she managed to reconcile to some small degree the horror of the shipwreck and her near drowning, the memory of that mysterious woman was never far from her thoughts. Each night she had the same dream, several times over, until sleeping became tortuous in itself. Then, without warning, three days after the visits stopped she was given the chance to leave.

With no thought to her future, Sally decided to head for the countryside of her greatest happiness, that being her beloved Wessex. It was there she had experienced her first step into adulthood away from her parents and siblings in Midford, becoming an independent woman teaching at the small school in Westkings. It was in this hamlet that she had first met James Elvington, a married man of lofty position who had taken her into womanhood. She had presented him with a son, her wonderful Edmond, whom she had given up to James' care and who was now heir to the Elvington estate. The thought of Edmond gave her a warm feeling. For, whilst she knew virtually nothing of his life, she had seen him fleetingly before her voyage to Africa and he had become a fine, proud, young man. Of course, he hadn't known who she was and had treated her only with the politeness afforded to a guest.

The train pulled into Cudwick, where she alighted carrying one small bag of newly purchased clothes. Most of her belongings rested at the bottom of the sea, with the remainder stored at Midford.

"Next stop Cudwick Junction" came the call.

The train hissed and puffed. With wheels spinning for grip, it began moving ahead in a cloud of steam.

"Sir," Sally called agitatedly as she ran to the station master. "Isn't this Cudwick? I need Cudwick."

"In a manner of speaking it is. This is Cudwick New, built

just a few years back. I expect you wanted Cudwick Junction. You would know the Junction alright, it has the Railway Inn, my favourite watering hole. Get a good quart of ale there . . . a proper job. Where's your final destination to be?"

"My destination? Wherever I can get a job, I suppose. Perhaps a larger town. I was a teacher."

"Educated? I thought as much by your voice. Look, you best get yourself off to St Jude's. The vicar there will help you find a place for the night. If there's no room anywhere else, he'll offer you a bed at the vicarage. He's kind like that. You won't get any further along your journey today."

Sally thanked him for his help and listened to his directions. She remembered seeing a beautiful church with a tall tower while hurtling along the railway embankment, the open fields with hilly backdrops offering excellent views of a church nestling among a small enclave of stone terraces and some grander dwellings.

The directions took her along The Sprint, a narrow passageway that emerged by the village wheelwright, close to St Jude's. Outside the church stood a 14th century stone cross, moved from the churchyard to the village square a hundred years before at a cost of a few shillings. Ancient, the cross had not weathered well. In contrast, St Jude's was nothing short of magnificent, its chancel of blue lias dating from around the 13th century and the remainder built two centuries later using stone brought from Wells. Sally entered.

She was at once in awe of the ornate roof, with twelve highly carved trusses and angels to the centre and sides. Although heavily varnished, it was clear that the roof had once been brightly decorated before the sombre values of the present era. Eight more angels emerged from the wooden pulpit, while the tower carried six ancient bells.

"You like our little church?" came a soft voice from a distance.

Her stare dropped. "Wonderful. I hope it was alright for me to walk in unannounced?"

"The door to God is always open. I'm Fry, by the way."

She took his hand in welcome. "Sally Ayres," she replied.

"Mrs?"

"Plain *Miss* Ayres, I'm afraid."

"Well, if you want to be formal, I'm actually The Honourable Alexander Ethelred Fry. Quite a mouthful for any village vicar." He smiled kindly. "Don't be embarrassed, we venerate spinsters here. Let me show you what I mean."

He guided her to a small stone tablet set into the wall.

HERE RESTETH THE BODYE OF ALIS BENNETT
WHOM WAS BORN AND REBORN INTO GOD'S GRACE
AND WITH HIS SALVATION BY WATER ON 15 DAY OF
APRIL 1553 AND DECESED A VIRGYN 8 DAY OF
SEPTEMBER 1578 – AGED 54

"It's a strange epitaph, not least because the mason clearly couldn't do his mathematics."

"What does it mean?"

"Nobody knows. I've always assumed baby Bennett stopped breathing, but was revived. I can see no other explanation. I suppose she was hurriedly baptised, just in case. She may have become prone to lunacy through lack of air at birth. Anyway, as you see, Miss Bennett was a virgin pronounced for all to read into eternity. A truly righteous state."

'If you only knew', she thought. "Actually, I need a bed for the night. My destination is elsewhere. I was told you might know of somewhere."

She placed her bag on a chair in front of the pulpit. He leapt forward, snatching the bag and holding it high off the seat.

"No, please, put your bag in my care. It cannot be left there. This seat is our Glastonbury Chair. Of great importance and not to be used in any way."

Sally weighed her apology carefully. The vicar caught her surprised expression.

"No, it's me who should apologise. I clearly startled you. The chair is normally covered by a cloth, but it's being washed as we speak. Let me explain my actions."

"Please do," said Sally, taking her bag from him and placing it on the stone floor. "It's alright here, I suppose?"

"Of course," he replied, flick-dusting the wooden seat with his handkerchief and peering for even the slightest scratch. "As I said, this chair is very precious. Its design was based on an original belonging to the last Abbot of Glastonbury Abbey, who was hanged in 1539. You should understand that Glastonbury Abbey was a rich Benedictine place of worship and moral guidance, and it was because of this spiritual connection that this type of seat became popular throughout the remainder of the 16th century, even commonplace. Our example might look ordinary to the unknowing eye, but it isn't."

"How so?" enquired Sally, her dark eyes settling on his look of complete reverence.

"See the circle set into the back?" he asked, pointing to an ornate ring of carved leaves that would have made the chair uncomfortable to use. "It's said the wood for that came from a Crataegus oxyacanthoides. You could know it as the Holy Thorn tree."

She shook her head.

"No matter, it's easily explained with a little trip into biblical history. The account goes that, after the crucifixion of Christ, Joseph of Arimathea asked Pontius Pilate for Jesus' body to stop it hanging on the cross overnight. Incidentally, that was an incredibly brave act on Joseph's part, as Jewish law forbade anyone who had been executed from having an honourable burial. The gesture did not go unnoticed, however, and came back to bite him later. Anyway, after wrapping the body in fresh linen, he placed it in his own prepared tomb."

"Joseph had his own tomb while alive?"

"Being prepared for the next world was a completely ordinary thing in those days, for the well-to-do, that is. Hot climate made rapid disposal of bodies essential."

"I see. Please continue."

"Now, Joseph was a rich Israelite and an honoured member of the Jewish supreme court, plus a town councillor for Jerusalem. But, more importantly to us, he was not only a secret follower of Jesus but was the Virgin Mary's uncle."

"Is this true or faith?"

"You shouldn't ask a vicar that! To me, all faith is real. However, as you ask the question, it is historically accurate. As I said, giving Jesus his tomb had its consequences and it is believed that he was temporarily imprisoned by the Jews for orchestrating the burial. Now, the significance of all this is that, after his release, he eventually left the Holy Land and journeyed to Glastonbury in England as the leader of a small number of missionaries, carrying a most precious cargo."

"Which was?"

"The Holy Grail, no less, used during the Last Supper."

"Oh come on! Isn't that a bit far fetched? I know we like to think that all roads lead to the British Empire, but bringing the Holy Land to England is going a little far."

"Listen to the man," thundered a strong voice, echoing along the nave. Even in the dim light she knew the owner instantly. His tone was engraved in her mind.

"What are you doing here? Can't you and your kind ever leave me alone?"

Russell Thackeray stepped forward. The vicar lit a candle and held it to his face.

"Who are you, Sir?"

He ignored the advance and kept his glare fixed firmly on Sally. "If you hadn't kept your acquaintance with Cudwick from me, I wouldn't have bothered you now. I had you followed. I was waiting nearby to see where you went."

Sally looked askance. "I beg your pardon?"

"A pity, for your sake."

"You, Sir! What is your business?" enquired the vicar once more.

"My business, you ask?" retorted Thackeray. "Why, the same as hers I shouldn't wonder, and perhaps yours too if your meeting today wasn't by chance."

"Mine, Sir? What can you mean?"

"And for my part," added Sally abruptly, "I've absolutely

no idea what you're talking about and no settled business to discuss. I've never been in Cudwick before, yet you followed me and say I have. What for? I know where I've been, better than you."

"Oh, but you do know something. I'll admit you might not appreciate it yourself at the moment, but, believe me, you do know something I need to understand, even if this place *is* new to you as you say."

"Is this mischief of the devil?" cried the vicar.

"No devil, but a plight."

"A plight, Sir?"

"Just so. Now Vicar, you were talking about Joseph of Arimathea."

"I have no more to say until I grasp what monkey business you want to make of it."

"No more games" roared Thackeray in sharp contrast, indicating alarming impatience. "Have my name and be done." He pulled out a small printed card and handed it over.

Holding it to the candle, it was examined. "Government!" The vicar hesitated before handing it back. "I see. At least, I know who you are and from where, but at that point my comprehension ends."

"Then, let me take over the story-telling. It's significant to our investigations and we think equally important to Miss Ayres. Time is precious."

Thackeray led Sally to a pew, where they sat. She was bemused and more than a little frightened. The vicar followed.

"Now, let me see. Oh, yes, you were feigning surprise at there being a connection between the Holy Land and England."

"Not feigning. Stop saying such things."

"My apologies. For the moment, then, I will accept your plea. You indicated to the vicar that it's merely national egoism to believe this geographical connection between Joseph of Arimathea and Glastonbury. In your position I would be sceptical, too. But, in this case you must see past any such high-minded ideals and look at the facts as I present them. Judge them only then."

"Do I have to listen? I would far rather go and never see you again."

"I strongly suggest you don't try to leave. In fact, I absolutely insist on it. Not just for your own well-being, but for the good of others."

The vicar shivered at the chill atmosphere. "Are you threatening her, Sir?"

Thackeray made no reply. He raised his foot onto a kneeler to block the way. "It would be as well to take me entirely seriously. If not for yourself, then for the nation."

"What!" she exclaimed. "First for the good of others and now for the nation! If I'm suspected of something, some wrong-doing, for goodness sake tell me now so that I can clear my name."

The vicar dropped to his knees, hoping to still his pounding heart with a moment of silent prayer. In this state of quiet meditation he suddenly caught a sound from the balcony. He looked up. Nobody.

High above, Fairbourne ducked below the fascia. Thackeray alone caught a glimpse, promptly taking up the story to mask the sound of his colleague crawling out on all fours.

"Do get up, Vicar! Knees are made to articulate the legs, not to brave the hardness of wood and stone."

"Amen and peace to all God's children," said the vicar as he lifted himself back onto the pew.

"Amen to that," added Sally, who looked fiercely at Thackeray.

"Oh, yes, amen if you like! Now, let's get on. I haven't got endless time. I shall continue apace. Historically, Miss Ayres, The Church of England came about in King Henry VIII's time, declaring himself supreme head of the English Church in 1531. Of course, there were dark plots behind the announcement. Best remembered among romantics was his wish to end his long marriage to Catherine of Aragon by divorce, so that he could marry Anne Boleyn two years later, who was by then carrying his child. This was in direct defiance of Rome and the Pope. But, did Henry care? Not a jot of it. He was used to getting his way in all things material, so having his way in all things godly was no less daunting, if it served his kingly purpose."

"Sir, you speak of a Monarch of England."

"I speak of a spoiled boy grown to be a spoiled man, an over indulgent one at that and someone in an untouchable position who was completely intolerant of others." He turned to Sally with an air of marked superiority. "Less remembered, Miss Ayres, was Henry's other need that didn't involve his loins, that being to replenish his war chest. However, that's more interesting than important, so I'll say no more about it. Of course, it did sweet Anne no good to trust him. Married in 1533, her head came off to the sword of a French executioner just three years later, allegedly for adultery, but then Henry would say that, wouldn't he. It suited his purpose. As the blade cut through her flesh, he was already openly flirting with Jane Seymour. Anne's other sin was to give birth to a daughter. He demanded a son and, with the next child miscarried, he considered his misfortune to be the judgement of God on an unholy marriage."

"I really must protest at this shameful attempt to . . ."

"Calm yourself, Vicar. I'm finished with fat Henry's love life. I now return to biblical times, for it is that era we need to examine. You see, Miss Ayres, Joseph of Arimathea was a trader used to travelling to far-off lands. People tend to forget the huge distances traders were willing to cover in centuries past, but that doesn't make such journeys any less real. Look at Marco Polo, as a later example. Venice to China, and not just once. As we now think in weeks and months, so they thought in years. Anyway, it's documented that Joseph had *previously* journeyed to Glastonbury and elsewhere in the West of England, bringing his niece's child with him, the young Jesus. The connection to Glastonbury is seen as real."

"That part's true enough," reflected the vicar. "We know so little of Jesus' young life, but his great uncle's credentials are faultless and recorded. As I said before, after the crucifixion Joseph is said to have returned to Glastonbury with the chalice, The Holy Grail, and eleven disciples. That would be AD63, making him a very old man, or perhaps it was nearer AD34, depending upon the ancient calendar used. The group were given twelve 'hides' of land by King Arviragus."

"Hold it there! What's a 'hide' of land?" enquired Thackeray.

"Don't you know? I though you knew everything!"

retorted the vicar sarcastically, receiving a warning look by return. "A hide is an ancient measure, roughly based on the land needed to support a family and its dependents. I would say anything up to 120 acres, but it could equally be half that."

"So twelve hides were a great deal?"

"Very much so. A princely gift, so to speak. Up to 1,440 in modern acreage. It was . . ."

"Now we're getting somewhere," interjected Thackeray, demanding no further interruption. "In Glastonbury, Joseph constructed a simple place of worship. This was known as the . . ."

". . . Wattle Church," said the vicar with a smile.

"Yes, that's correct," snapped Thackeray angrily. He looked to see if he was going to be allowed to continue, alone. The vicar shrank into the pew. "It was built of interwoven willow sticks, made solid and lasting with mud daub."

"Of course," threw in the vicar once more, unable to resist demonstrating his better knowledge of local events, "before the birth of Christ, the whole of Glastonbury had been little more than small settlements of mud and thatch, some built on artificial foundations of timber and branches. This was because the area was one of peat bogs and watercourses, where every winter flooding turned Glastonbury itself into a high-ground island. Yet, these waters were still navigable for trading. The Pagan Celts called the area . . ."

"Stop! Who cares what the Pagan Celts called the place."

"I thought it was interesting and you would want to know. That's the impression you leave. On this subject, you know little compared to me!"

"And I know least of all," added Sally in vindication.

"Damn it. Go on, then, if you must. But keep it brief!"

"Moderate your language, Sir. This is a place of God."

"Fine. Sorry," he sputtered. The vicar was unmoved. "I said I'm bloody sorry. Now, get on with it!"

"I will address only you, Miss Ayres, until our visitor shows proper respect for his surroundings."

"Go to hell," shouted Thackeray through clenched teeth, standing to thrash his gloves against the pew. "All may be calm in your world, but mine's in turmoil. I've not come all this distance to play dinner parties, and you'll be well advised not waste any more of my time."

"Calm your outrage," pleaded Sally. "No harm or insult was meant." She turned to the vicar, who cowered below Thackeray's staring eyes. "I beg you to continue, but quicker if you please to get this interview done for all our sakes."

"The Celts," trembled the vicar, "called it Ynys-wirren, meaning the island of Glass. Of course, Summer Land, as this part of Wessex later became known, was eventually drained to produce an area of year-round agriculture, as it is today. But, in ancient times, the winter flooding produced fertile land for Summer growth, temporarily destroying its romance as the legendary island of glass."

"Go on," entreated Sally.

"It was in the Wattle Church that Joseph baptised the first Britons to Christianity, so beginning the fall of the old religions that predated Christianity in the area by a thousand years."

"So . . ." began Thackeray.

"Please let me finish," requested the vicar in timid tone, while bracing himself for further scorn.

Thackeray shook his head in resignation.

"When the Saxons overran this part of Wessex in the 7th century, the Wattle Church was supposedly still standing and occupied by Celtic monks. Legend says the Saxons thought the church to be built not of man but prepared by God. Indeed, the hand of God was undoubtedly upon it. Records then talk of the Old Church, which must have been on the same site. All I can tell you is that, today, the existing Lady Chapel of the otherwise quite ruined Glastonbury Abbey was erected where the Old Church stood before it, and that Lady Chapel was the first part of the Abbey to be built. Lady Chapel is also known as St Mary's Chapel."

"Correct," said Thackeray. "I'm gratified our accounts merge, speedily."

"And the significance to the chair, Vicar?" enquired Sally. "You still don't tell me."

"I'm coming to that. At a place called Weary-All Hill, close to the Tor, in that time just after the main Roman invasion of Britain, Joseph drove his staff into the soil. There it is said to have taken root and grown into the Holy Thorn tree. This blessed creation only blossomed at Christmas and Easter, Christ's time of birth and resurrection, the seed of Christianity."

"Is it still there?"

"Alas, Oliver Cromwell or one of his henchmen had it cut down, believing it was an idolatrous icon. But, unbeknown to the Ironsides, many cuttings had been taken and these once flourished in several parts of Wessex. Just as anamorphic images were cleverly devised to allow Royalists to keep paintings of King Charles I without the enemy knowing, by seemingly random splodges of paint on a board forming a picture when reflected in a concave mirror, so it is said a section of the Holy Thorn tree may have been embedded in this oak chair. For a time, Glastonbury had been the heart of Christian worship in England and remains today a place of great mystery."

Thackeray rose, pulling on his leather gloves. "I didn't know about the chair. I suppose that was worth waiting for. Is there anything more you would like to add before I go?"

"I don't believe so. Please go in haste."

"Then, I fulfil your wish and bid you goodbye."

"Ah, I might whet your appetite with one more trifle that has come to mind. Such a thorn tree still exists. A descendant, that is."

Thackeray stopped and turned. "Where?"

"At St Patrick's chapel. It is said to have grown from a cutting. There are others dotted hereabouts, too."

"Interesting, but it hardly helps me."

"It's proof of the story being genuine."

"Maybe, in your view!"

CHAPTER 3

A world in crisis

Thackeray strode purposefully from St Jude's and climbed into a carriage, where Fairbourne waited anxiously.

"Was I seen?"

"I don't think so."

"And did you discover anything of interest? I caught none of what was said. His voice was too soft to hear from way up high."

"Nothing particularly useful. All that stuff you told me about the beginnings of Christianity in Britain came in very handy, though. I sounded quite the expert."

"Was it helpful?"

"It was. I'm the first to admit, Fairbourne, that my general knowledge is quite fearful. I remember as a young man suggesting at a dinner party that Paradise Lost was a cricket result, and feeling extremely foolish when castigated through torrents of laughter that it was actually the name of Milton's poem! An epic, no less, so I was told. Even now, I can see in my mind's eye their look of derision. Sadly for them, I was working my way up the tax department at the time and had the means at my disposal to deal with their cachinnation."

"With Miss Ayres, I meant?"

"I know. I was reminiscing, that's all. As to your question, little bits of information come together, but I'm still blind to any common significance. As for Miss Ayres herself, I could detect nothing in her manner to indicate that she is holding back on us."

"Sir, with respect, it would help me a great deal if I knew a bit more about the Government's concern over the so-called Predicted Nine legend, and its basis. You've given me so little to go on, but expect my help in return. Frankly, I don't know what I'm looking for and I can't be sure I would recognise anything of importance, even if it stared me in the face. What's more, you're taking all this so seriously that I'm beginning to feel a little frightened."

"I've told you all I should, Fairbourne."

"But, Sir, if I'm to assist you properly you've got to trust me, on an equal footing. I need to know everything you do. For a start, why would any modern government concern itself with legend and prophecy? British history is stuffed full of that sort of thing, but nobody takes any of it seriously. Why is this different?"

"The prophecy of the Predicted Nine, itself, isn't secret at all. References to it can be found in any number of books on folklore. But the proofs we have that could turn it from legend to reality are."

"Are what?"

"Secret! Have you ever heard of the 'dark box', Fairbourne?"

"Rumour in shady corridors of power only."

"What do you know?"

"It's an eyes-only chest that's held in a repository under lock and key, going back a hundred years or so. I don't know what it contains."

"The chest is much, much older than that, Fairbourne. Importantly, it stores documents going back centuries including, among other papers, the only known authenticated references to a prediction claiming potential catastrophe for England should the last of nine particular drowned people rise from the dead. What would otherwise be considered fairytale is, in this case, now being taken extremely seriously."

"Can you tell me why?"

"Because of Miss Ayres, of course. It would seem that the prophecy is possibly far from nonsense *if* her experience can be proven to be true. No, let me rephrase that. It's my job to *prove* to the Government that the prophecy *is* nonsense, as you say, or alternatively dreadfully real. If we could've shown that Ayres was only the seventh or eighth woman to have had such an experience, then we could relax. But, it's gone way beyond that now, thanks to your research."

"You've already lost me, Sir. How can a prophecy have believable provenance regarding what it predicts? They are *non sequitur*."

"How can I explain what is known in simple terms? I'd best start in the year 1660."

"Sir?"

"In that year, after nine years in exile, King Charles II returned to England to restore the monarchy. With me so far?"

"Of course."

"Good. In August that year the Scots were given back the power of self-determination, after nine years of military occupation by Cromwellian forces. By then, Oliver Cromwell, Lord Protector of England, had been dead almost two years. Now, this is the important bit. In 1662, the new Royalist parliament, sometimes known as the Cavalier or Restoration Parliament, set about ridding the nation of a great deal more unpopular and militarist Cromwellian legislation. Under Parliament's own orders, many documents were burned publicly, including the Solemn League and Covenant, the much-hated and one-sided alliance between the English and Scots. There were others."

"I know a bit about that, Sir, from my school days."

"Bear with me, Fairbourne. It's important to do this systematically. As a result of the 1662 burnings, a great deal of paper-shuffling had taken place. No doubt, seemingly unimportant papers were burned alongside those dealing with flawed legislation, in order to give the public a much-exaggerated sense of a fresh start to parliamentary rule."

"Showmanship."

"Just so. Then, in 1665, with the plague at its height and tens of thousands of Londoners dying, the King, his Court and Parliament fled to Oxford, together with many clergymen and doctors, leaving the ill and poor to their horrific fate. Certain items of national importance that couldn't be secured or carried away were, instead, placed in hiding. Everyone knows that the Great Fire of London in the following year destroyed hundreds of acres of the city. But, as every cloud has a silver lining, so the fire destroyed the plague and its causes. St Paul's cathedral was among the victims of the flames, tons of roofing lead falling like a molten waterfall."

"And?"

"And, now we get to the crux of the matter. When normality resumed the best it could after such devastation to the infrastructure and population of London, among lost treasures being sought for recovery was an ancient chest. When found, it was burned and blackened. That's why it became known as the dark box."

"I'd always imagined 'dark' meant something secret."

"It was an unfortunate choice of name, as it brought attention to the fact that it *did* hold a secret. Who rediscovered it and where, are matters lost to time. It's generally agreed that the chest must have originated as the property of an Abbey, no doubt plundered during King Henry VIII's reign. Anyway, although charred, its contents were examined and found to be preserved, among them a metal cross that had vanished after its discovery in Glastonbury centuries before. I'm not saying the chest originated in Glastonbury, although it may have, and how it ever got to London is anyone's guess. Inside was a mix of historic and seemingly religious stuff, plus papers of parliamentary origin. That's why I asked you to find out about Glastonbury. I thought it might help. It was a bonus when you told me about early Christianity and made me sound so knowledgeable."

"Does the cross still exist?"

"I assume so. I've never seen it for myself. Now, retracing a couple of years, something monumental had happened in 1663 that was of sufficient concern to the Cavalier Parliament to have it written down for future record and placed inside that chest for safe keeping, which thereafter took on almost mystical importance among the great and the good in government. Hence, why it was so revered. Remember when you mentioned 1663 while we were at that hospital?

He nodded eagerly.

"Spot on. Unfortunately, nowadays nobody can make much sense of that particular 1663 document, which still survives intact, as the earlier papers it mentions and refers to had been burned in 1662. I can only suppose that the author of the 1663 document had been the same archivist who had been placed in charge of going through all the pre-1662 papers prior to burning. He must have known what had been sacrificed to the fire. Only after, in 1663, did anyone realise the significance of their loss. By then it was too late, of course, but some restitution was made by his vague reference to the earlier, burned documents. Any further concurring knowledge was taken with him to the grave."

"So, it's a blind alley?"

"No, not exactly. What we do know from the 1663 document is that the burned papers correlated to Arthurian legend in some respects, and that they involved prophecy based around the so-called Predicted Nine. Maybe, the cross was once part of the same package. Who can tell? Popular Arthurian legend has two central pillars, both supposedly twaddle. One relates to the search for The Holy Grail and the other predicting that the dead king will rise to help England at a time of crisis, 'the present and future king', so to speak."

"And, that's it? All this fuss over 5th and 6th century legend? I took my task seriously, thinking it was based on a firm footing. And, now, all my hard efforts seem to have been a complete waste of my time."

"No, Fairbourne. Don't treat the rest of us as idiots. Remember above all else that the 17th century was puritanical, not given to actions outside of strictly religious and moral behaviour. That, alone, gives such prized documents an element of credence. You should be made aware that among the sentences of the 1663 document are references to the 'previous three', as I said, all in extremely vague terms. The only *certain* common factor is that each woman supposedly drowned but survived, as did the woman mentioned in the 1663 paper itself, which he called the 'prophecy fourth'. The writer was most clear about that."

"A Government secret going back centuries that has taken on legendry status in its own right."

"I will ignore that gibe! Now, according to *your* research, the author of the 1663 document was wrong, claiming only three previous experiences, whereas there had been four, plus 1663. Given the period of history, such a mistake is forgivable. Now, three more followed before Miss Ayres came onto the scene."

"Making nine in total!"

"According to you, yes. In fact, other than 1663, the dates 1773 and 1828 had been the only positively documented times for survivors the Government had, prior to Ayres herself, that is, until you managed to piece together the missing dates. I suppose you found the Adams and Lawrence files in the Government archives?"

"Yes, Sir. Shouldn't they have been in the dark box with the rest?"

"I suppose so. But look on that positively. If they had been, you wouldn't have accessed them. Tell me, Fairbourne, what more did you find out about Nancy Adams?"

"Her case came to public attention quite accidentally, as it happens. All because the Government that year passed a new Act of Parliament to force ship owners to provide more space on board vessels when carrying some of the tens of thousands of emigrants leaving Scotland for a new life in North America. You see, many ships had been providing slave-trade style accommodation for the transatlantic crossing from Clyde. On board one ship in 1826, everyone who arrived in Nova Scotia had typhus."

"Everyone was diseased?"

"To a man. Then, what brought it to a head was the story of Adams herself who, it is said, had paid thirty shillings to a ship owner for just three square feet of room on a lower deck. Already forced from her highland croft, this poor woman had to wait weeks around the docks until the ship was full and only then would embark. Many people died on that particular voyage including, remarkably, Adams, who was buried at sea. Although this case highlighted what was going on, it was ship conditions in general that encouraged the new Act of Parliament."

"I don't understand. Are you going to tell me that she wasn't dead after all?"

"Not at all. By all accounts she was as dead as a doornail when she was put over the side, but she arrived back in England on board another merchantman weeks later having said she revived after hitting the water, only to drown again. She couldn't understand how she returned to life for the second time, but she said she was helped by a woman in the sea, who she took to be another passenger. Yet, records show that nobody else was lost overboard at that location. It was suggested in the newspapers that she had suffered sleep apnoea, whereby a victim stops breathing and appears to have died, but actually hasn't. Of course, that doesn't explain the other women in the water."

"How could she be pronounced dead by accident? From my little understanding of sleep apnoea, it usually doesn't last any time at all."

"If the captain thought she was diseased, he wouldn't have wasted a minute pitching her overboard, believe me, to save his own skin. Disease on board a cramped ship becomes rampant far more quickly than on land. I know how callous some captains could be, especially those just out of slave trading."

"Are we getting anywhere?"

"In understanding the victims, perhaps we are. As to what it all means, then the simple answer to that is, *no*."

"We must understand everything. Soak in every small detail, however insignificant it appears, just on the off chance it helps. We are, Fairbourne, ships without rudders, heading for the rocks without the means to steer away."

"Sorry, Sir, I don't understand!"

"I mean, if we are to take the Predicted Nine prophecy seriously, and it's a big *if*, then we have to decide what *can be* found out."

"Sir?"

"I've given this some thought. It seems to me that we have three possible lines of enquiry. Firstly, we can follow Miss

Ayres. Up to now we've struck a blank with her. She seems to remember nothing, but that's not to say the clues aren't embedded deeper in her mind, or could be revealed through her future actions. However, I must alert you to a big problem here. The prophecy states that catastrophe to England could happen *when* the last of the Predicted Nine appears, presumably allowing some kind of last minute prevention or rescue. Now, should that be taken literally? Does it mean at that exact time or soon after?

"It could be either, surely, Sir. Translations or word-of-mouth often introduce variations of meaning. However, if we believe Miss Ayres is the Ninth, and nothing untoward has already taken place, then it can't mean 'immediate', can it?"

"Good thinking, Fairbourne."

"So, she must be followed. You mentioned a second line of enquiry?"

"Yes. We must find out everything we can about the legend itself. I think this will only be possible by looking into the life and times of the king called Arthur. This will, of course, also encompass known searches for The Holy Grail, and anything else associated with it. There's no knowing what there is to discover. So, we must investigate these, too, even if they cover centuries of British history."

"British?"

"Yes, Fairbourne. We must find British connections, which I suppose must include all we already know about Joseph of Arimathea. What intrigues me is that the more I hear of the history and legends of the West Country, the more I feel we could trip unknowingly onto an answer, including perhaps Miss Ayres' alleged entanglement with events to come.

Several small matters, individually seemingly unrelated and unimportant, appear always to point to the one place. Glastonbury, I believe, will be the key to solving our enigma."

"Don't you mean possible events to come? Much of the Government remains sceptical about our findings so far."

"And rightly so." He banged on the window with his stick, meaning for the journey back to start. "Superstition has no place in modern politics. But, it is our job to prove or disprove a link. The Cabinet is hardly known for acting decisively to head-off problems, so our mandate must indicate a genuine level of discomfort. I put it no more strongly."

"That's how I see it, too. Oh! Stupid of me! At last I begin to understand your tactics."

"Do you, Fairbourne?"

"You think that if this Glastonbury town has any significance to the Predicted Nine prophecy, then, by Miss Ayres knowing something of the historic background of the place, it might trigger connections in her mind that could speedily reveal any complicity to doom and destruction, whether consciously or subconsciously. That's why you got so hot and bothered when she journeyed here to Cudwick. Glastonbury's just around the corner."

Thackeray smiled in self satisfaction. "That's the card I'm playing. I've no other jokers up my sleeve. But, listen. Under no circumstances must we alert her to the prophecy itself. At best she would think of us as lunatics, at worst she would be too frightened to follow her instincts."

"And the third? You said there were three possible lines of enquiry."

"Quite right, I did. The third you have already started, I

hope. We must try to assess the nature of any possible threats to our nation, surmise what may be heading our way. War, plague, disaster. Take your pick, but something is amiss or we're all being led on a fool's errand. The Prime Minister wants answers."

"Didn't Gladstone himself once say: *you cannot fight against the future. Time is on our side?*"

"But, in this case, Fairbourne, I'm not so sure how much time we have."

"Perhaps this might help." He opened his briefcase. "Assuming any catastrophe to our nation doesn't have to be on our sacred shores, I've drawn-up a long list of possible crisis points, as you asked. Of course, there's nothing even remotely connected to prophecy, or Glastonbury for that matter. In fact, my list comprises almost exclusively dangers on foreign soil within and without the British Empire." He handed the notebook to Thackeray.

"I see the Balkans is top of the list. Why?"

"Since Russia imposed a punitive peace treaty on Turkey in 1878 and humiliated us by ignoring our wishes, despite the Royal Navy being anchored off Constantinople, the Russians are seen as a threat to British influence in the Mediterranean and our sea route to India. Austria-Hungary and the German Empire back our position, but for their own self-interest."

"Is the German Empire currently friend or foe?"

"The consensus is that the Germans would fight alongside us, but only if they gained dominance over Russia in the area. Conversely, the French would be worried at any such alliance that could result in greater German influence anywhere."

"Next, I see you have Southern Africa."

"This is a growing foreign policy problem, with the Zulus under King Cetewayo massacring whole columns of our troops. We now also have to square-up against the Boers as a separate political issue, which might boil over in the future."

"But even the most pessimistic outcome couldn't envisage the possibility of it spilling outside of Africa. Zulus and Boers up Pall Mall are hardly likely. In reality, Southern Africa can be no threat at all to our homeland, unlike the Balkans could become."

"Then, Sir, you will see I list Ireland. Charles Parnell and Michael Davitt of the Irish National Land League."

"I admit to knowing little about Irish politics. But, from the trifle I have read, surely they argue only for the rights of poor tenant farmers during the rural depression? What can be wrong with that?"

"Sir, some of the Cabinet take the opposite view. They think it's the Fenians stirring up trouble. A couple of years ago militant groups were organised in an attempt to prohibit land being harvested that had been taken over from evicted tenants."

"Boycotting the land. Yes, I heard of that."

"Named after Captain Boycott, Lord Erne's land agent. Orangemen were used as temporary labour on that first publicised occasion, guarded by a thousand police from the Royal Irish Constabulary. Since then, these protests have grown alarmingly in number. Why, only in 1881 Parnell and 35 supporters of home rule were suspended from the Commons. It could easily spread into an armed struggle over wider issues, encompassing the whole question of Irish politics."

"But I understood the Peace Preservation Act gave Irish tenants the lawful right to fair rent, fixed tenure and the ability to sell a tenancy at the market value?"

"Yes, Sir, but it wasn't supported by Parnell or other leaders of the Land League, and so trouble erupted. They were later thrown into Kilmainham Prison, until the Government agreed a secret deal with Parnell to let the Act lapse and major rent arrears be cleared. Unhappily, that wasn't the end of it. Not content with the contrived outcome, some of the Government resigned, but, just as dramatically, Parnell has recently come under attack from a number of his own former supporters. I believe Ireland may develop into a very serious problem, with ever-increasing levels of violence until home rule is achieved. The mischief could even spread to the British mainland. Only last year the so-called Irish Invincibles killed a Minister and Under-Secretary to Ireland in an ambush, to Parnell's horror. Five Invincibles have been sentenced to death."

"All very sad, but not one for us to dwell on, surely? Are there other problem spots?"

"With respect, I beg to differ. Even Gladstone said: '*these gentlemen wish to march through rapine to disintegration and dismemberment of the Empire, even to the placing of different parts of the Empire in direct hostility one with the other*', or words to that affect. I have to admit, I don't know what 'rapine' means."

"Where's your education, man. Plunder, forcible taking of another's property."

"Is that so?"

"It's a pretty black list. Yet, there remains another written, I see."

"Yes, the Suez Canal, opened less than a decade and a half ago and already causing us problems. Ottoman sovereignty over Egypt is little more than words, as we British monopolise Egyptian politics. This vital trade route has been under threat from Colonel Ahmed Arabi, who is a self-proclaimed champion of Islam. As I understand it, his forces massacred fifty Europeans in Alexandria, for which the Royal Navy bombarded his strongholds in the city until he withdrew. A land battle followed at Tel el-Kebir, with our army gaining ultimate victory. But, even more serious is Sudan, where a jihad is being lead against unbelievers by the Mahdi, Mohammed Ahmed. The Government's view is that the Egyptians may be incapable of governing the region, even with our political and military help, which might lead the army to defeat. What the Government doesn't want, almost at any cost, is for Sudan to step-back to its past, ravaged by unchecked slavery. Similarly, the Government doesn't want anybody trying to suggest that British interest in the region is modern crusading against another faith group. Diplomacy is the watchword."

"The actual Canal itself isn't under any great threat though?"

"No, and it will never be allowed to pass from British control. That is certain in my lifetime."

"That's everything on the list? Nothing else to report in our troubled world? Nothing even closer to home?"

"If you like I could add Crofters in the Scottish island of Skye who are protesting violently over further Highland evictions by land owners. Then there are property developers who are unhappy at Epping Forest being made into a public park. Next, we have the Queen amongst others concerned at London's horror slums, which are fermenting unrest. Oh, and Australia won the cricketing Ashes for the first time, which caused more outrage in the Commons than Sudan!" He slammed his notebook shut with gusto, smiling at his wit.

Thackeray sat back and closed his eyes in despair. There was a long journey ahead to endure and a long list of trouble-spots to consider.

For some moments after Thackeray's departure, the church fell into silence, as if reassurance was needed that he had finally gone. Presently, Fry took the candle and snuffed out the wick, joining Sally outside in the early evening air. She had watched Thackeray's carriage disappear into the distance.

"That was all a bit scary," he said. "What do you make of it?"

Sally merely shrugged her shoulders, hiding the anguish she felt. "My life has been turned upside down since my return to England," she said in soft voice that was almost a whisper. "I hope he now realises that he has the wrong woman and that I'll be left alone from now on."

"Where will you go?"

"Glastonbury," she mused. "Yes, that will do."

"Dare I ask whether you will be visiting family or friends, if you don't mind my prying?"

"Not family or friends. I have nobody who needs me hereabouts. Work is what I need. I'm a teacher."

"What happy fortune, Cudwick is in need of such as you. God be praised that you were sent here. We have a small

school, not a stone's throw from where we stand. Would you
be interested?"

She looked across the churchyard at the small stone
building clearly dated 1842 and the almshouses close by.

"Kindly, I think not. I've a mind to try my luck in
Glastonbury and get away from here. By the way, I didn't ask
what happened to Alis Bennett."

"I don't know the circumstances of how she eventually
died. She may have been young, she may have been old. The
epitaph gives nothing away." He shook her hand. "I'm
disappointed to say goodbye to a teacher. Still, good luck and
Godspeed. You'll find a comfortable room at The Drum Inn."

CHAPTER 4

The merry month

The next morning was the first day of May, the start of the Merry Month, abundant in pagan rituals. For country folk living amongst nature and dependent upon its many moods, the seasons were not measured so much in calendar months as by creation's own bountiful signs. Yet, certain celebrations had fixed dates no matter what the weather held, May Day being one, shared by those living on and off the agricultural landscape.

It was a time of change, when the bleakness of the colder months gave way to the warmth of new life and a fullness of bright colour. Catkin-bearing trees had already shed their pollen to be spread by the wind blowing freely through the open branches, and were now coming into rich leaf. In the shady woodland floor, already thickening with carpets of bluebells, fox and badger cubs began to emerge from earths and setts, and hedgehogs avoided both while foraging for their own prey.

Elsewhere in the undergrowth, deer hinds looked for cover

to protect their newly-dropped fawns, hiding them for the first few difficult days of life, returning occasionally to suckle. In the air, bees were on the wing, among them queen bumblebees laden with pollen and nectar to make into bee-bread for the egg-laying cycle at their chosen nest sites. Other insects were plentiful too, enjoying the proliferation of wild flowers. But, away from hidden nature, it was mostly a time of birdsong, celebrating the forthcoming summer.

There were few places in England that were more perfect for peace of mind than the region of Wessex known in ancient times as Summer Land. Here, among the gentle rise and fall of the fields, never to any great height or any great drop, a person could lose themselves in a timeless beauty that feasted the eyes with endless pleasure. Pretty villages and hamlets were plentiful, yet so distinct in their own character through the use of local stone for buildings and the layout of the crooked streets and paths, that they were separated from each other by more than the intervening open fields.

Sally emerged from the Drum Inn in the early light of morning, having breakfasted heartily on the freshest of eggs, bread still warm from the oven and milk so rich and creamy that she declared it was fresh from the cow. Whereas the pastures of Devon were best suited to turning out milk for clotted cream, the low and lush grasses hereabouts were ideal for high milk yields to satisfy a growing population. The butter she had spread on the bread had come stamped with the pattern of a dairy cow, as carved on the ornate butter print applied last after the farmer's wife had beaten the butter into shape. The date 1881 left by the print recorded when she had won a bronze medal for her produce at the sixth Frome Agricultural and Cheese Show.

To the farmer's wife, it was more than mere butter. It was her escape to a little independence, pin money of her own that was not accounted for within the income of the farm, but hers to do with as she liked. The same was true of the small quantity of cheese she sold locally, and the eggs. She believed, and it was generally agreed, that her poultry laid eggs of particular taste, her secret being to feed the hens with warm food in poor weather, each meal containing a small portion of uncooked meat. When it was coursing day, though, she would hold back a small pat of butter to rub onto her dog's throat, sure that it enhanced its breathing and improved its performance.

Sally was left in awe at the tranquillity of the place at this early hour, where only birdsong broke the silence and seemed almost intrusive. At last, with her mind rested from the previous day's events, she believed she would now be free to get on with her life. Looking in each direction, there was nobody to be seen, the milkmaids and field workers having already trudged their way to the farms and any general street life had still to emerge.

Then, as if by script, across the street a man came choking from his terrace, door flung wide open. He had lit his black tortoise stove with turf peat blocks and damp coke. But, when the window had been opened, the breeze had fanned smoke back into the room. He smiled to Sally as he leaned forward to clear his lungs.

"I'll be glad to get to me pigs. They might eat everything in their path, from beechnuts to beetles, but they don't wallop me like she do indoors. She'll get her own later, though, you just see." With a friendly wave of his hat, he made an unsteady path for the fields.

This singular event now seemed to signal the true start of the day. A horse-drawn cart carrying churns of milk came into view, several small children wearing flower garlands over their best clothes running out of their houses to meet it and jump on board for the ride. The milkman seemed unbothered, filling his customers' jugs. A shaggy dog cocked a leg on the cross before barking around the playful children, while an elderly woman carrying a basket of horsetail plant cuttings knocked from door to door, offering them as pewterwort pot and pail scourers.

Many miles away in Westkings stood 'Samain', the manor house of the Elvington family who were viewed by the locals as the nearest thing they had to rural aristocracy. In reality, although owning goodly land and exhibiting well-bred ways, the Elvingtons were of low noble title. But, this accident of birth was not allowed to dent the pride Charlotte Elvington displayed publicly as a wealthy land-owner, nor that of Edmond, her son by default.

If ever three people had altered over the years in personality, it was the Elvingtons. James, as head of the dynasty, had earned at an early age an enviable reputation as a hard worker and fair employer. Skilled at running his estate by example and not ascendancy, he had also been widely admired for his generosity of spirit. But, Charlotte's infidelity had led to the birth of Christabel, an event that had changed everything. It had turned James temporarily into a madman who had plunged his own arm into a fire during a drunken rage railed against his wife. Passing years had healed his temper, if not his body, but had not reinstated any wish to continue running the estate, which he willingly left to his son.

In turn, James' indifference towards Charlotte and his insistence all that time ago that her baby daughter had to be sent away if she was to stay by his side, had changed her from a beautiful young woman of pleasant nature into a bitter and twisted middle-aged matriarch who saw family advancement as her only remaining ambition. Separated from Christabel soon after the child's birth, she had instead lavished all her love and attitudes in equal measure on James' own illegitimate son, Edmond, whose forming character had been gradually perverted to her will. Yet, beneath the skin, the young man had retained a good deal of his father's earlier ways, sometimes well hidden by a reckless enthusiasm for aristocratic pleasures, but never too deeply buried when a steady mind and kind heart were needed for important matters.

Westkings had once been a place of great significance to Sally too, but now in Cudwick she hadn't expected the past and the present to converge so unexpectedly. She turned to the sound of carriage wheels coming from the opposite direction, slowing from a trot to fully stopping by the church. The door opened. A man appeared. Even before he had fully alighted, he caught sight of the woman standing alone.

"Miss Ayres, Sally. Look, it's me, James Elvington."

Sally looked aghast as she recognised the caller, the intervening years having changed his appearance only in small measure. Now, she wanted above all else to avoid him, but could not with any civility. She stood her ground. He could see she stared at his stump arm.

He walked over with dignity, raising his hat and smiling in a friendly way.

"I tried to see you in hospital. It was only after you were discharged that Schofield told me the direction you were heading. I'm his biggest client, but, even so, I had to apply a fair degree of pressure to get him to spill the beans. He won't even talk to Charlotte, for obvious reasons."

"You guessed I would be here?"

"I had a slight idea you might be, that's all. You wanted to use this railway line before, when I gave you a ride instead. Don't you remember?"

A nod was the only reply.

"I tried several of the stations down the track before someone told me a stranger of your general description had arrived here yesterday. Anyway, now that we're reacquainted, we have much to talk about. Would you join me in the carriage?"

"Is Edmond with you?"

"No, but Charlotte is. Indeed, that woman I have the dishonour to call my wife is so full of remorse that I'm surprised she could face you at all. I think she only came to ensure we weren't left alone."

"I don't understand. What do you mean?"

"Not here, my dear. Take my arm."

They walked to the carriage, where the coachman held the door open and lowered the step. She entered, followed by James.

Sally sat opposite both Elvingtons. In the awkwardness of the situation nobody spoke, the two women eyeing each other for signs of intent.

"My dear Miss Ayres," said Charlotte presently, "have you heard my Edmond is to be engaged?"

She replied that she had not.

"Oh, yes. A little young in my opinion, but, nonetheless, a fact."

"Should I know to whom?"

"No, I doubt if she would be known to you. Her family is of an entirely different standing. The youngsters met last Michaelmas. He brought her to the manor to show her the place and she was so delighted that she stayed a fortnight."

Sally nodded acknowledgement.

"You are not told this because of your connection with Edmond," Charlotte added in haste. "Only that you being here in Wessex makes it proper that you should be acquainted with the facts and realise the importance of being circumspect. We . . ." she looked at James, ". . . I mean, I wouldn't like to think you intend to see him. He is *my* son."

"You flatter me with foresight." She lowered her head in self-pity. "In truth, I admit I do often think of Edmond. Why wouldn't I? You say he is *your* son but, in truth, he is *mine* and we all know it. He is of my blood and that of your husband's. But, this knowledge is caged as a fond memory rather than a future prospect. If Edmond is happy, and you clearly say he is, then my intervention into his life would bring nothing more than scandal."

"We think as one, then," replied Charlotte, feeling the interview had now ended. "I'm sure you can get wherever you're going by public carriage. And, before you ask, we can't spare a servant to accompany you, even if that means you must travel alone."

"Such a favour hadn't entered my mind."

James was far from pleased with the direction the conversation had taken and wasted no time in expressing his anger.

"Damn this, Charlotte. Are you fevered to act so irrationally? You know this isn't the reason for our being here." He leaned forward, just holding back from taking Sally's hand. "You have been much misused."

"How so?" asked Sally in all innocence.

"You really know nothing of the circumstances of your tragedy?"

"I know my husband and I wanted to take a mission to Africa and you kindly provided the means."

"Your husband?" blustered James. "You were married?"

"Of course she was," grinned Charlotte, pleased at having the upper hand.

He sat back, perplexed. Did he have the right to think that she wouldn't marry, ever, just because they had shared a brief dalliance many years ago which had resulted in a son? He wondered at the wisdom of going too far, after all, as immediate perceptions had changed. Yet, the air had to be cleared.

"Yes, as you say, *the means*. But it was Charlotte who made the arrangements for the ship. Truth be told, I was mainly ignorant of them. Anyway, those *means* turned out to be a disaster which nearly cost you your life and, as I now comprehend all too clearly, cost your husband his.

Understandably, I feel under an obligation to you. We should make some recompense, more so now."

To James' conspicuous dismay, she declined most politely.

Charlotte looked entirely pleased. "Then, we all accept the matter is closed. Now we must talk of Christabel. There are issues here, too, to be resolved to avoid unnecessary harm. Edmond is all we have and he is ignorant of any connection to her."

"Who's Christabel?" asked Sally faintly.

"Good heavens, of course, why should you know? She was the child I gave birth to."

Sally remained perplexed. "You still say more I don't understand. Are you saying the little baby I helped the doctor deliver all that time ago at 'Samain' was named Christabel, or has there been another child since?"

"There was but one. She died."

"No, it was the other baby who died. The little boy."

"What! What mischief is this?" demanded Charlotte, with James in close unison. "What baby boy are you talking about, you wicked woman? I had a girl."

"Oh God! I didn't mean to say that."

Charlotte slapped her face, intent upon wringing the truth.

"It was the doctor's idea," said Sally, holding her burning cheek. "He said we shouldn't tell you of the still-born baby, as you had another on the way. It was gently wrapped up and removed from the room before you realised what had happened."

"I had twins? A boy as well?" exclaimed Charlotte, barely able to take it in.

"He meant only good to come from secrecy. He was a kind

man in all ways and thought only of your best interest. I was too young to argue."

James, too, was now in deep shock. He couldn't think straight or guess how to comfort his wife after such an unexpected disclosure. He remained angry at her hard ways, but such thoughts mellowed in the face of her obvious distress.

Still stunned, he instead took Sally's clenched fingers, which showed white at the knuckles, and gently caressed them, saying: "What Charlotte was about to say was that Edmond has never been told of the family connection between himself and Christabel. He knew her all right, but not as family."

"When did the baby girl die? Little Christabel, as you called her."

"Not for many years after. She knew womanhood."

"Such a pretty little thing. A beautiful baby."

"I hardly noticed," offered James defensively. "She was born and gone so quickly. That's when we first met, if you remember. Schoolteacher-cum-midwife, and all in such a pretty young frame."

"James!" prodded Charlotte. "Is it your intention to vex me to my grave? My nerves won't withstand any more ruffles today!"

"Your nerves are as known to me as my own feet, Charlotte. I know how far they can travel without adverse effect!"

Sally formed a smile, which she tried to hide.

"You really mean to hurt me."

"No, Charlotte, I merely want to lift you from the

melancholy that comes from delving into the long past. Your baby son, as he would have been, never took a breath of air. You must accept that there was a reason under heaven why he wasn't given to your breast."

"You're right, James," she replied, with anguish miraculously leaving her voice, "it would be foolish to mourn now."

"Just so, Char. Anyway, the matter under discussion is how can we make up for the suffering endured at your hands by Miss Ayres?"

Charlotte could hardly believe her ears. She might have protested that her own distress should not be considered secondary to that of Miss Ayres, if it had not been for Sally's own sudden intervention. In quick succession, Sally said that she did not want any hand-outs, bade them to leave her alone and stepped from the carriage in one determined bound.

James, stunned by her quick departure, jumped out after her. He quickly caught her up, only stopping her determination to put distance between them by grabbing her shoulder. She turned, oppressed to have his company.

"Look Sally, now that we are free to talk, I know Edmond *would* like to see you again."

She stared into his eyes. "What new mischief is this?"

"It's true. He came with me to the hospital. Don't misunderstand. He doesn't know you are his natural mother, at least not yet. But, when he found out that you were the stranger he had once met in the conservatory, and then what had happened to you, and that Elvington money was involved, he showed great concern. After all, he now runs the estate and controls most of its finances. What Charlotte did in hiring that dreadful ship, that accident waiting to happen, affected him greatly."

"And what of us in this intrigue? And what of Charlotte if she found out I met up with Edmond? If truth be told, I'm sick of hearing her name, especially if you say she knew the ship was flawed and wanted rid of me. I've been told since that the ship was in poor condition, but that's a far cry from Charlotte knowing that it would almost certainly sink. Is that what you're saying? She wanted to kill me, but killed my husband and a ship full of sailors instead?"

He looked aghast. "No! I suppose I went too far. Even Charlotte wouldn't plan that outcome. I won't believe her capable of it. Lots of other things, *yes*, but not that. Never manslaughter." He let go of her arm. "Look, Sally, I'm a broken man. I have nothing you would want. I know it from your eyes and it's probably for the best. But my son, our son, deserves better than to live his life as a lie. Knowing the truth about his mother could, I suppose, cause him great harm, even lose him his future wife. But, isn't that a trifle in comparison?"

She put her hand on his cheek, softly rubbing her thumb on his flesh.

"You are kind and honest. If things were different, your affliction wouldn't bother me at all. But *our* time has passed. When I thought I would die, I felt nothing but self pity. When I lived, I saw the world in a new clarity. I can now tell right from wrong. We were wrong, James." She kissed his cheek with a gentility of touch, like the warm brush of a breeze. "Between us can exist only friendship, a trust forged by my experiences and your openness to make amends. If it was ever necessary, I know I could depend upon your firmest reliance. In that I am satisfied."

"Where will you go?"

"Glastonbury, I believe."

"You wish me to take you? It's no long journey by carriage but a healthy distance on foot."

"Thank you, but no. I'm told there are village events taking place here this morning and I shall stay long enough to see them."

"Then, it's goodbye again."

Instinctively, he kissed her hand, turned and walked back to the carriage, where Charlotte waited anxiously.

"Is she done?" she asked sternly.

"She is."

"You are too good to me, my dear James. A capital husband. We can be at peace in our lives." Her kiss to his cheek was rough and quick.

"Perhaps," he muttered, glancing sideways into the street.

The first of the village events Sally had been told to expect was scheduled for mid-morning, allowing the excited children to attend school in a calmed manner that afternoon. By the ten o'clock chime of the church a goodly crowd had gathered in the square.

Right on schedule, a group of small children appeared, the smallest, the May Queen, dressed in white and wearing a wreath of flowers around her bonnet. The other children, among them those who had played on the milk cart and wearing flower garlands of bright colours, followed behind. They paraded through the street and stopped at an open space, where a maypole awaited, its coloured ribbons hanging loose. To the accompaniment of an accordion and drum, they danced in and out and circled merrily until the pole had been fully plaited.

Then, to great gasps, the chimney sweep jumped out from behind a bush, dressed as Jack-in-the-Green. Wearing a wicker frame adorned in green foliage, only his beaming face remained uncovered. Last of all came a knight in paper armour galloping from the doors of the inn, a cardboard horse suspended by braces from around his waist. The comical legs dangled from corners of the horse, each too short to reach the ground.

Finally, upon a signal, all the performers gathered around the knight for a photograph, barely able to contain their excitement as they stood completely still for what seemed an eternity. Food that had been prepared on trestle tables was now uncovered, and with great gusto it was swallowed greedily. Tankards of beer on trays came from the Drum Inn, the adults making merry in their own fashion.

An hour later, and the once presence of food being recognisable only by birds walking on the table tops to pick at the crumbs, the festival had ended. Yet, merriment had far from abated. There remained another spectacle to come, of somewhat different nature but, nonetheless, a cause of huge anticipation among the expectant onlookers.

To the sound of singing and shouting, crashing of iron pots and blowing of horns, the choking man she had seen earlier appeared from one end of the village, carried aloft on a pole lifted high by a number of his friends. While holding on tightly with one hand, he banged a hanging kettle with a stick and began singing something that was almost inaudible but ended with:

> *'She struck him so hard, and she cut him so deep,*
> *Till the blood run down like a new stuck sheep'*

From the opposite direction attended his wife, carried high in a wicker basket supported by older men. She was laughing merrily. A fiddler played by her side.

Sally asked what was happening. A woman of cheerful manner grinned, her tone making it clear that no malice was involved.

"Why, it's old Percy the pig man and his missis, of course. They're Riding the Stang. All a bit of fun. If taken seriously, it's meant to bring to public attention a woman who beats her husband, to shame her. Does no good in this case, though, as we already know she hits him daily. Of course, she loves the old rascal too, so no harm's done. Piggy Percy took her in when she was homeless, but she still insisted that he had to marry her before she would stay overnight, even as a housekeeper. He always had a fancy for her, so the demand was no real hardship for him."

"Did she love him in return?"

"I doubt it. Appreciation I expect is what she felt at first. Gradually, though, appreciation turned to friendship, friendship to care and care to love. Anyhow, it's the Stang you want to know about. It's a custom not usually known hereabouts. Think it originated in the north somewhere. But, somehow, in years gone by, people heard about it from a traveller or some such and took a liking to it. If we haven't had a Stang in a while, why, we women go about in a gang with willow sticks hitting our men folk until one is called. Daft, but nobody gets hurt. I've ridden it twice.

"And, what of the paper knight?"

"Oh, that's wicked Mordred, who legend says was King Arthur's nephew. The story goes that it had been foretold in that ancient time that Arthur would be killed by a boy born on May Day. So, apparently Arthur cast adrift in boats all the babies born in his kingdom that day. But, Mordred survived and became a treacherous man, only to be killed by Arthur at the Battle of Camlann when he rebelled against his uncle while allied to the invading Saxons. Unfortunately, Arthur was mortally wounded in the mounted combat and died. So, prophecy was realised."

"And you celebrate that?"

"It's only pretend. Just another excuse for a bit of fun, to brighten our festive day."

By chance, or so he said, James arrived back in the village just as Sally began her way on foot towards the Junction, the merriment finished. He had dropped Charlotte back at the estate in Westkings, but had immediately turned around and left again before she had time to object. Sally's disapproval at seeing him was tempered by the thought of the miles of road ahead.

As she climbed on board, her heel stuck in the folding step. At that moment two riders came galloping from around a blind corner. James grabbed her arm with considerable force and pulled her in, leaving her broken shoe behind. Panting, she lifted herself from the floor, where they had both ended in a heap.

"I think you saved my life."

"Don't thank me; it was your purse I was after! Saving your life was a dividend."

They laughed as she took another pair of shoes from her bag. He stopped her throwing the broken shoe away, instead putting the pair under his seat.

"We don't need to talk, Sally, if you feel disinclined. Just enjoy the ride." He stared at the passing fields. "This certainly is a pleasant place." He smiled guiltily. "Sorry, I said I wouldn't speak. I was just thinking . . ."

Despite the small event that had made them sociable, Sally remained a wounded soul in his company, feeling strangely alone and finding nothing in her heart to reawaken any of the passion she had once known for him. Yet, as she bemused, he was much the same man as before, except for his arm. Admittedly, he was a little heavier set, but in general he was the same. Nevertheless, that spark had gone and she was pleased. Now, she could look fully and squarely upon him without fear of kindling any renewed entanglement. And, if truth be told, he too felt more that it was his duty to help her, rather than any genuine attachment or romantic ambition.

The carriage continued at a steady pace. After ten minutes, he could take the silence no longer.

"I wanted to write to you, but I was mostly drunk and incapable. Of course, that's of the past and most of the time now I'm unhealthily sober. Edmond is doing a fine job with the estate, except when he's out socialising with the beautiful people. Although early days, I think the Elvingtons will survive among the great and the good and it will be all down to the boy."

"I'm relieved to hear that," she answered.

"I can't understand why I don't provoke a little more interest in your son?"

She looked down at her hands, only raising her head after some seconds of thought, the slightest tremble to her lips.

"Because, he's not my son in any real sense. Oh, I gave birth to him, but that's where I ended as a mother and you and Charlotte started as his parents. It's time that can't be recaptured and, thereby, shouldn't be recalled. I would do him a disservice if he knew. No, he's so much better off not knowing and I'm free to live unloved again." The sincerity in her face, in her voice, moved him greatly. There was absolutely no self-pity, just a gentle acceptance of the facts. She continued. "Maybe, one day soon, I will have a reason for living. Until I find out what it is, I must survive day to day, keeping my own company and not dwelling on the lost past."

"Does that include forgetting that husband of yours?"

"Of course not! And nor shall I ever forget Edmond. I meant that no good can come from dwelling on things that can never be revisited. I sometimes find, when sitting alone, that I think more than ever of my parents who used to give me cuddles and cake on my birthday. If only I could return to those secure days. If only I had appreciated them at the time. I can't even remember them ending. What happened to my life that I should end like this?"

James said nothing. She had made him think of his own violent past with Charlotte, days that were irretrievable and marked by pain of conscience. Nothing could erase those bad days, but he could try to make the future better for everyone dear to him.

"And your purse, dear Sally, is it wanting or full?"

"It is, as it is. I don't wish to tell you, as my life is so entirely separate from yours. I won't look favourably at your interest, though no-doubt kindly meant. I ignore from now on any conversation of a personal nature, regarding as proper only that of a general type."

"Well, that's me put in my place, along with my heartfelt wish to know that you're provided for. I would do the same for a milkmaid formerly employed, if down on her luck. You know, Sally, you have a stubborn pride that's not necessarily beneficial to your wellbeing, but reminds me greatly of a precious gem I once knew."

"You mean Christabel, don't you?"

He nodded.

"Of her, I *will* talk, if you wish. She intrigues me. It must only be twenty years or less since she was born. And your wife said she is dead. How can that be?"

"Actually, with respect, she's someone *I* can't speak of, other than to say that I wronged her greatly when, in essence, I was trying to hurt only Charlotte. I failed in every manner to save her. If I'm honest with myself, I'm haunted by Christabel's memory. You must believe that I didn't know who she was when she first came back to my home as a fully grown young woman. I hadn't seen her since she was a babe in arms and was given up by Charlotte, at my insistence, into the permanent care of her rogue father who was responsible for wronging my marriage. All those years later, and not knowing her from 'Adam', I had made fun of her while she worked rough for me in the fields, just as her father had before her. But, she withstood it with a graciousness unbefitting her position in life. When I was finally told who she was, by Charlotte no less, who had been as surprised as myself in discovering the truth but had held the secret for fear of my temper, it was too late to make amends and too late for Edmond. She had left."

"For Edmond? I don't understand. She must've been a long-lost half-sister to the boy."

"That's the rub. Edmond was my son with you, and Christabel was Charlotte's daughter with a fieldworker. There were no blood ties between them at all. But, Charlotte and I were foolish when, all those years later, the two youngsters showed a fondness for each other in their ignorance of the state of things, having met merely by some accident of chance. Both were entirely unaware of any linked family lineage, and we left it that way for too long. Indeed, Edmond still knows nothing of it. You see, in our complicity to protect Edmond, who Charlotte and I had nurtured together throughout the years into manhood, we ignored the needs of the girl we hardly knew at all, although of Charlotte's womb."

"You didn't enquire of her during her formative years?"

"Not to any extent. As far as I was concerned, I had provided a stable home life for her in Shalhurn, and the land needed to support her, and that was an end to the matter. Charlotte was not permitted to know anything of her life or whereabouts. Matters were handled by our solicitors."

"The good Sir Schofield?"

"Exactly. For years we remained in happy ignorance of Christabel's fate and were content in that nescience. But, in so doing, we didn't understand anything of her desperate plight. Not until it was too late did I discover the unpalatable fact that she had been turned off the rented acres following her father's death, or even that he had died. Indeed, I only found out what had happened when I realised the rent I had been paying on their behalf was no longer being collected. You see, I had already salvaged my conscience by providing that land in the first instance and wanted no more contact with any of the Meres. In the event, as I later discovered, I had done far too little to protect her. Then she appeared in Westkings, unannounced. For whatever reason, she eventually left the estate again with little warning, travelling alone and on foot and we could do nothing more to help her, although by then Charlotte and I were agreed to do so." He sighed. "Now, having relived a time that pains me, I can say no more. It's a big hurt and a memory that I'm cursed to live with for all my remaining days. So, as I said, like you with Edmond, Charlotte and I hadn't seen Christabel between being a baby and a young adult. That's how I know you surely must want to see Edmond now, before it's too late."

"Not so," she insisted, gazing out of the window in defiance of the suggestion.

"Why, for pity's sake?"

She turned with forceful expression. "Because Christabel was poor and needed help in her young life. She needed a help up. Edmond is rich in comparison and I would only drag him down. That's the difference, which I see all too clearly." She turned once more to the window. "We will talk no more on any subject."

For the remainder of the journey to Glastonbury, Sally was as good as her word. James was merely awkwardly compliant to her wish. On the outskirts of the place, where the high Tor dominated the view to the left and the ruined abbey lay ahead, Sally asked for the carriage to stop. She alighted with her bag at Market Place, where a spired market cross stood ringed by iron railings. James, who had stepped onto the road to help Sally down, again offered her a few gold coins. They were refused.

"Look, take this." He scribbled a few words on a scrap of paper.

"What is it?"

"Not much, but it may help."

He watched as she put the paper in her purse without reading it and walked away up the small incline to the shops. As the carriage turned, Sally listened for the sound of retreating hooves before chancing one backward glance. Now free of him, she opened her purse and withdrew the note.

CHAPTER 5

The mystical Isle laid bare

To Sally's surprise, the little scrap of paper merely held names and the start of an address. There was no accompanying explanation, just the words *Ella and Ernest Browning at 'Little Thatch'*.

After a number of enquiries and the passing of an hour and a half, Sally found herself at 'Little Thatch', although, for all to see, the house of that name was neither little nor thatched. She knocked. The door opened to a woman of about her own age, who strangely invited her in before she had any chance of explanation.

Inside, she was led to a large and pleasant room that was full of talk, there being several ladies and just two men casually dressed among a dozen or more officers from the West Somerset Yeomanry, one civilian being James. He bowed his head slightly towards her. She responded, puzzled but not altogether surprised at seeing him again so soon.

James turned away, finishing his drink alone as Ernest

made his apologies and marched over with hand outstretched. Ella introduced Sally to her husband, but allowed no further conversation before guiding Sally into an adjoining room, where the doors were closed behind them. They sat. There was a bang as the front door slammed and James left the house. Sally could see him walking past the window. Ella followed her stare.

"I was once James' bit of business in Glastonbury, nearly twenty years ago."

"Good gracious!" was Sally's immediate reaction to such bluntness, but she recovered quickly. "So, he was straying before he met me. In fact, now I think on it, he must have been on his way to you when he took me instead! I remember him saying something about going to Glastonbury."

Ella could tell that Sally was more than a little offended and dropped her accompanying smile. "You shouldn't look surprised, my dear. Once a man like James has had a mistress, he's bound to have others. It's as natural for some men as going to work. If anyone should be put out, that person should be me. I was the one left in the lurch that day without so much as a by-your-leave."

"You speak as if you're condoning him for having multiple affairs. What about a woman's lot in this intrigue, this choice of lifestyle?"

"Oh, come now. You don't need me to answer that. Our gender can't have lovers and that's an end to it, or so it must appear publicly. Except that, of course, for every man straying there has to be a responsive woman. In Glastonbury, that woman was me. Somewhere else it was you."

Sally was shocked. "I didn't say . . ."

"No need to, dear. I know much more than you think. James and I remain the closest of acquaintances. My dear Ernest would have a heart attack if he knew my past, and I do mean *past*."

"I shouldn't wonder," was Sally's only reply.

"Anyway, you haven't come to talk about James, although you should know he came here just before you, but only to tell me of your likely arrival and why. And, much happiness you have brought to me."

"How so?" she asked.

"Why, my little cherubs need someone to look after them, as a nursery nurse, and you come recommended."

"A nursery nurse? Surely he told you I'm a teacher?"

"Nursery nurse, teacher, what's the difference? In either position you're responsible for children, though mine sometimes vex me to a point that I believe them not to be of earthly creation. Oh, I can see from your face you think I'm joking. Well, maybe I overstate the case, but they're no angels of Wessex, more like gremlins of Glastonbury! Do I have your agreement?"

"To what, pray?"

"To look after them, of course. You are recommended by James and that is reference enough for me. Anyway, we need you as much as I think you need work. What's your answer?"

"My answer is, yes, and thank you!"

While arrangements were put in hand and a shabby spare room hastily redecorated in preparation for the purchase of a new bed, Sally was billeted at The Planet, an inn a little way from the high street, where she was to remain for ten days.

Then, on Sunday week, she was to take her belongings to 'Little Thatch' and accompany the family to church.

During this vacant time, Sally acquainted herself with Glastonbury, while also receiving a visit from Ella on the first day. This visit was duly returned on the second, providing an opportunity to look around the house and take tea together. Sally's pleasing ways, soft tone and obvious accomplishments quickly endeared themselves to Ella, although Sally found Ernest as vexatious and intolerable as Ella had described her own children to be and hardly worth speaking to.

"Once you are in our employ and live with us, you will have to be called Miss Ayres and I am to be Ma'am or Mrs Browning to you, as Ernest here will be Mr Browning or Sir. Thinking upon it, you might as well begin now. That, you must agree, is only proper between a mistress and her employee."

Sally agreed.

"Good. In the meantime, you must tell me woman to woman if James still admires you. It's generally evident in his care for your welfare that he must."

Sally considered a reply. "I believe you've misread the situation, Mrs Browning, and assert feelings that no longer exist. I believe him to be kind, that's all. I do not see in him any false pride that would cause him not to speak his mind or act differently from his nature."

"His pride has always been of wonderment to me. If ever there was a man who had cause to carry pride before him, that man should be James. He has a beautiful home and estate, and he treats his field-hands well, even joining them for hard labour when he was younger. Yet, he maintained such respect and dignity among them. It's a rare ability indeed. Oh, I know he's had his moments with Charlotte Elvington, but, then, I see he had reason, even if he's now in self-denial."

"I agree with that," stammered Earnest through a mouthful of scone and cream. "If I was as rich as him, I would let the world know of me and be damned at the consequences. And, as to that wife of his, why, she's as hard as nails and has an ego to match since she and Edmond began hosting grand balls at the manor. She has pride and isn't afraid to show it."

"I believe you to be wrong, Ernest," added Ella, wiping crumbs from his chin with a napkin. "For Charlotte demonstrates vanity, not pride." She turned to Sally. "You see, my dear, for someone of great achievement, pride is an acceptable consequence if held at a moderate level as not to offend or oppress others. It is even understandable and mustn't be seen as a vice. I'm thinking that a person's level of pride must equate to their level of achievement, other than when it is pride in another, say for a child. But, even then a pitfall is present, for if pride in another person is made obvious to those about in general, then again it has to be earned by the recipient and not merely the false boasting of a doting parent. No, Charlotte has vanity. My Ernest, here, on the other hand, remains a moderate soul and someone I find little cause to boast about. Isn't that correct, dear?"

He nodded obediently through bites of rich Dundee cake, now that the last of the scones at been eaten.

During a solitary walk on the first Sunday in Glastonbury, Sally passed little groups of people making their way to and from the churches of St Benedict's and St John's, prompting her thoughts to occasionally and unexpectedly return to James, wondering what he was doing at that moment and whether he might be in the company of Edmond. But, there being so much to see and interesting places to visit, such considerations were generally fleeting. Nonetheless, she found herself staring sideways into the distance as she stopped to look into the windows of closed shops, always finding nothing of him but with a feeling of being followed.

It was on the fourth day of her sojourn at The Planet that Sally felt loneliness for the first time and more than a little surprise and disappointment at not yet having met her future charges, the Browning children. Then, as she prepared for another outing, there came a knock at the door. She opened it to find a small boy and girl holding hands.

"Hello, I'm This and he's That," said the pretty little girl politely.

The boy pulled off his cap. "Miss and Master Browning, she means."

"Is your mother with you?" enquired Sally, looking past them along the corridor.

"She's outside with Father. We aren't allowed to stay because of the market. Mother said we were to introduce ourselves." They turned to leave.

"Before you go, what are your real names?"

"I'm Esme and he's Edward, but everyone calls us This and That."

"Why, pray?"

"Because Mother found it hard to cope with twins when we were very small. So, when we were fed and cleaned, she would say to Father *you do this one and I'll do that*. For a long time we thought they were our names. Goodbye."

With The Planet sited along a side street, Sally had been unaware of the preparations taking place for a special post-Christmas annual grand market, postponed for the first time in living memory from the previous December because of a cholera scare. The town had previously been subjected to a cholera epidemic in 1866, due to the appalling state of the sewers and the contamination of water supplies. The virulence of the disease had taken the town authorities by surprise, yet their subsequent actions to prevent future outbreaks and improve the over-crowded, damp and poorly ventilated living conditions of the poorest of the poor in their cottages that might also help ward-off consumption, pneumonia, scarlet fever and diphtheria, had fallen woefully short of requirements. Indeed, a good deal of the consequential improvements had been privately funded, some by enlightened landowners who had only recently finished laying pipes to farms and cottages under their patronage.

In reviewing the causes of the epidemic, it had been found that a number of sewers actually ran below the floors of houses. Dramatically, it had also been discovered that water collected by the poor from a handful of public conduits fed by springs and four well-pumps sited in the town included one or two already known to have been unsafe for human use. Even some private wells were situated next to outside toilets, allowing contamination of the drinking water.

With memories of 1866, when the streets and market squares had been doused with carbolic acid and chloride of lime in the hope of containing the spread, and the evening sky illuminated by blazing pitch and tar against airborne disease, it had been an easy decision to postpone the December event. Equally vivid was the memory of cholera sufferers themselves, passing watery diarrhoea and vomit, while writhing in acute pain from cramps.

But, as quickly discovered, the new scare had been a false alarm. Nevertheless, the grand market had been rescheduled for Spring, to fit in the calendar between normal monthly market days. Of course, health reasons alone had not caused postponement. It had been widely reported in the press of 1866 that the Glastonbury Fair immediately following the epidemic had been a resounding flop, as the many thousands of dealers, farmers and public who normally attended simply stayed away in their masses, despite all attempts to hush-up the extent of the cholera outbreak. And so, after due deliberation by local businessmen and the town authorities, it had seemed the lesser of evils to take no chances where money was concerned and delay the event.

With May upon them, the grand market was at last in full swing and very well attended. Cattle were gathered in large number, but these were in visibly poor general condition due to the harsh winter. Despite this, buyers outnumbered the sellers and so the animals were fetching good prices.

Particular interest fell upon an auction held by the Featherstone brothers. They offered a brood sow, four dairy cows in calf and suited to milking, twelve bee skeps of twisted straw, four fifty-gallon tubs for turning surplus milk into cheese, a wooden 'follower' to imprint an elaborate design into each truckle of cheese made, four lots of twenty apple saplings for cider orchards and a cider press that had to be collected by the buyer.

Elsewhere, the thoroughfares were bustling with local town folk and those from the surrounding villages, enjoying the festive occasion. Merchandise, stalls and exhibitions were abundant, seemingly occupying every available nook and cranny. Refreshments were the dominion of the Temperance Society, and the Glastonbury Friendly and Benefit Society. The Temperance ladies, dressed in white, preached abstinence with every non-alcoholic libation offered, while the men of the Friendly Society handed out drinks and notices while standing beneath banners advertising their own Feast Day procession and lunch on the last Thursday of the month. Elsewhere, oysters were among the treats offered as ready snacks.

By the time Sally left the inn, Magdalene Street itself had become a sheep market, with pens blocking the road. At Market Place and along High Street, pigs and more sheep were penned to the west side, keeping the pavement clear for walkers, with larger beasts to the east, behind railings. The centre of High Street echoed to the trotting of horses being traded.

Before a much-anticipated three-shilling festive lunch at an inn for ticket-holders only, the Town Hall became the venue for the distribution of annual cash premiums, intended to encourage hard work, long service and good behaviour among agricultural labourers and domestic servants. A few additional cash prizes of several shillings to two pounds were to follow for the best show of potatoes, parsnips, onions and carrots grown in allotments, and for the best fat pig reared on a smallholding.

For those low-wage winners, the months of unexpected delay had been worthwhile, that is with the exception of one labourer who had been given a silver tankard valued at four pounds for bringing up the largest number of children to an age of ten years without parochial relief. He grumbled at not being offered the cash equivalent. At least, having been distinguished with a premium, he was entitled to a free lunch.

His grievances were duly noted, but it was pointed out by the committee that premiums were not given as rewards for lives of virtue and sobriety, which should be expected, but as expressions of goodwill on the part of the benefactors. Indeed, in addition to maintaining good character and loyal service, the awards were aimed at encouraging a good relationship between employer and employed, and between the poor and the better off. All these characteristics, it was said, favoured the British in their affairs and were the envy of other non-English speaking nations across the sea.

As the sun became lost below the distant horizon and the afternoon brightness gave way to the first signs of twilight, Sally made her way through the thinning crowds and back to The Planet, where a hearty meal awaited. She had enjoyed the day, the more so for being unexpected in nature.

On her way back she had seen public notices advertising a large Circus with one-hundred horses and bare-back riders, acrobats, jugglers, clowns and contortionists, followed by the band of the 10th Somerset Volunteer Rifle Corps and fireworks. Although tempted to purchase a ticket for the following day, she had decided not to spend the one shilling entrance fee. Later that evening, while sitting at the dining table for a late supper, she recounted her day to the landlord.

"The day I recall as being special for entertainment was two years back, at the Assembly Rooms," he replied, with more than a little pleasure in his voice. "If you'll permit me, I'll sit with you and tell of it?"

She bade him take a chair.

"I've never seen anything like it, before or since. I can't say I've any liking for the disabilities of others, but if the entertainer makes much of his own afflictions as part of his act and makes a goodly living from it, I suppose I'm in no position to feel uncomfortable."

Sally was intrigued and asked him to continue.

"It was February in the year 1881. I can remember as if t'were yesterday. I was sitting in the sixpenny Third Seats when this little fellow came out dressed as a military General. He was perfectly formed, but in complete miniature, not a dwarf you understand, but a proper little gent the size of a sparrow. As God is my witness, he could only have been two feet tall and yet a fully-grown adult. He was introduced as General Tom Thumb, the smallest man in the world and a proper jester to boot. With him was Commodore Knott, just thirty-two inches high, can you believe. Together, they paraded in a miniature Brougham four-wheel carriage, pulled by goats."

"I'm not sure I would like that," remarked Sally once he had finished. "It all seems a bit cruel."

"Not a bit of it. I only wish I had his money, though kept in the pockets of trousers with longer legs." He laughed. "Anyway, what will you do for the rest of your stay?"

She really had no idea and said so.

"Then why not make yourself known to one of our schools hereabouts. I'm sure you could be useful to them on a temporary and voluntary basis."

"I might," she added with renewed enthusiasm.

"Just one stumbling block. As church schools, you will need to be dedicated to the church, or the governors will prevent it."

It was fortunate indeed that one governor was discovered to be no other person than Ernest Browning. When a note was hurriedly dispatched to 'Little Thatch' informing him of her intention, a letter was quickly returned giving his complete approval without need for the whole committee to know, due to her teaching credentials. Apparently, a teacher had recently left following a school report by an Attendance Officer, who had singled her out as 'wanting in spirit', the warning notice being sufficiently damning to send her packing, leaving the staff below required levels.

Sally read the reply with glee, wishing the contact had also offered another invitation to the house. As it turned out, the school of his connection was not that attended by his own children.

The school for ninety young pupils was found to be fairly close to a church bearing the same name, reached by a narrow pathway that eventually led on to open fields beyond. It was a dark affair, with thick stone walls and high mullion windows to prevent the children being distracted by events outside.

The inside was divided into two large rooms, with cupboards holding books sited around the walls. Ceilings took the high pitched roof-line, thinly coated with lime plaster. Just four black stoves fed with peat blocks provided heating, which went out if the wind blew from the wrong direction. In this way, there remained a damp and cold atmosphere until Summer brought natural warmth, when the stone walls would provide a welcome coolness. The younger children sat in long rows on hinged wooden seats that were carried on iron frames, with narrow working tops above. Older children in the second classroom had slightly higher seats and larger tops for their slates and chalk.

Each day started with a three-quarter of an hour scripture lesson, and from the outset Sally was instructed to take part. She found this simple and much to her liking. The prayers on her first day included one for a former pupil named Leonard Pope, who had recently left at the age of eleven having attained Standard IV in reading, writing and arithmetic, including a basic understanding of long-division. Having been given his Labour Certificate, he had gone straight into fieldwork, where he had caught his fingers in the workings of a chaff cutter, slicing three clean off. Another prayer went out to the seven children who were obliged to remain at home with ringworm.

The noise once general teaching began was uninterrupted. Children had been divided into smaller groups within each open classroom, and the chanting of times tables, reading from books, instruction on needlecraft, singing, the scraping of slates and more became a cacophony of discordant sounds. Yet, despite the hubbub, each teacher continued as if alone, unaware of any distraction caused by another. Silence was only visited on the proceedings when the bell rang for a break, or during the occasional inspection by the vicar, who would give encouragement in all things or chastise a girl for having poor deportment, whereby a wooden foot-stock would be fetched to force her to stand with toes pointing outward. In this obedient chaos, the next few days passed quickly for Sally.

Then, one morning, when she had been assigned playground duty, a huge roar of laughter pierced the air. She ran to the source, close to the boys' and girls' partition toilets where each had a wooden plank with a suitable-sized hole cut into it. Waste dropped into forked peat. Close by, the boys causing the uproar stood in a huddle, using a separate latrine and laughing while relieving themselves. Urine from the latrine ran out into a soak-away filled with peat, there being no drains.

"What's all the commotion?" barked Sally, staring among the innocent-faced children and looking for a volunteer.

The tiniest boy was pushed forward. "It's Pee Man Duckett, Miss," he said with a red face, knowing his friends would be giggling behind. "He comes once a week."

"And?"

"He wheelbarrows out the soiled peat and poo, Miss, and replaces it with fresh peat. Then he takes the smelly stuff to his vegetable allotment as manure"

"And?"

"Well, Miss, he didn't shovel it up properly today and he slipped backwards into the soak-away. He had overfilled his barrow too, Miss, and it tipped on top of him."

Sally smiled gently at the conjured picture. "Is that what I can smell?"

"Yes Miss. He's just gone. He's very wet and pongs rather a lot!"

"What about the mess he's left behind?"

"He's left his broom, Miss. I think he'll come back to clean it up."

Sally patted the boy on the head and said that she would add a good-conduct star to his record for coming forward. There were groans from behind.

All too soon Friday afternoon came and her short time at the school ended. She had spent most of that day under a cloud of concern for three young boys from one family who, she knew from the register, were regular in their attendance but had been absent now for three days. She just had to check on them. Accordingly, after the bell had rung out, she walked hurriedly to their two-bedroom cottage on the edge of town.

The children's mother, burdened with other people's laundry to supplement the family income, directed her to various parts of the smallholding where the children could be found.

"Don't hold 'em up, mind," was her parting comment.

The youngest, aged just six, was busy collecting and chopping firewood, while his brother of seven had finished attending the poultry and was now watching over a small number of dairy cows grazing in the only field owned outright by the family, the remaining acreage and the cottage itself being rented. The eldest brother, a boy rather large for his age, led a horse over a field of furrows, the sandals he wore borrowed from his mother and now caked in mud despite the circular plates under the soles to elevate his feet. She waved as he struggled with the beast.

Satisfied of their healthy state, Sally strolled back to the cottage. "You have three bright boys, Mrs Millar, who really should be at school."

"And then, pray, who would help Mr Millar, who is sick and taken to his bed?"

"But their education? Don't you think they might have better prospects by achieving the required Standards?"

"And do what, when they leave with Standards? Go to work in Street at Cyrus & James Clark's shoe factory instead of the land? What would happen to me and Fred? We couldn't keep the farm going without help. It would make us homeless, with no rent money and no food for our bellies."

"But the boys would support you, surely. It would be good work and reliable income."

"Until they married or moved away, independent in income from our acres. We wouldn't try to stop them getting on, bless me no, but it would be the death of Fred and I'd finish in an almshouse for poor widows. Is that what you want for us? That's what happens when the land gives up its hold on the young."

Sally couldn't argue with the logic of the case and gave her apologies. Perhaps she had been too narrow minded in her belief in education above all else. For the poor in agriculture, reliant on free or cheap labour to scratch even a basic living, such high-minded values were not necessarily appropriate. She had to admit to herself that she was wearing a pair of Clark's laced boots, which lived up to the reputation of making walking a pleasure. As promised to her on purchase, they had not deformed her feet or caused corns and bunions because of the attention paid to correct fitting and size. Yet, she had noticed the footwear of the Millar family and it was hand-me-down and mended, with no concern for comfort and style and little worry for size either.

The experience of her visit was liberating and more than a bit humbling. Yes, it was decided in her mind. On Saturday, the day before she would join the Browning family, she would see if she could be of any help to the Millars, careful not to appear patronizing. Maybe, if Mr Millar was feeling better, she could ask to be allowed to have a short time with the boys to show them what they had missed at school, while taking along a basket of food to enjoy with the family and an old pair of her everyday shoes for Mrs Millar.

As she lay in bed that night, Sally reflected on her first days in Glastonbury, that place supposedly of legend and great mysteries. The days had laid bare such preconceptions, exposed by the legitimate mortality of man and the precious thread of life that so many of the poor had such a tenuous grip on.

It was all very well for the Government of the great British Empire and Queen Victoria herself to express grave concern for the poor in the slums of London, when those in the countryside died in equally torrid ways from foul water, chronic disease and starvation. What she now realised was that any person removed from poverty by their social standing could not truly be aware of the depth of despair many families felt daily. Or, if they became aware, they were still able to shut themselves from it and live a galaxy apart. It was wrong, unenlightened and corrupt, and she resolved to do something about it.

CHAPTER 6

A quest for understanding

At this time, many miles away in London, Russell Thackeray waited impatiently for David Burgerhout, a Dutch academic living in England who had been called to the offices of the Board of Trade. As an expert on Hebrew history, he had been summoned on many occasions to assist the Government with timely advice. Now, he was needed again.

Burgerhout travelled to London using an economy ticket bought under the newly instituted Cheap Trains Act, intended mainly for workmen but, nevertheless, available to all. After all, he gave his time and advice free of charge, but claimed expenses from a prudent government.

He arrived at Baker Street on the Metropolitan Railway as his first ever experience of the Underground, relieved to have arrived safely. He had feared for his life, expecting the steam trains to offer up a suffocating smoke with no place to vent. The actual experience had been very different. For public safety, the gas-lit engine had exhausted its smoke and steam into a rear tank through a great many pipes, leaving the platform either side of the twin railway tracks full of healthy people. Much to his delight, the station tunnel was so large as to render the whole experience of travelling like a worm to be intoxicating and not in the least claustrophobic, although still better to be over with. From there, he engaged a horse-omnibus for most of the remaining journey.

Burgerhout was no young man for such new experiences. Indeed, he could be said to be on the cusp of late middle age and old age, with the skin texture of extreme old age. Nevertheless, although feeling light-headed and more than a little dizzy, he walked determinedly towards his final destination, needing to divert only once inside the building to a washroom near the far end of the carpeted corridor, to freshen up and catch his breath. Splashing cold water onto his hands and face, he pulled out his handkerchief. The note beckoning him to London fell onto the floor. He unfolded it. It said nothing he had not already read several times before. It intrigued him. He was irresistibly drawn to the words *Capel Seion*, which he had circled in ink, transfixed by their significance that only a very few people understood.

Thackeray stood as he entered, thanking him for coming and offering a cup of tea.

"How could I resist your letter," beamed Burgerhout, taking Thackeray's hand and shaking it vigorously. "You intrigue me, dangling so little that offers so much."

"We could think of nobody else. Above all, you are known by the department to be trustworthy, if you understand my meaning."

"Discretion, of course. But why here, at the Board of Trade of all places? It's not where we've met before."

"It was Fairbourne's idea, to maintain secrecy from the public and press. Nobody is in the slightest bit interested in what the Board of Trade gets up to, unlike the Foreign Office, Ministry of War and so on. It's seen only as the boring side of government. Ideal place for us to establish our headquarters, don't you agree?"

He replied that he thought it was. "You know," he continued, "I wouldn't be here at all in a government building if it wasn't for Benjamin Disraeli. He was responsible for abolishing the law that kept Jews out of Parliament thirty or more years ago. Without such acceptance of our culture, you wouldn't ever get my co-operation. It's amazing how the tables have turned, now that you need us."

"Wasn't Disraeli a Jew? I thought he was," enquired Thackeray.

"To that I answer, no and yes! He was by blood, but his father had embraced Christianity when young Benjamin was nine years old. Without such foresight, his son wouldn't have entered the House of Commons in the first place, let alone become Chancellor of the Exchequer and Leader of the House. Incidentally, these dual roles made him the first person since Pitt to be both without first having held any previous government office. Personally, I find it interesting that Lord Derby's cabinet had only two members who had held any office at all! Such foolishness, such inexperience. Little wonder there followed such chaos, if politics are run like a club for novices."

Thackeray became noticeably edgy.

"What you say is very interesting, but discussion for another time, I think."

"Do you know," said Burgerhout, taking absolutely no notice of Thackeray's suggestion, "Disraeli once told me, me of all people, that he was descended from a distinguished family of Jews in Spain who had made a fortune centuries before as merchants operating out of Venice. Ha! He couldn't fool me, not for a minute. That story could no more stand-up to investigation than the claim that his forebears had made up their own name."

"Does it matter?" asked Thackeray, ready to get on with more important issues.

"I can tell you, there was no mistaking his Jewish ancestry, especially as a young man when he had all that curly jet black hair and dark eyes. I've missed the old rascal the last couple of years. Laughing to the grave, he was. Do you know what his last words were?"

"No," replied Thackeray in submission.

"Gravely ill with bronchitis for the last time, and in reply to being asked whether he would like Queen Victoria to pay a visit, he smiled back and said '*No, it is better not. She would only ask me to take a message to Albert!*' Such a joker. Maybe Prince Albert appreciated the humour from heaven." He grinned in lingering thought. "Anyway, enough of that. You waste too much of my time. If you want to know more about his views, read his novel *Sybil*, which portrays the fulfilment of Judaism via the Anglican Church in a society torn between the have and have-nots. Such foolishness, such inexperience."

Thackeray's gaze upon him was now more through admiration than irritation. This man was, indeed, learned and should be left to ramble.

"I asked you to come because we have a bit of a flap on

here. I can't be specific about it, unfortunately, but what I can say is that Fairbourne and I are taking the view that to make sense of the current problem, we first need to brush up on our history to understand the ancient times and events from which it originates. See if we can establish genuine links between ancient people and present events, times past and historic places, to assess the likelihood of any of it being real."

"I'm intrigued! I understand nothing you say, but I'll do what I can."

"Tell me, what do you understand by Capel Seion?"

"Ha, straight to the point, I like that. So rare among Gentiles. Before I do, tell me first how you come by the name?"

"Quite by accident, as a matter of fact. As usual, it was my assistant. He was researching Avalon, Glastonbury as it is now and, of course, the Abbey is foremost in the place. Well, we all know Fairbourne to be thorough, and so a paper chase began. Certain events that supposedly took place on the Glastonbury site have direct links to other parts of the country, most notably with Wales. Once he started looking for connections to medieval legend, lo and behold, Capel Seion crawled out of the woodwork."

"Has he found something?"

"Such as?"

"Come on, don't treat me like an idiot. If you link Glastonbury with Capel Seion, it can only mean one or two things. The cup of Jesus, known to Christians as The Holy Grail, or persons with British connections to it."

"I can promise you we've found nothing. It is answers we want."

"Oh! Is that all? I thought you had discovered something new that would interest me."

"You should've known I wouldn't presume to teach you anything, my dear fellow. You're the expert."

"That, of course, is true. But still . . . Oh well! Fairbourne is quite a man. He sticks his nose into corners others leave alone. If he worked for me, I'd be at the end of my quest."

"Which is?"

"Never mind. That's my personal business."

"Now I think of it, how come you mention The Holy Grail?"

"I didn't. I called it the cup Jesus may have used, known to Christians as the Grail. Why shouldn't I?"

"Because you're Jewish. You don't believe Jesus was the Son of God. Therefore, without the Resurrection, which is the cornerstone of Christianity, the Last Supper when The Holy Grail was used would be meaningless."

"You're quite right, of course, my friend. But should that mean that I wouldn't know anything about it, academically, from the viewpoint of trying to understand other faiths and their beliefs?"

"I suppose not."

"Of course not. You know a little of what I believe, and I offer the same courtesy in return. However, most Jews believe Jesus was a prophet. I share that view. We too believe he was executed, but then we part company again. We believe that his body was hidden and buried. I won't argue the theological point. We do not seek converts to our faith, but neither do we agree with many of the views expressed by Jews who convert to Christianity."

"Jews don't try to convert others? Christians have spent hundreds of years trying to spread their faith."

"And, look where it's got you. You see, we have our own written Law, but we are still taught that God will look kindly on the righteous of all peoples and find a place for them in the world to come, in the Royal House of David, when the Messiah appears. To you Jesus was Christ, the Son of God. To us, the anointed one of God, the Messiah, is still to come."

"I understand, I think. So, I repeat, why do you show interest in the Grail of the Christian faith?"

"And I repeat that I call it merely the cup Jesus used, and leave the full term 'The Holy Grail' to Christians who view its importance differently. However, in answer to your question, it is because a scholastic life is my world. I am not a practising Jew in any truly devout sense, but I keep the faith in my heart. Academia and faith can be difficult bedfellows. So, I sometimes think outside of the usual. I take the attitude that if Jesus existed, and we all accept that he did, then the cup used during his last meal probably existed too. The rub comes when its importance is debated. As an academic, I'm fascinated by it. As a Jew, it merely holds interest as an artefact of history, a vessel of a prophet."

"I see. Can we progress to Capel Seion?"

"Fairbourne is a remarkable researcher. He's now one of the few people to fully appreciate the interconnection between Wessex and Wales, both in fact and legend. I congratulate him. However, sticking to the matter in hand, Seion . . ."

Before he had time to continue, there was a knock on the door. A tray of tea was brought in and he took a cup, waiting until the clerk left before placing it on the table. He opened his case.

". . . Seion, a place a few miles east of Aberystwyth, one of several *Capels* in that area of Wales."

"Just so. And?"

"And . . . 'Nanteos' stood there, an early mansion where Cistercian monks from the nearby Strata Florida Abbey fled to at the time of the Reformation in the 16th century. They carried with them something they believed to be a religious treasure for safe keeping. Of course, the elegant mansion there now isn't the same place at all, being built in the eighteenth century."

"Explain Cistercian, if you would. I need to understand everything."

"I think the best description would be the formal meaning, a monastic order dedicated to religious contemplation. Originated in Cîteaux, France, by reformist Benedictines at the close of the 11th century, taking their name from the medieval Latin *Cistercium*.

"Go on."

"The Abbey itself, according to my notes here, dated from Norman times, originally 1164, but shortly after moved to a new site. They had chosen a rugged place, but one entirely suited to their lonely contemplation, in the hills of Tregaron."

"The treasure you mention. Tell me about that."

"It was widely known as the Healing Cup of 'Nanteos'. I can't tell you whether the item taken to 'Nanteos' by the monks was originally whole, but it certainly isn't now."

"A cup?"

"More of a mazer, a wooden drinking bowl, actually."

"The difference being . . ."

"An important one." He raised his tea cup. "A cup may be nothing more than a cup, like this one, or another much older.

A mazer is normally wooden, although sometimes metal to confuse things, and ornamental. If of sufficient historic importance or one used for the Christian sacrament, a mazer could even be elevated to the status of chalice, depending upon its origin and owner. I would expect a metal vessel of this sort used by or held in an abbey to be a chalice, and a wooden vessel from a minor abbey to be a mazer, whatever popular name is given. The word chalice comes from the Latin *Calix*, usually taken to be a goblet with a stem and base or a bowl without handles for holding the consecrated wine of the Eucharist, the Christian sacrament initiated during your so-called Last Supper and in memory of your Christ. You would know it as Holy Communion."

"The blood of Christ?"

"In your faith, yes."

"And you think . . .?"

"I think nothing and I infer nothing. The Cup of 'Nanteos' is an ancient piece of ceremonial mazer, that's what I think because I have no evidence to the contrary, although that opinion has to remain completely open. More importantly, in my view it is most likely to date from somewhere between the 11th and the 16th centuries, nowhere near the right age to be connected in any way to the beginnings of Christianity, as is sometimes claimed for it. However, I should make you aware that a great many people over the centuries have believed it to date from the time of Jesus. That's not my interpretation, but it's valid for others to think. Indeed, so sure were some believers of its healing powers, supplicants chewed off fragments from the rim until it became a mere remnant of the original mazer, as it is today. What is left is, in my opinion, probably no more significant than any religious relic from the Middle Ages. Sorry if that isn't what you wanted to hear."

"So this Priory of Sieon no longer exists?"

"Nor did it ever, as it wasn't a priory. You need to understand the difference between a priory and abbey. A monastery governed by a prior is called a priory. Strata Florida was an abbey, run by an abbot. There's a distinct and vital difference. Moreover, Sieon is the town where the 'Nanteos' mansion was located, not where the monastery stood. You're manipulating the facts to suit a legend."

"One last question, if you don't mind. Tell me, what do you make of the legend of the Predicted Nine? Has it anything to do with people drowning?"

"That old cherry! Arthurian myth and nothing more, with connections to Glastonbury and Wales. An elaboration of a fairy story from the imagination of people like Geoffrey of Monmouth in 1136, the drawings of Dante Gabriel Rossetti and others who together managed to turn a genuine Briton cavalry warrior fighting the Saxons and Picts into a mythical king who undertook imaginary and fantastic adventures. Via Arthur's knights came a search for the Grail itself, in the stories, that is."

"But, what of the Predicted Nine women themselves? You don't tell me!"

"Nine weeping maidens, or weeping queens in Rossetti's painting, led by Morganis, who was related to Arthur, were said to have crewed a barge to carry Arthur's mortally wounded body to Glaston, on the Isle of Avalon, following the Battle of Camlann, so that his wounds might be healed. Needless to say, he died. These mystic women were as real to history as the mischievous Bogeyman. The maidens were Arthur's 'Nine', but when and why the 'Predicted' part came into the legend, I just don't know. I never understood the connection, as the only prediction in most of the medieval tales has always been assumed to involve only Arthur himself, who would rise up again to help his country at a moment of mortal danger. The Predicted Nine legend somehow transferred this visitation to the women, but in what form and by what means was never told, even in stories. The appearance of all nine, or perhaps the last in line, would herald immediate danger. You must understand that even legends become exaggerated with the passing of time."

"How could Arthur ever rise up, when he died in fact and legend? Perhaps the women were needed to fulfil the Arthurian prophecy?"

"And nine 5th or 6th century maidens could? It's all stuff-and-nonsense. We're back to Bogeymen!"

"But the Bogeyman *was* real. Napoleon, wasn't he the Bogeyman of Europe, a name used by parents to scare children to go to bed?"

"Now you waste my time. That really is outside my studies. I graduated with a First in Hebrew and Greek, not witches, wizards and fantasies. I now specialise in Roman to medieval Palestine. If you seek something tangible, like the resting place of what Christians call The Holy Grail, for example, if that's your quest, then I will happily help you out by casting an eye over any new evidences you discover, on the strict understanding that my belief in such an object would be entirely different from yours. In fact, the words Capel Seion brought me here in anticipation of you having stumbled upon something new and of academic interest, believing you wanted to pick my brains. In that, I'm very eager to help if I can. But, if it is Arthurian fantasy that you're interested in, or other such erroneous figures associated with the mythical Round Table and Camalot, I'm very much *not* your man. Truth be told, I too once studied such tales and their relevance to the real warrior, just in case folklore had any basis in historical fact. Word of mouth, and all that. Thankfully, I was able to throw the whole lot out as bunkum. I suggest you do the same."

"I'll note your advice."

"Anyway, what is the British Government's interest in folklore?"

"Oh, just one of several matters we're looking into."

"Goodness knows why. Has it something to do with trade and profit, or land claims?"

"Maybe! Thanks for coming."

"That's it, is it? All this way and returning empty handed."

"You'll be paid for your expenses. But, before you go, answer me one more thing. Specialising in Palestine, how come you know so much about Christian abbeys?"

"Because they're the physical remains of a lost period of historic importance, some having direct connections to the Holy Land and the Semitic people. After all, the Christian faith stems from people of original Jewish origin. Christian relics sometimes display that link, not only because of Joseph of Arimathea, who I wouldn't expect you to know much about, but because of the so-called Holy Crusades in Palestine from 1096. Even you would know about the later Third Crusade against Saladin."

"Of course."

After Burgerhout left, Thackeray instructed Fairbourne to

prepare a short treatise on the Crusades, just in case it turned up anything of relevance.

Some days later, while still sweating on the treatise, Fairbourne came rushing into Thackeray's office, armed with a letter and breathless with anticipation.

"It's from Burgerhout. He says he has given the matter much thought and wants to point us in a different direction. It will save me so much work if we take his advice."

"Couldn't he come here to tell me in person?"

"Apparently not. He didn't like the early train enough to want to do it again and he hasn't received his expenses from last time. Anyway, he has a cold and intends to stay at home."

"*Such foolishness*," commented Thackeray sarcastically. "What does he say?"

"He says that if we are genuine in our wish to find connections between Arthur and abbeys, we should concentrate our enquiries on the 12th century, but not the Third Crusade and Palestine as he mentioned in passing, which are irrelevant to everything you discussed together. We should restrict ourselves to 12th century England."

"That makes sense."

"He intends to provide a list, suggesting that there could be, after all, places of interest to us if we go to Glastonbury ourselves."

"Glastonbury again! Anything more on the prophecy of the Predicted Nine? Has he had a change of heart about that, too?"

"He doesn't mention the Predicted Nine as such, other than to point out that we may have made a fundamental mistake. He suggests we are barking up the wrong tree. He says he had barely given a thought at the time to you mentioning *drowning*, realising only on his way home that it was meant to be a serious question. His belated answer is 'no'. As far as he is concerned, any weeping maidens in that story of pure make-believe were there only to transport King Arthur safely across the water to Avalon. Nobody in the stories drowned on the way to Avalon, of that he's pretty certain. What's more, to prove it's all fiction, he says Arthur would have needed to die in AD474 or thereabouts to match contemporary events that are chronicled. Yet, he says, his death is often written in the fictionalized fable stories as having been in the 6th century. He says such errors are inexcusable for any genuine historian."

"And, you conclude from this?"

"I go along with Burgerhout. We must think afresh. Could it be that our nine 'humans', who claimed to have drowned, but lived, aren't important after all? Perhaps we've allowed ourselves to be misled. Don't you remember what Miss Ayres said in hospital? It wasn't *her* weeping. She was content to drown and believed she had. It was someone else in the water with her who wept, someone not listed as being on board ship. I've had a flash of inspiration, Sir. What if *all* nine real women were accompanied by weeping apparitions as they drowned, then we could surmise that the women in the prediction wouldn't be Ayres, Adams, Lawrence and the others at all, as we supposed, but those 'things' in the water with them."

"For goodness sake, Fairbourne, where's the logic in that?"

"Yes, Sir, I know it sounds improbable. But just suppose I'm right?"

"Even if I went along with it, there'd be absolutely no way of ever knowing."

"Maybe there is. I have an idea. We keep saying weeping women, but Burgerhout made a point of saying the legend is about nine weeping *maidens*. And, remember, Burgerhout has never seen the dark box, which alone proffers some real evidence that might substantiate aspects of the prophecy, although still hearsay. So, in my estimation, it could help to find out if Miss Ayres is a virgin. If she isn't, then she couldn't possibly be a predicted *maiden*."

"Which would mean?"

"That the 'Nine' are either the apparitions in the water, or Miss Ayres isn't one of them after all."

"And how in God's name could we accomplish that?"

"You can leave that to me. I have a plan that's foolproof. Sir, we can still rely on the Contagious Diseases Acts, if we hurry. These allow the police to pick up any woman suspected of prostitution and take her in for medical examination. However, the Acts won't be tolerated for much longer and repeal is in the air. Josephine Butler, who has led the campaign for repeal over two decades, now has the support of the House since it was realised that the figure for men in the armed forces with venereal disease hasn't dropped a jot since the Acts came into law in 1865. It remains a quarter of all servicemen. But, as I say, only if we act quickly can we make use of the Acts."

"But, if she isn't, what then? How would we proceed?"

"I haven't got a clue. Could it be that the self-proclaimed drowned women, including Ayres, were merely the messengers of the dead, the beacons that drew the appearance of weeping maidens, so that the warning would be heard?"

"It's all getting a bit weird."

"Of course it is. We knew from the outset that we might be

dealing with the paranormal. We don't have to believe any of it, just prove to the Government with our findings that the paranormal *doesn't* exist and that England *isn't* headed for catastrophe."

"Did Burgerhout say anything else?"

"Yes. He added as a postscript, *Faith is the substance of things hoped for, the evidence of things not seen.* I looked it up. It comes from Hebrews in the New Testament. As a Jew, he wouldn't be expected to quote that. I can only think he believes the sentiment has some relevance to all faiths."

"What does he mean by it?"

"I can only guess. Maybe he's warning us not to be swayed by the beliefs of others, the medieval monks and so forth."

"Or perhaps that we shouldn't be put off if we can't find hard evidence. I have made my decision, Fairbourne. We must go to Glastonbury and finish the business without delay."

"Burgerhout has pre-empted us! He writes that he knows a good place to stay in Glastonbury, called The Queen's Arms. He will send another letter there, with a list of things to look at."

"Make the arrangements, Fairbourne. By the way, has anyone found Miss Ayres? We must make sure we know where she is at all times and what she's doing."

"My informant tells me she's already in Glastonbury."

"Can he be relied upon?"

"Absolutely."

CHAPTER 7

That sacred place of pilgrimage

Glastonbury, that mystic place of many legends and great deeds, was no disappointment to Thackeray. Both he and Fairbourne had arrived on the Somerset and Dorset Railway, known locally as the 'Slow and Dirty', but were, from that first moment, in awe of the place. It oozed history from every street corner. From High Street that descended in steep fashion to Market Place, every space was occupied, ancient buildings cheek-by-jowl with more recent in-fills. Thackeray lost no time in heading straight for the Abbey, the high Tor standing majestically as a backdrop.

Fairbourne, who was equally anxious to get started, had been ordered to The Queen's Arms in High Street to pick-up Burgerhout's second letter and check them into their rooms. Much to his annoyance, though, his progress was temporarily delayed by a fire that had broken out in the draper's shop next door. A gas lamp had ignited the stock. The volunteer fire brigade, with its base close by, rapidly controlled the outbreak, preventing the flames from spreading beyond the premises.

With precious moments lost, by the time Fairbourne entered the Abbey grounds Thackeray was already sitting on the grass reading a newspaper. Faced with ruins spread over a large area, he had at once realised that he had been simplistic to the point of absurdity. There was nothing here that could be understood merely by standing and looking. The pillars, bits of wall, fallen stone and crypt, all overgrown and with trees breaching the arches, offered no meaning in themselves. All the treasures of the place, and everything else that could be confiscated or auctioned off, had been plundered hundreds of years before to swell King Henry's coffers. Even the leaden roof had been ripped away and melted down, and the doors and locks sold off, leaving just a stone shell exposed to all the elements and finally laid to waste by looters. Yet, despite the devastation, enough of the ornate stonework remained to inspire any onlooker. Thackeray had been suitably struck by the scale of the Abbey, but he needed explanation for what he saw, a reason for looking.

"I said you should wait for me, Sir. I have Burgerhout's new letter. This all makes perfect sense."

Thackeray looked up, bewildered.

"Let's see what he says." He unfolded the letter, which ran to several pages in large handwriting, with a rough drawing at the bottom. "Ah, the building over there, away from the rest of the Abbey, is the Abbey kitchen. Now, where we stand is Lady Chapel. He says this is important for being built in 1186 at *Vetusta Ecclesia*. That means the Old Church, which was destroyed in a great fire two years before construction of Lady Chapel began."

"I knew some of that. The vicar at Cudwick said the same."

Fairbourne sensed impatience. "Right, well let me go on. He says it wasn't originally linked to the rest of the Abbey, but in the 13th century the Galilee Chapel was constructed to connect it to the nave of the Great Church."

"Galilee! That's biblical, from the Holy Land. What does Burgerhout say about that?"

He scanned the pages. "Nothing. Anyway, it seems a crypt was excavated by Abbot Richard Bere in about 1500 and was used as a shrine to Joseph of Arimathea, who is the patron saint of Glastonbury. Oh, and this is interesting. It seems Bere was responsible for the construction of almshouses for ten poor widows, and also for another chapel on the site that wasn't finished before he died in 1524."

"We're not here for a sightseeing holiday, Fairbourne."

"No, Sir. Sorry. Anyway, Burgerhout says that his successor, Richard Whiting, was the last abbot before the dissolution of the monasteries. Glastonbury appears to have been the last surviving abbey in the region, finally pounced on by Thomas Cromwell's Royal Commissioners in September 1539. That poor soul was hanged, alongside two other Glastonbury monks, and all for 11,000 ounces of precious plate and some furniture!"

"An enormous fortune."

"Was it? I wouldn't know."

"Anything nearer to the point in hand, Fairbourne?"

"Oh, my goodness, yes," exclaimed Fairbourne. "In 1191 monks unearthed the bones of a man and women from a deep grave just outside the Abbey walls, in an ancient cemetery, buried inside a coffin cut from a hollowed oak. They believed the bones were the remains of Arthur and his second wife,

Guinevere. Burgerhout says a lock of golden hair from the woman fell to dust when it was touched. He says that disintegration would be expected, as each strand of hair preserved in an air-tight grave can form a hard crust, while the core breaks down completely. The slightest pressure and it would be gone. The monks wouldn't have known how to handle it safely. With the bodies was a lead cross carrying the Latin inscription HIC IACET SEPULTUS INCLYTUS REX ARTURIUS IN INSULA AVALONIA. Wow!"

"We must get a full translation."

"No need, Burgerhout has done the job for us. It means '*Here lies buried the renowned King Arthur in the Isle of Avalon*'. It's our first real connection between the 12th and the 5th to 6th centuries. Surely this means that we must give some thought to all the events of the Middle Ages that could have a bearing, not just bog ourselves down to Arthur's ancient time. After all, that's exactly what Burgerhout suggested. You see how clever he's been? He's given just enough detail for us to decide that for ourselves."

"You mean enough rope to hang ourselves!"

Fairbourne grinned. "Exciting, isn't it!"

"What are you saying, exactly?"

"That, if my schooling doesn't let me down, we must look at the entire period between antiquity and the Renaissance, from AD476 to 1453, and possibly not confine ourselves to Britain. We must look to Europe and, perhaps, beyond."

"Oh dear!" was Thackeray's only reply.

"And there's more!"

"I was afraid of that. Sounds like bloody hard work over a lot of nonsense."

Fairbourne ignored the outburst. "Avalon in Celtic lore was a mysterious fairy island and the meeting place of the dead. A fitting place for Arthur to be taken when dying. We, at last, have a clue. All roads from Joseph and Arthur meet at the Abbey."

"Steady, Fairbourne. You're jumping way ahead of yourself. Burgerhout says the shrine was 'dedicated' to Joseph. I can't see how that helps in the least. Lady Chapel being constructed on the same site as Joseph's Wattle Church is much more significant, except that it has no bearing whatsoever on our weeping women. Tell me, why do we concern ourselves with Joseph at all? I just can't get that clear in my head."

Fairbourne drew a long breath. "You're right, Sir. Burgerhout says much the same further down. He says St John's Church in the town has a huge stained glass window that is also dedicated to Joseph of Arimathea. I was a bit hasty in my enthusiasm. Sorry."

Thackeray put his hand softy on Fairbourne's shoulder. "Listen, we must take this business step by step, or we too will start believing the unbelievable. Let's be entirely rational. If we assemble the facts, a conclusion will show itself. Take my word for it."

He nodded in agreement.

"Let's review what we have. The weeping women, or maidens as Burgerhout calls them, are connected to Arthur's death, although not necessarily to his pledge to assist the country at a time of peril unless we believe the Predicted Nine prophecy. We know Arthur was a real cavalry warrior but probably not a king in the accepted sense. By the way, that needs more research. I don't fully understand any of that period and we should be clearer in our understanding of who Arthur really was, what he got up to, and whether we can glean anything from folklore."

Fairbourne took notes.

"I'm even less clear about Joseph of Arimathea. What *is* he to us? Why does his name keep popping up, when he was alive five centuries before Arthur and has absolutely no connections to the Arthurian ladies."

"Isn't his connection to do with The Holy Grail, which Arthur's knights also sought?"

"No, Fairbourne. That's the trap, and you have fallen straight into it. All that stuff about Arthur's knights searching for the Grail is balderdash. Pure myth. No, I think we should put Joseph out of our minds and concentrate elsewhere. Now, are we finished here?"

Fairbourne looked to the next paragraph. "Burgerhout says Arthur and Guinevere's bones were reburied close by, but were disinterred at the dissolution and lost for ever."

"And the cross?"

"That too was lost in the 17th century, but not before a copy had been made. However, Burgerhout suggests the cross may have been a fake. He thinks it was probably made by the monks who found the original grave in the 12th century, and who placed it in the new grave for later identification. You know, that makes sense. We know it still exists, fake or not. It's in the dark box."

"So, we have finished here."

"Yes, but he says we should also go to a place called Cadbury."

* * *

Elsewhere in Glastonbury, Sally Ayres too was finding the place a trial. On the Saturday evening, the night before she was due to join the Browning family for Sunday church, she received an unexpected invitation. It was from Ella and Ernest, asking whether she would care to join them for a musical evening. Despite being emotionally bruised from visiting the Millars and not feeling in the least sociable, she nevertheless accepted and returned a note to that affect.

When she reached the house later that evening, the door was already open. She stared inside, unsure whether to wait or step forward. The large hallway was bathed in a soft white light from a ring of candles on a circular table, with flowers draped around the candlesticks and half-way up the stems.

She called out in gentle tone, but nobody came. Taking two steps inside, she could hear muffled talk from the far end of the corridor, where a brighter light emerged from the crack of a partially open door. Again, she called out and again nobody came. Realising that she risked being accused of unreliability if she quietly left, she removed her cloak and placed it on an easy chair before heading for the activity. As she reached for the handle, the door swung open. She stepped back.

"My pardon. Did I make you jump," enquired a young gentleman of kind face and quality apparel, barely looking at her as he pulled on his gloves.

"No, Sir. I'm fine," she said, recovering.

"Are you quite sure?"

She said that she was. He nodded, placed a hat on his head and left from the front door.

As she stood looking at the space left by him, a rather large gentleman with a red complexion stepped forward, took her hand and led her in, squeezing her fingers rather too tightly.

"I'm Digby Ellis, by the way. My friends call me Busybody, for sticking my nose into other people's private affairs. You must be my surprise partner for the evening," he joked.

Following a number of polite introductions, Sally extracted herself from Digby and sat by Ella, she being alone as the only other woman in the room.

"Now you know why I sent for you," whispered Ella, looking around. "I have been that bored by them that I was about to retire early to my room. Nothing now can revive me."

"Are all these gentlemen your friends?"

"Goodness, *no*. They are Ernest's acquaintances from the council and a proper stuffy, self-interested bunch they are too. But you miss the point. Didn't you recognise the young man just gone?"

"Of course. He was Edmond Elvington."

"Another reason for asking you here. Call me meddling, but I thought you two should meet again, so I cooked up a plan for his visit. Fortunately, I found he was in town anyway. My good intentions have been foiled by timing, though. Is your heart not stirred?"

Sally turned towards the door. "It is," she said.

By the time Sally's attentions returned to Ella, the hostess had already moved on to other matters.

"I have played thrice on the piano for their entertainment, but they're best pleased when left to drink and talk among themselves, so I shall play and sing no more. But, you must."

"Oh, no, please, I beg of you. I play so little and have such low ability in my voice as to be embarrassed if asked. Please, don't ask!"

"No, my mind is made up. If I'm to be ignored by the men, then you shall interrupt them and break their pleasure. All the better if you are bad."

She stood briskly, clapping her hands. "Your attention please. Miss Ayres, who is charged with bringing This and That into a civilised existence from tomorrow, has agreed to perform." She turned to Sally and smiled. "Pray, let me hold your glass."

The men parted in silent entreaty not to play, exposing the instrument at the far end of the room as they stepped back. As she passed through, each smiled and bowed slightly, but with pained expression.

"What will it be?" asked Ella.

"What would you like?"

"The music is there, my dear. Pick your own."

Sally lifted the lid, leaving the sheets in their pile.

"I will sing this."

She began thumping at the keys, singing a comic number from Gilbert and Sullivan's *The Pirates of Penzance*. She spared nobody from her raucous tones and strange expressions. At its end, the room fell silent. Then, suddenly, after a few seconds, wild clapping and cheering broke out. They shouted for more, gathering around the piano. Next came a song from *Trial by Jury* and a third from *Iolanthe*, the latest operetta, with Sally gesturing as a winged fairy between notes.

As her hands swept across the keys with the flow of a

shuttle on a woollen loom, she caught 'a look' from Ella. The meaning was obvious and her theatricals ceased, completing the song in a softer manner. Then, without a noticeable break, she played straight into a waltz as her finale, with singular elegance of touch. At its end, she closed the lid and rose. Ernest escorted her back to his wife. Sally smiled in the hope of making light of her performance, hoping above all that she still had a job.

"You misled me, Miss Ayres. You play and sing beautifully."

"Thank you, but I feel I don't. I never play in public, other than to the children in my care at school. Pray, would you play once for me?"

"I have no intention of doing so, and if you announce me I shall sack you on the spot. Anyway, it would be futile to try and enliven this lot." She looked past Sally, annoyed at seeing the men noticeably brightened and the party better for it. "No, they don't appreciate our gender."

Sally thought it best to change the subject and enquired about the children. "Shall I see them tonight?"

"They're where they should be, in bed. You'll see them tomorrow."

"I look forward to it."

The ladies smiled to each other, nodded and turned away. Silent seconds passed. Sally searched for something else to talk about.

"Ah, I had a most enlightening experience today. I went to see . . ."

". . . the Millars. Yes, I know. We saw you coming from their cottage on our way back from Chalice Hill."

"That's a place I haven't heard of. What's there, if it's not personal?"

"Why should you? You've only been in Glastonbury five minutes. As a matter of fact a water spring and well are at its base. Ernest goes there to taste the water, which he's sure helps heal his arthritis. Secretly, I think he believes the water inspires him, but I can vouch that it has no such affect!"

"Heal?"

"It's a chalybeate spring. The water is high in salts of iron and has a strong taste. Many people believe it has healing qualities."

"How so?"

"It's symbolism mainly. It used to be known as the Blood Spring, because the water leaves a slight red residue on everything it touches. The water well it feeds was known as St Joseph's Well, after Joseph of Arimathea, who is said to have placed the Chalice from the Last Supper and two bottles containing blood and water from Christ's crucifixion in the hill. Some people think that's why the water runs red, never dries up and remains at a constant temperature. Whether that is believed or not, the place does have a calming atmosphere on everyone who goes there to sit in peace and quiet, or to drink or bathe. It has 'energies' that I can't explain. By and by, the well is now known as Chalice Well, but it has no depth anymore. It is lined with stones taken from the Old Church that was burned down."

"Are there more places of interest in Glastonbury? I'm fascinated to know."

"There are, in plenty, for those who look for themselves."

Ella's reluctance to expand the subject was duly noted.

For the next fifteen minutes the ladies talked a little, drank in sips, but mostly sat quietly in subdued boredom. Amongst so many men, they were not once asked for their opinion on any matters and felt unable to express a view from their seated position, away from the thrust of conversation. Again, Ella's eyes began to flicker with tedium. Sally yawned discreetly. She wanted to go, but felt she should stay for at least another thirty minutes.

"Well, I'm for my room. I can stand this no longer." Ella stood and held out her gloved hand for Sally to touch. "We will meet here tomorrow at ten of the clock. You must stay a while. Don't mind me."

Whilst not a direct command, Sally felt unable to make her excuses and leave as Ella had so elegantly managed before her. With a sigh, she sat back. She pretended not to listen to the conversation around her, yet it was impossible not to. The manner in which the men talked of women held her attention, so fixed were they in their general ridicule of the sex. Yet, hardly a worse example of manhood and chivalry could be found in the whole of Wessex, with only one or two exceptions.

"Oh, come now, surely you admit there were at least three pretty ladies among them to dance with, of a very pleasant disposition. I found the occasion quite a pleasing experience and would not hesitate to return."

"On the contrary, Hubert, it was merely a gaggle of geese gathered to pleasure us and cluck around our ankles. I found no beauty and little fashion, and even less reason to take to the floor in a polka."

"But, you rascal, I saw you dance with Miss Peters, and more than once."

"A sweet girl, I admit, but knowing her family as I do, I could no more make love to her than bugger her brother!."

A huge round of laughter erupted among them. "You're far too choosy, Douglas, for I would, perhaps to both!"

"Maybe, but I'm selective regarding in which ink well I dip my pen!"

Sally looked archly and turned her head away in disgust. Her gesture was noticed by Digby, who mischievously invited her opinion of men, adding that there was much they spoke of that any decent woman would be absolutely ignorant of knowing anything about.

She stood with perfect indifference to Ernest, her employer, who appeared to agree with his friend.

"That is undoubtedly the precise difference between us," she began, feeling rather too angry to be guarded. "I would never assume any worldly man to know little of the opposite gender, unless so proved by remark and conversation. On the other hand, it is clear some men would stifle similar discussion among women, by pronouncing that if such knowledge was known among them, then those women were not of good character. Is that what you believe, that a woman leaps from first acquaintance with a man to fondness, from fondness to love, love to engagement, and engagement to marriage and children, without a by-your-leave thought about the physical pleasure their marriage might bring to both?"

"You speak beyond the pale, madam," said Douglas, another of the gang. "A deal too far."

"I speak with politeness and the authority of being a woman. The fact that I don't agree with your vision of perfect womanhood is a difficulty you will have to bear and I will forgive."

"But surely," interrupted Hubert with grave propriety, "a lapse in the moral behaviour of a woman is immeasurably worse than in a man? I can see every distinction of difference."

"A woman's mind is rapid, not cloaked and silenced. We see the same world, read the same reports in newspapers, and hear the same screams of ladies attacked for their purses or their chastity. We know the difference between love and lust, because we have to deal with it on a daily basis. Yes, perhaps it may be argued reasonably that we spend too much time on our appearance and thereby appear frivolous, and that by our liking of a modest degree of scandal in fashionable evening dress we invite such attention, but it is that very attention we receive, and reject, that makes our knowledge of such things so rich and personal. To have knowledge isn't wrong in itself, but to act improperly upon it would be. Only by physical actions of impropriety should different women be judged, not as a collective whole of womanhood, but as individuals, as miserable and wretched or as wise and good as individuals can be."

"Bunkum!" shouted Douglas. "Be silenced, madam."

Sally glared at him. "We women may be stifled in our public opinion of men, but you may be assured from the bottom of my heart that a woman thinks equally badly of a man who is an incurable rogue. A woman with a fallible husband may appear to forgive him outwardly, whereas a fallible wife would be thrown out of the marital home and abandoned. But, the reason for the difference isn't one of different outrage. No, it is more that a woman has to consider the consequences of her leaving a husband and having no means of support."

"Maybe she has something there," retorted Hubert. "I've seen gentle women walking the quays of our seaports, trying to encourage ladies of the night away from vice and reclaim their lives. Some prostitutes, being too rotted, had no future and jeered and scolded the fine women, but others took the pledge and listened to the gospel message. Nobody could suggest that these ladies meeting for the first time at the water's edge were not different in class and standing, yet all knew what life among the servicemen meant."

Sally stared softly into Hubert's eyes. She took his hand and squeezing it gently between her long, slender fingers. "Thank you."

"Ho, ho!" bawled Douglas in slurred tone, "I think little Carrot-Top has an admirer at last." He inhaled the last of his cigarette and stubbed the remainder into a half-eaten cake.

Hubert winced. Sally took a step backwards towards the sofa, where she picked up her purse. Hubert fetched her cloak.

"I'm sorry my friends embarrassed you. I'm used to it, being a short-house and ginger headed. But, it wasn't fair to mortify you. By the way, I'm Hubert Smith. You may call me Hubert, if you like. Everyone else does, when they're not being rude to me, that is. I already know who you are. May I walk you home to make amends, Miss Ayres?"

"Dear Hubert, your conjecture is incorrect. I'm not in the least embarrassed. And, no, I will walk myself home."

He looked hurt.

"I will walk by myself only because I'm a mere stone's

throw away from my room. If you feel so inclined on the next occasion we meet, I would happily welcome your attention. You are a dear and kind man."

With that said, and having expressed her apology to Ernest for leaving so early, she left.

Emerging from the building, Sally made her way along High Street, where not all the lamps had been lit by the lamplighter from the Gas Company, leaving a shadowy patchwork on the path. Magdalene Street was still in virtual darkness, with the lamp-lighter gradually making his way from lamp to lamp a full two hours after sunset. She now wished she had accepted Hubert's offer.

The lamp-lighter, having over four miles of streets to light, had began an hour before sunset but was tasked with an impossible job to illuminate the town before dark set in. Those living in Benedict Street had the longest to wait. Sally could hear the poor man mumbling as she passed, saying that the company should employ a second lamp-lighter for a place as large as Glastonbury.

Eventually, through the gloom, she could finally make out brightness radiating from The Planet. It was a welcoming sight. "I need a bed," she said out loud and increased her walking pace.

On the left side of Magdalene Street, where the Abbey Kitchen could be seen behind and above a long wall with brick columns crowned with stonework that looked very much like a row of bishop's mitres, two policemen stood in a walkway. The darkness of their uniforms and the lack of public lighting made them almost invisible. Sally, who had not seen them, jumped in terror as they called out to her as she passed. Her legs turned to jelly. She would have fallen to her knees had she not been grabbed by one of them. For a few moments Sally was beyond reply.

To Sally's surprise, as her breathing became more regular and her pulse slowed, the grip was not loosened. Still believing it to be a normal situation, she tried to wriggle her arms free in the least provocative manner. This only caused the grip to tighten further.

"What's going on?" she entreated, a small panic setting in.

"We would like you to accompany us to the station, madam."

"Why, for pity's sake?"

"Come quietly now, Miss, if you please."

Unable to resist, and still believing it to be a huge mistake, she walked with them, back out of Magdalene Street in the direction she had come and left into Benedict Street, passing the Church of the same name. An open area of grass stood in front of the wide, two-storey police station and police houses, looking more like a grand country house than a place of crime and punishment. As she entered through the central lobby, still in restraint, it all seemed surreal, dreamlike.

At a desk, Acting-Sergeant Murry was scribing entries into a ledger. He was recording the taking of one shilling from each of three boys who had confessed to stealing sprigs or knots of flowers, *nuts of May*, and was about to deal with a tramp who had been arrested for begging in the market place. The tramp would serve one week of hard labour in Shepton Mallet gaol. Her turn arrived.

"Your name please?"

"Sally Ayres. What's this about? I've done nothing."

"Mrs or Miss?"

"Miss."

"Very good." He looked up with stern expression. "You have been arrested under the 1866 Contagious Diseases Act."

"I beg your pardon?"

"We have reason to suspect that you are involved in soliciting. Under the law, you now have the choice. Either submit to medical examination for venereal diseases or face imprisonment. Which will it be?"

"For pity's sake. I'm a school teacher, nothing else."

"Employed?"

"No, not as a teacher at present."

"Got any money?"

"I have some, but not much."

"So, you needed to make some, quickly?"

"No! Tomorrow I'm to be a nursery nurse for the Brownings, a local family."

"Yes, I know of them. Nevertheless, you must decide which you want, examination or custody."

Hardly believing her first ever meeting with law enforcement could result in possible custody, she submitted to examination, on the promise of it being quick and by a woman.

Late that night, she was released. The examination by a nurse had been a hard experience, but less so than for a genuine prostitute. For, having sent word to The Queen's Arms that Miss Ayres was not a virgin, it was ordered that the farce should end at once. Consequently, she was taken back to The

Planet by police cart, after a caution not to loiter again in the evening hours. She was further warned that her unusual views on womenkind had been recorded, as told to them by Douglas Cox, who had himself just been arrested for disturbing the peace and had noticed her name above his in the ledger. In his drunken state, his tongue had wagged merrily.

In the quietness of her room, Sally burst into tears, her face buried in a pillow. Her dignity had been stolen and her belief in justice had gone too. She was a different person, in a place she now hated. But the trauma was not over. At two o'clock in the morning there came a knock at her door. She asked who it was.

"Jim, the proprietor," came the reply.

She pulled the bedcover over and bade him enter. She knew him to be kind and was not afraid. He entered meekly. He was very apologetic but at the same time emphatic that she must leave, at once.

"Leave?"

"At once. It's come to the notice of some hotheads that you've just been arrested for soliciting. They demand I force you out or they'll set my hotel ablaze. What am I to do, other than meet their demands?"

"But, how can that be? I'm innocent in all things."

"I know it and that's why I'm going to help you. I'll return in five minutes. Please dress in these old clothes without delay and I'll then take you to my sister's house, where you can stay for the night in safety. After, when you're well out of it, I'll come back here to confront the trouble-makers and ensure my hotel comes to no harm. I can show them around the rooms if necessary. Please hurry if you would, for all our sakes."

In the darkness, Sally was spirited out of the back door and to a tiny cottage in Hill Head, well away from the town centre. Here, she spent a troubled night, not falling asleep until dawn and not waking until after ten o'clock, making her late for church with the Browning family.

Gingerly, Sally crept into St John's, noticing an empty space at the end of the same pew the Browning children occupied. As she sat, Ella and Ernest turned from the pew in front. He was clearly amused, but she was quite disgusted and indicated as much. Sally mouthed that she was sorry and would explain later. There would be, indeed, much explaining to do, with little cordiality.

Ella turned to Ernest and whispered into his ear: "See, this is a poor start to things. She is unabashed at letting us down. I cannot say she will do for me, no, not at all can I say that."

"Shush, dear, or she'll hear you. I'm sure she will give a reasonable account. If it's genuine and you can excuse her, then you'll realise how wise you were not to jump to early conclusions. After all, you do need her help."

Ella turned once again to look at Sally out of the corner of her eye, but was shocked to see her undisturbed, now standing and gazing up at the stained glass window, her face showing only amazement. For there, ahead of her captured in glass, was the huge image of Joseph of Arimathea, cloaked in blue, holding a staff in the right hand and two small bottles in the left.

From the very back of the church, Thackeray and Fairbourne watched Sally's unique reaction to the window. Their suspicions about Sally seemed more real, their darkest fears about her complicity a possibility. They now knew Sally was not a virgin and, thereby, she could not be with any reasonableness the last of the predicted nine weeping maidens heralding national peril. Yet her self-acclaimed drowning *was* the ninth recorded. It was clear – the significance of her drowning just had to be, instead, in the mystic woman in the water with her. The presence of weeping maidens had been recorded in only a tiny number of the cases, but it was possible similar experiences had overtaken all nine.

"Come on, Fairbourne, we have work to do," he whispered. "I've an uneasy feeling that we're missing something that stares us in the face."

"Sir, I have an idea," he replied in equally low volume. "Well, to be honest, it isn't mine, so much as Burgerhout's. It's wild, but plausible. At the end of his letter, he wrote as a postscript that in the early 1440s some of England's monasteries and convents were suspected of being corrupt. It was claimed in contemporary accounts that far from being places of prayer, purity and self-denial, a significant number were rife with feasting, drunkenness, fornication, gaming and worse. So-called virgin nuns were said to have had babies, sometimes fathered by clergy, and even the Mass was sometimes incorrectly chanted. Now, just suppose we could transpose the 1440s for a more exact date, say 1443, what does that tell us?"

"Suppose you tell me?"

"Don't you remember? 1443 was the date of the first self-confessed drowning. Now do you see?"

"No, I don't. It's too insubstantial to be credible. Anyway, you said that date was the least certain."

"I accept that, but, in a leap of faith, couldn't it have been monastic heresy that triggered the appearance of the first of the weeping virgins, mourning the corruption of the church and its beliefs? As we're dealing with the possibility of fantastic things, couldn't we accept that the nine appearances at exact intervals are timed to give a precise future date for spiritual catastrophe, which has arrived?"

"That's ridiculous. There's nothing much wrong with our present-day religious institutions. No widespread corruption or any threat that I know of. Future predictions, my foot! This is the 19th century, soon to be the 20th. We can't believe in goblins and gobbledegook. All that Nostradamus-type prophecy rubbish!"

"Strange you mention Nostradamus, Sir. Burgerhout even mentioned him."

"Who?"

"Nostradamus. Like Burgerhout, he was versed in Greek and Hebrew, as well as Latin and much else. Like Disraeli, Nostradamus's father was a Christianised Jew. I think that's what attracts Burgerhout to his prophecies, written in France in the 16th century."

"And your point is?"

"Burgerhout says Nostradamus wrote about the destruction of Christianity. He quotes a Quatrain."

> *In a short time sacrifices will resume;*
> *those oppressed will be put to death like martyrs;*
> *there will no longer be monks, abbots or novices;*
> *honey shall be more expensive than wax*

"I'm totally lost," admitted Thackeray. "Surely, Fairbourne, you don't really want us to try and make any sense out of that gobbledegook? It could be applied to anything, from the dissolution of the monasteries that had already just happened when he wrote the Quatrain, to our present troubles with Islamic jihad in the Sudan. The Quatrain is complete rubbish."

"Is it? Just give me a minute. Joseph's Wattle Church was erected on the same site as the present Glastonbury Abbey, within one hundred feet of Arthur's grave. Now, if we try to extract myth and legend from fact, what are we left with?"

"Nothing at all!"

"We are left, Sir, with one indisputable common factor, Joseph and Arthur's link with the area now occupied by Glastonbury Abbey, built hundreds of years after each of them walked the earth. It has to be a religious connection." Fairbourne suddenly froze. "Good Lord! Didn't you notice?" He turned to the stained glass window. "Look. Joseph carries his staff that grew into the Holy Thorn Tree and two bottles. But where's the chalice, The Holy Grail? That was probably what Miss Ayres noticed and why she was so transfixed. Don't you see, perhaps the Grail used during The Last Supper isn't as significant as the two bottles holding the blood of Christ and the tears of passion from the crucifixion. In fact, perhaps the term Grail should not be applied to the chalice at all, as is always supposed, but to the bottles holding the most precious of all possible contents. Or, perhaps, the missing Grail itself serves as a warning."

"Of what?"

"To be mindful of blood and tears, the alternative Grails, perhaps?"

"Meaning?"

"I don't know! Self-sacrifice and forgiveness, martyrdom and compassion, or, conversely, the effects of wrong-doing such as tyranny and oppression, ignominy and . . ."

"Ignorance?"

"Yes, that sort of thing."

"This is pure, outrageous speculation of the wildest kind, without any foundation whatsoever."

"But it has," he insisted. "The sins of the monasteries, Arthur's pledge to be pure and his legacy to defend England at a time of crisis, the Glastonbury connection to all the main players, the burial place of Joseph's bottles, and the birthplace of Christianity in England. They all point to just one conclusion."

"Which is?"

"That the future harm to England *is* real, but it isn't political, war or plague at all, as we thought possible. It's an attempt to destroy England as we know it by bringing down the building blocks of the Christian faith, the very foundations of our national institutions, from the church to the monarchy. The Queen is the Defender of the Faith. Arthur the warrior didn't have to come back himself to help us. His weeping maidens brought his warning. It's the same thing!"

Thackeray thought hard and long. "No, it doesn't work for me. It's hard enough accepting conclusively your calculated dates for the self-confessed drownings, but, even if we do, you said yourself you had matched only two of the nine with definite apparitions in the water. The prophecy isn't for the Predicted Two. I still think we must concentrate on the humans. Can you give me one other indisputable contemporary proof that a woman survived her own drowning on one of your calculated dates and in the company of a weeping companion? You can't, can you?"

"Yes I can. 1663. Alright, I know nothing specific is said, but it had to be a 'near miracle' to gain such an important place in the dark box after the others had been so recklessly burned."

"My goodness!" exclaimed Thackeray, thumping his head between his palms. "I've been a complete nitwit! We have a third, even without 1663. When I was in the church at Cudwick I saw a large epitaph on the wall. It was to some woman or other who had died aged fifty something, yet there was only twenty-five years between her birth and death. It said she had been born and reborn with salvation in water, and died in 1578. I thought it meant baptism, and that a mistake had been made in calculating her age, but now I'm of a different opinion."

Fairbourne did his maths. "Twenty-five years old in 1578 means she was born or reborn in 1553."

"Exactly. *She* fits your pattern of drowning dates. Her name was Alice someone. I can't remember."

"Bennett. It was Bennett, wasn't it? I found that name. Folklore claims she spoke of well-nigh drowning in her young years. Sir, we have been warned by the tears of phantoms, brought to our mortal attention by nine real people in distress in the sea. What could be more poignant to a sea-faring nation? Onward Christian soldiers and all that! Rule Britannia . . ."

When Britain first, at heaven's command;
Arose from out the azure main;
This was the charter of the land;
And guardian angels sung this strain.

"Sir, we must look to ourselves as much as abroad. It could be an enemy within."

CHAPTER 8

Arthur's tale

Thackeray helped himself to a cup of coffee from the lounge bar at The Queen's Arms. He sat in a corner, where two club chairs provided privacy. Fairbourne joined him, spreading papers over a small occasional table nestling between. The fervour of their enquiries seemed to ebb once away from the trappings of mystery and back among ordinary surroundings. No longer did Arthur's warning from the grave seem to be such a credible conclusion.

"You know, Fairbourne, when you consider what we've found, it doesn't actually amount to a pile of corn! Yes, it's true that Miss Ayres was involved in a tragic shipwreck, but everything else that's followed or we've found has been nothing more than speculation or conjecture. What if we took the view that she *did* nearly drown, but that's all? What then?"

"Then, Sir, I guess that would be an end in itself. It was only her being the ninth survivor of a self-confessed drowning that forced us into this investigation. I see what you mean. I think you're saying that if her accident is taken in isolation, then there's no conspiracy to foil."

"Just so. I mean to say, does anything around here or in London look to be on the verge of catastrophe? No! Now take this weeping woman Ayres claims to have seen, why not accept her as nothing more dreaded than a hallucination, brought about by the lack of oxygen to her brain." Thackeray sat back in the deep chair, sipping from his cup. It was hot and sweet. For the first time in a while he was relaxed. "You see, Fairbourne, how easy it could be to pack up and go home. All it takes is one ounce of common sense. After all, aren't we guilty of making conclusions on evidence that just doesn't stack up, looking for a conspiracy that just doesn't exist? Conspiracy theorists. Yes, I might coin that phrase for people who pervert facts for their own advancement. I'm beginning to think that's exactly what *we're* doing."

Fairbourne put his cup on the floor and began sifting through the papers. He picked one out.

"You asked me a while ago to produce more background on Arthur. I haven't had time to finish it, but we could look at what I have, if it helps. May I read a note or two?"

Thackeray sighed, but agreed. "Here we go again. Fairbourne, for God's sake I warn you, give me something plausible and solid. No more humbug."

Fairbourne rubbed the inside of his stiff collar, giving himself extra breathing space.

"I started by looking into Britain at the time of Arthur. This is all factual, I assure you. According to my research, the Romans had cleared out of Britain by the close of AD409, leaving behind a changed society that was in partly based on the Roman way of life and the rest slowly entering into a new Dark Age. It must have been chaos countrywide. Anyhow, the Romans had previously fortified England against barbarian attack, for defence against the Picts, Attacotti and Scots. Then, after the Romans left, a good deal of peaceful immigration took place, including the Angles and Jutes from Denmark and the Saxons, a Germanic tribe. Of course, there had always been the threat of massive invasion and, duly, peaceful migration gave way to bloody invasion by hordes of these Germanic peoples wanting to grab more than a place to settle."

"Nothing new there, then!"

"No, Sir. It appears our country was under real threat of being overwhelmed by new cultures. It was left, as usual, to the people themselves to rally to the challenge, many having already been forced to leave their land and take to the hills and forests."

"And this is where Arthur comes into the picture?"

"Sort of. With the Romans gone, the country turned into a patchwork of small kingdoms, for want of a better phrase, run by local leaders. Chieftains, so-called kings and that sort of thing. Earthwork hill forts that predated the Romans, plus abandoned Roman sites themselves were hastily repaired into strongholds to be occupied and defended against the invaders."

"Places of resistance?"

"Absolutely. Among the best of the resistance leaders was somebody named Ambrosius Aurelianus, a Romano-Briton prince who was successful in holding onto parts of the south and west of England against the Angles and Saxons, while elsewhere in Britain the invaders were achieving considerable inroad. The Angles established the kingdoms of Northumbria, East Anglia and Mercia, eventually founding the Anglo-Saxon race with the Jutes and Saxons."

"And is it now Arthur comes in?"

"Please, a little more patience. One of the most influential invaders was a particular Saxon leader known as Hengist, who, with his son Asc, had destroyed an army of 4,000 Britons in Kent in AD457, followed in AD465 by the massacre of twelve Briton chieftains at Wippedesfleot in the south of England."

"Bloody cheek!"

"Quite! Anyway, Hengist was killed at the Battle of Mount Badon. The opposing victorious army had been led by either Aurelianus or an Imperator named Artos, otherwise known as Arthur. Whoever was in ultimate charge, it was Arthur who had united the defenders from a squabbling bunch of small units into a unified army of resistance. That was Arthur's *coup de grace*, effectively holding back the invaders in the south-west for many decades. He was particularly effective because he led horsemen, whereas the Saxons fought on foot."

"A cavalry force of knights, with Arthur as its leader?"

"Just so. Mount Badon was Arthur's twelfth and final major campaign of resistance. Now, this is the interesting bit. Because his mounted force could move rapidly, he had fought the Saxons, Picts and others all over Britain, from the South of England to Northumberland and Lincolnshire, and even Scotland, which might explain why local legends say that Arthur and his knights found their final resting places in Northumberland, Wales, Cheshire and Scotland, to name a few claimed locations."

"You earlier said 'Imperator'. Meaning?"

"It's a Roman title for a conquering commander-in-chief."

"A hang-over from the Roman occupation?"

"Exactly, Sir. It appears that after Mount Badon, Arthur and his wife and cavalry-knights settled at South Cadbury, a pre-Roman hill-fort about twelve miles from Glastonbury."

"Cadbury. Didn't Burgerhout say we should go there?"

"Yes."

"Shall we?"

"I think not."

"Well done, Fairbourne. I like your style. Carry on, dear boy!"

"South Cadbury was an earthwork site which had been heavily fortified with stone and timber defences. It covered a staggering eighteen acres of ground. Geoffrey of Monmouth, a Welsh churchman who wrote a history of British kings in the 12th century, called the hill fort Caerleon-on-Usk."

"How much of what you say is true and how much folklore?"

"As far as can be confirmed, all I have said is factual. I think the fort at Cadbury can safely be regarded as the headquarters of an army commander, rather than the castle of a king with a court. We can most certainly dismiss the whole Round Table bit, with Lancelot and the rest. That *is* pure fiction."

Thackeray looked up with surprise. "So, if Lancelot goes, so must Guinevere and all stories of their affair which destroyed Camelot and the Order of the Round Table."

"Not completely, with respect. Lancelot is fantasy, but Guinevere was real as far as can be discovered. Don't forget the bones and hair found by the monks of Glastonbury

Abbey, alongside Arthur's remains. By the way, the monks at Glastonbury found Arthur had the physical signs of nine wounds to his bones, plus another that hadn't healed before he died. Nine old wounds . . . nine weeping maidens. Make of that as you wish. The last unhealed wound was probably the blow from his nephew Mordred that fatally injured him at the Battle of Camlann. Interestingly, it is said that, even before Camlann, Arthur had come out of retirement to defeat the Romans at Gaul, after the Roman Emperor Lucius had demanded tribute. He might even have marched on Rome itself had news not reached him that Mordred had joined the Saxons in open rebellion.

"And Guinevere? You still leave me without an answer."

"I think it's safe to assume Guinevere may have been the daughter of a local king, often quoted as Leodegrance. The story goes that the King had given Arthur a huge Round Table as part of her dowry, the significance being that a round table has no head position. Clearly, he didn't give that table, as it never existed. But, consider this. As Guinevere was supposedly the daughter of a king, could that explain why Arthur was elevated into becoming a king himself in stories? Of course, as Arthur was born into Celtic nobility, he might equally have inherited such a title. Who can tell? I prefer to consider him only as an army commander."

"What of Guinevere's fate?"

"Tales abound of Guinevere being abducted by Melwas, King of Aestira Regio, *Summer Land*, and Melwas holding her prisoner on top of the Tor at Glastonbury Castle. Because the area was marsh, Arthur couldn't mount a successful rescue attempt. In the end, her release was negotiated by the Abbot of

Glastonbury. Still, whatever the truth, when Arthur died, it is thought Guinevere joined Amesbury convent and subsequently became Abbess. That alone might help explain why she and Arthur finished up at Glastonbury Abbey, although Arthur was possibly initially buried at Cadbury Hill. It's equally likely that his bones were later moved from Cadbury to Glastonbury in great secrecy, to avoid the Saxons discovering that their greatest adversary was dead. As far as they would have known, Arthur may have survived Camlann. There was no military gain to be had by declaring the demise of the commander-in-chief of the best Briton force."

"Hang about, Fairbourne. If Arthur was first buried at Cadbury, doesn't that dismiss the nine weeping maidens at a stroke? After all, they only come onto the scene to carry his wounded body by barge to Avalon."

"I've puzzled with that myself. I haven't got an answer. All I can suggest are the obvious conclusions, that either he *was* taken straight to Glaston after all, or that the maidens were involved in his reburial, perhaps to join Guinevere."

"Ha! I looked for a small chink in your armour and found a bloody great hole!"

"Yes, Sir, I know. More so when I tell you that some ancient writings suggested that he would return one day as a future king because he *didn't* die of his wounds."

"And, your conclusion is?"

"That we must accept that folklore changes over the centuries by its telling. Any conclusions we can make could only be, at best, pure conjecture. Truly, I don't see that it matters. Whatever the circumstances of his burial, because he must have died at some stage, we are interested only in the supposed appearance of the nine maidens, in whatever role they took."

"Going back to the Round Table, you said it never existed. Yet, aren't I right in thinking that such a table hangs on the wall of a church somewhere?"

"Not Arthur's Round Table, Sir. I can only suppose that, after Edward III created the Order of the Garter in 1348 to represent the fellowship of the Knights of the Round Table, only then was such a table constructed, or at a later period. But, it's not a 6th century table that exists, that I can promise you."

"And your summary is, Fairbourne?"

"That we should carry on a little longer," he said quietly, trying to subdue his enthusiasm.

Thackeray winced. "Do you know something? You have the most annoying habit of convincing me to do things I don't want to do."

CHAPTER 9

Burgerhout's revenge

$\mathcal{A}$t home, and now worryingly aware of Government interest in matters that could cut across his own investigations, Burgerhout had pursued his own agenda with renewed vigour. He viewed Thackeray and Fairbourne's attentiveness to detail as dangerous, not to themselves and certainly not to the country, but to his *own* research.

For the past twenty years he had been quietly searching for the cup used by Jesus during what Christians called 'The Last Supper', a gathering which held very little religious significance to his faith beyond its attendance by a prophet of the Jews. To Burgerhout, though, the cup was more than just an artefact of history. It was a Rubicon.

He had saluted, rather than mourned, the death of Charles Darwin in the previous year, believing Darwin's academic book *The Origin of Species by means of Natural Selection* to be an abomination to his own spiritual beliefs and loathsome in suggesting that mankind could have evolved in any way other than through God's infinite creation. In his estimation, finding the cup would be the greatest blow against the modernizers, those who sought to undermine the power of any faith by scientific means. For him, its mere existence could be capable of subduing agnostics and make those who remained undecided come down on the side of religion, in whichever faith they chose. For, the righteous of all peoples would find a place in the world to come, in the Royal House of David.

He did not suggest modernizers were evil in any way, just misguided and more than capable of deluding others. To take away the hand of God from the evolution of man and woman, was to cast as false so much of what faith meant to the praying masses of many religions.

And God said, Let us make man in our image, after our likeness; and let them have domination over the fish of the sea, and over the fowl of the air, and over the cattle, and over all the earth and over every creeping thing that creepeth upon the earth . . . Male and female created he them

His research had taken him to both England and the Middle East. He was convinced that the pot of gold at the end of his rainbow would be a cup of incalculable historic interest and, therefore, priceless beyond diamonds if authenticated by the greatest living experts, of which he considered himself to be one. He had been careful to disguise his own researches under the umbrella of being available to help others in whatever professional capacity he could. As a Jew, he thought his private enquiries would not arouse suspicion.

But, it was just that, a ruse, to access everyone else's

findings and carefully guide them away from places he deemed most likely to hold the treasure. This was easily done, and Palestine was an area he guarded above all. Conversely, offering to others such convincing titbits as Chalice Hill also suited his purpose. Having exhausted the place himself as a likely site, his enthusiasm that others should do their own digging around had two beneficial effects. It gave him respect as a philanthropist, while providing others with the chance of discovering something he might have missed, certain in the knowledge that he alone would be the academic asked to view any new findings. That way, he gave second wind to areas he would never again visit. As cynical as this appeared, it was not altogether egoistical. For he believed the cup used by the prophet belonged to Palestine, and he would return it in triumph once rediscovered, to be marvelled by visitors of any sect.

Burgerhout's own researches had allowed him to dismiss a long time ago Arthurian legend associated with the cup, or 'Grail' as Arthur's knights supposedly called it. As a learned man of reason, such stories were merely folklore and nothing else. Joseph of Arimathea was an entirely different kettle of fish, though. Here had been a real person of both Jewish and Christian connections, who travelled from the Middle East to England carrying some of the most sought after artefacts the world had ever known.

He, too, had once been concerned that ancient references to Joseph burying the 'Grail' and bottles at Chalice Hill had not been authenticated by the stained glass window at St John's, or, indeed, the age of the Chalice Well itself, which was thought to date from the 13th century. Such blatant discrepancies always caused him serious concern, having learned long ago to take due notice of ancient ballads and illustrations in whatever form they took, understanding that these were the means by which history was passed through the ages among a general population ignorant of reading and writing, Latin and Greek. But his faith was strong and he believed that, if he had missed something, the truth when discovered would put the pieces of the puzzle neatly into place and explain any discrepancies in chronology as mistakes by those mortals recording events of a much earlier period. After all, the bottles could have been buried in Chalice Hill centuries before a water well was dug by man.

He felt vindicated at having told Thackeray not to bother with the Crusades, which had historically begun in 1096 when knights set out on the First Crusade to wrest Jerusalem from Moslem control and restore a Christian state. It had been a deliberate attempt to stop others pre-empting his own research, which had thrown into the cauldron the stories of those warrior monks, the Knights Templars and the Hospitallers, and their untimely demise. Anyway, he had a gut feeling Thackeray was looking for something entirely different, although what it was had been kept pretty much a secret from him.

In his determination to leave no stone unturned, Burgerhout had even researched the meaning of Friday the 13th as an unlucky date because, perhaps, it referred to the day when Pope Clement's orders were carried out to begin the destruction of the Knights Templars by torture and fire. Yet, like so much else, the suggested link between Friday and the 13th and the warrior monks appeared to have no foundation in historic fact, beyond the wish of those wanting it to be so. He knew Friday to be the day of crucifixion for Jesus. Perhaps, also, Adam ate the forbidden apple offered by Eve on a Friday. Stranger superstitions included a taboo from starting any job on a Friday, believing it was Tip Tod's Day, or Devil's Day, and any work begun then would never be completed. Similarly, sailors would not willingly set sail on a Friday, and at some boatyards new vessels would not be launched.

As for the 13th, the number 13 referred in Christian terms to Jesus and his twelve apostles at the so-called Last Supper, thereby making it an unlucky number. That was why many people across the world wouldn't sit thirteen at a table. Better to have fourteen and leave a chair unoccupied. However, with more research he had equally found that the belief in unlucky 13 predated Christianity itself. Putting the day of the week and date together for the convenience of a story dating from the 14th century seemed incredibly dubious, to say the least. No, without any doubt in his mind, the superstition of Friday the 13th in modern thinking had to refer to the Christian interpretation of events and nothing else.

At his home and under pressure, Burgerhout began shuffling through his papers, trying to make sense of old notes written years before, but never properly collated. He knew somewhere among his files were references to the Knights Templars being the guardians of a secret, which had been found during excavations. His unbelievable rediscovery of that ancient secret had not become a clue in his quest for the cup of Jesus, as he had hoped, but had put into his possession an artefact second only to the cup itself. All written references to it had to be obliterated, fearing that they could now accidentally fall into the wrong hands and lose him his most prized possession.

Their work in Glastonbury wrapped up, Thackeray and Fairbourne planned their return to London. They would need Burgerhout's help once more, if only to lay bare particular facts needed for their report, and in the fastest possible time. Any questions Burgerhout couldn't answer as an academic and friend, Thackeray believed he could persuade Fairbourne to dismiss as unimportant. The end was joyfully in sight.

"You are aware, Sir, that Burgerhout isn't very likely to come to us at the Board of Trade. I think he'll say it's a waste of his time, and who can blame him."

"You have an alternative?"

"We should telegram ahead and go direct to his home."

Thackeray didn't much care for the idea, and said so.

"I understand your reluctance, Sir, but it might allow us to end our investigations once and for all, perhaps in a single afternoon. I can then prepare a report for the PM, which you will give as your own, and the whole untidy mess will come to a speedy conclusion."

This was music to Thackeray's ears and he agreed.

The telegram was duly dispatched late the next morning, but it had not arrived before they knocked on Burgerhout's door that afternoon, having made excellent time by train and cab. Burgerhout was noticeably shaken by their unexpected arrival, fearful of the meaning.

"My home was once a pump house and has a most unusual

layout," he explained, standing guard by doors he didn't want opened. He guided them into his office, a huge room on two levels, with a mezzanine gallery to one end that was reached by a cast iron spiral staircase.

"If you listen hard, you can still hear the water flowing beneath the floor. Indeed, it can be heard just as easily in the garden, deep under the lawn." He pointed to the upper level of the floor and led them to a large trap door under a loose rug, which he lifted. Just a few feet below, water cascaded over a stone slab and into a deep, dark hole beyond.

"I bet you've never seen anything like that before. Quite impressive, don't you think?"

They agreed that it was and the door was lowered. The noise of gushing water abated. The rug was kicked back into place.

"Now, as for the gallery, I use it as a library. It's pretty dark up there, being roof space, ideal for the safe storage of rare books. I have a paraffin lamp for reading. I keep my papers there. It's forbidden to all others and I ask you not to betray my hospitality by asking to see it."

"And all these cabinets around the walls?" asked Fairbourne, opening a glass-fronted door to peep inside.

"My treasures," he replied, uncomfortable at having them inspected. He pushed the door shut, turned the key and placed it in his waistcoat pocket. "Most gathered legitimately. One or two acquired, maybe, in more dubious ways. Artefacts from years spent in Palestine and surrounding regions. Collecting has its dilemmas to an honest man, you understand. In Egypt, for example, the stuff is lying everywhere, with expeditions from Britain, Turkey and elsewhere now sucking it up from where it has rested over countless millennia to be taken out of the country. Locals have cashed in on the harvest and offer antiquities to anyone of a different skin colour. What am I to do? If I don't take what is offered, where will it end up? At least I know its true aesthetic value and take it for study to broaden man's knowledge, rather than see such treasures treated merely as trophies on some rich man's mantelpiece, waiting to be knocked off by a feather duster and broken forever by some over-vigorous servant."

"Have you any one treasure that eclipses the rest, Mr Burgerhout?" enquired Fairbourne for no other reason than curiosity.

Before he had a chance to answer, the front door slammed and in walked a young woman of about twenty-five, her hair and eyes striking in their deeply dark beauty.

"Where are you, Papa?" she called, following the reply to the office.

She stood in the doorway, her figure silhouetted against the beech wood panelling. Burgerhout looked at her with understandable pride.

"My daughter, gentlemen. Helen, dear, this is Sir Russell Thackeray and his assistant, Wendell Fairbourne. They come from the Board of Trade." She shook hands. "They've come to see a few of my things."

"Have they?" she replied, looking to her father in bewilderment.

He winked towards her, but it went unnoticed. "They need my help yet again. They know I hold no secrets from them."

"I asked your father if he had one treasure prized above the rest," said Fairbourne smiling, wanting to engage Helen in light conversation.

"Oh, yes he does. Don't you Father. The Lance of . . ."

"Helen!" he exclaimed in determined manner to stop her continuing. He turned. "Please, gentlemen, forgive my abrupt tone. It comes from a lifetime of keeping my own counsel. I've always thought a man's personal business was for nobody else to know."

He looked at Helen with kindness, only transforming to a scowl once his features were hidden from his guests. She understood at once and apologised through her returned expression of submission.

"I must go. I have so much to do." She turned and swept away into the hall. Fairbourne was enchanted.

"Will we see you at dinner?" he called after her.

"Oh, yes, gentlemen," interrupted Burgerhout, not wanting Helen to be delayed. "Please forgive me for not thinking of it myself. Of course, you must stay for dinner and the night. I'll have two rooms aired and made ready."

They thanked him. Burgerhout left the room to make the arrangements. Once out of hearing distance, Thackeray rounded on his colleague.

"You bloody idiot, Fairbourne. Do I look as though I want to be here any longer than I need to be?"

Fairbourne stirred from seeing Helen disappear into a side room.

"Sir, it struck me that we won't learn much if we're too hurried to go. A few extra hours could be the difference between success and failure. We want to finish our work, don't we? Anyway, aren't you curious why he jumped down Miss Burgerhout's throat like that?"

"Balderdash! You like the woman. That's why you want to stay. Admit it, man! It's your trousers that are talking, not your brain."

"No, Sir, honestly." He knew Thackeray was right, but was quick-witted. "The lance she mentioned and then retreated. What was that about?"

"Do we care?" asked Thackeray, arching his eyebrows and curling one corner of his mouth.

"I think we should. Who knows what else we may discover."

"Shush, he's coming back."

Burgerhout re-entered and closed the door behind him. He took a seat at his desk and bade the others to join him.

"So, you need me again. What is it this time, Russell?"

Thackeray looked across at Fairbourne for help, but none was offered.

"We do, actually. It results from our time in Glastonbury," he said, taking the lead. "As absorbing as it was, and we found much to see of superficial interest, it didn't really help us one way or the other."

"Weren't my letters of value?"

"Indeed they were. Most useful and, can I say, educational. But nothing we found led us to a final conclusion. We can't yet wrap up our investigations and feel true to ourselves. We have lots of individual facts, but they form no cohesive pattern or conclusion. Fairbourne has a theory which I can't divulge, but we've found no corroborating evidence. Moreover, we can see not indications that his prognosis is actually about to happen."

Burgerhout's forehead furrowed. "If you think I've even the slightest idea of what you are talking about, please take it from me that I don't. What are you trying to find out?"

Thackeray again turned to Fairbourne for guidance, and again he was disappointed. He continued: "We can't say, but if you would be good enough to answer our questions on trust, we might discover the missing links, or not, which suits us just as well."

"Oh, yes?" said Burgerhout in confusion, leaning back on his chair and taking a large cigar from a deep porcelain bowl with a lid. He offered the bowl to the others. Thackeray refused, but Fairbourne took a cigar, looking in detail at the container.

"You like it?" enquired Burgerhout, while snipping the ends off the cigars.

"It's a strange receptacle for smokes, if I may say so. That's all I was thinking."

"Tao-Kung Chinese, decorated with famille verte dragons."

"Looks very old!"

"Only to the untrained eye." He dropped it heavily on the table. "Made about 1850, I shouldn't wonder. It's no older than you are." He laughed, adding in an almost threatening tone: "You two are out of your depth here. You should know that. No good ever comes of prying." He leaned forward, resting on his elbows on the edge of the desk while he lit up. "Look here, Russell, I answered everything you asked me the last time we met. And a proper jumble of questions it was, too, without common thread that I could see. So, if your enquiries are on the same subjects, then know that I'm an empty vessel, drained of all useful facts." He sat back, drawing smoke and blowing it high in the air. "Be satisfied in the knowledge that your discovery has been that there are no conclusive evidences or connections to find, on whatever it is that bothers you. I may guess that it has something to do with Jesus' cup, or is it that the Government wants to track down privately-held artefacts for restoration to their country of origin? I'm only speculating, but am I getting close?"

He stared at Thackeray and Fairbourne, who gave nothing away by their expressions.

"Or, perhaps," he continued, "some nutcase is claiming to be Arthur back from the dead. Is that it?" Again, no reaction. "Well, gentlemen, whatever it is, make your final analysis accordingly. It's a perfectly sound academic judgement to make."

Fairbourne wasn't to be fobbed off so easily. He needed to reassert a degree of government prerogative. He scanned the other items on the desk.

"You have your pen nibs in a Derby crayfish sauceboat, circa 1750 I shouldn't wonder. The Meissen clock case must be of about the same age, while that pair of gilt and ebonised torchères are Venetian, if I'm not very much mistaken."

"Date?" asked Burgerhout.

"About the same as that bowl you didn't mind breaking."

"Bravo, Wendell Fairbourne, lad! You've truly surprised me, as was your intention, no doubt. But, you knowing a few such things will not alter any of my advice. Now, let me find something else that's more testing." He walked to a cabinet, unlocking the doors and searched for two pieces.

"How the hell did you know that?" whispered Thackeray, learning close to his ear.

"You'll never believe it, but my grandmother had a sauceboat and clock just like those, both cracked and chipped, of course. As for the torchères, I remember seeing a picture in the papers of a pair similar to those that had been stolen. I remember thinking at the time that they were extremely ugly, with the blackamoors scantily clothed and standing on a really fancy gilt base. The image just stuck in my mind."

Burgerhout returned. "Well, what do you make of this?" He placed a pointed metal helmet on the desk.

"Bronze."

"You don't know, do you? Its Etruscan of the Vetulonia type, made about 450BC. And this one?"

"A dagger?" He gave up. "It's no use me pretending. I haven't got a clue."

"An Ordos bronze dagger of the 4th century, BC. It's one of my passions, to collect weaponry from the time before Jesus."

"Talking of weapons," cut in Fairbourne, throwing caution to the wind, "Helen began to say something about a lance. What did she mean? Can we see it?"

Burgerhout froze. "Like all young women, she talks too much without thinking first."

"But, is there a particular lance here?"

He hesitated. "Yes," he said at last in a most reluctant manner.

"Can we see it?"

"Why?"

"No particular reason. Put it down to curiosity."

"I, too, would like to see it," demanded Thackeray, offering support to his colleague while smelling a rat. "Come on, it can't be something you can't show me. I won't steal it. On the other hand, if it's stolen, I'll keep my mouth well and truly shut, I promise. We both will, I guarantee. Of course, if you don't mind others enquiring into its legality, I can always get a magistrate to . . ."

"It's not stolen," he murmured, "just an object of huge historic importance."

Trapped, Burgerhout slowly opened a desk drawer and produced a small brass key. He left the drawer open. Walking reflectively to a cupboard, he unlocked the glass doors and pressed down on a shelf. At once the entire shelf and the pottery vases discreetly bolted to it were lowered on sprung hinges. The atmosphere was electric. From a recess, held in darkness, Burgerhout used both hands to withdraw a long object, wrapped in blue velvet. He carried it with utmost care to the desk, where it was revealed to be an archaic lance. There was silence, for the object on view appeared extremely plain but was clearly of huge significance.

"This, gentlemen, is the Lance of Antioch, to Christians 'The Holy Lance'. In concurrence with the Christian gospels, it is revered as the lance that pierced the body of Jesus during the crucifixion. Now you've forced me to show it to you, I'll have to kill you to keep the secret."

Thackeray and Fairbourne smiled, but were in awe of an object so steeped in historical importance.

Fairbourne raised his hand to touch the shaft. Burgerhout winced, but didn't prevent him. It was a life-changing experience, full of wonder and mystery.

"How do you know it's the real thing?" he said softly. "Lances like this must have been made by the thousand for the Roman legions."

"By the tens of thousands actually, when you consider the extent of the Roman Empire. But in answer to your question, I merely say that I have faith that it struck the prophet Jesus, and that alone tells me it's genuine. However, for good measure it's backed by traceable provenance. To understand, you'll need to know more about the Crusades after all. If I tell you what I know, I'll have to kill you."

"Again!" mocked Thackeray.

"You've been warned," he replied with a wink.

"Yes, yes! Now get on with it."

"There is much in faith that is misunderstood, even by those of religious conviction. As a simple example of something you would understand, Christians like yourselves celebrate the nativity at Christmas. You were brought up to believe that Mary gave birth to Jesus in a cattle shed because there was no room at the inn. Christians sing about it in joyous Christmas carols, and wooden depictions of the holy birth sit on mantelpieces. Yet, in Hebrew the word *inn* doesn't mean accommodation for travellers. It actually means the upper floor. It was commonplace for cattle to be kept at ground level, with accommodation for people above. Apart from being practical, it helped keep the accommodation above warm. So, the cattle shed of Jesus' birth was much more likely to have been the ground floor of a building, rather than a shed, barn or cave. In terms of the religious significance of the birth, it's unimportant, but from a historian's academic viewpoint it matters a great deal."

"And the lance? Is that proof of further false belief?"

"Far from it, my friend. It was discovered by a Provençal priest below the cathedral at Antioch at the time of the First Crusade. This is well documented. Check it out for yourself, if you won't take my word. There are plenty of references. I think, later, it may have been handed over for safe keeping to the Poor Knights of Christ and Of the Temple of Soloman, the Knights Templars as they were better known. Then, I speculate, it may have found its way to those other knightly monks, the Hospitallers, who probably kept it safe and hidden after the terrible fate of the Templars. Of course, I have discovered no conclusive proof of this. It is possible, but as yet undocumented and speculation."

"And you got it by . . .?"

"Chance. The right place at the right time. I acquired it from a Turk."

Thackeray questioned Burgerhout's innocent participation, but only in his mind. Instead, he asked: "How on earth would a Turk get hold of such a treasure, already safely held in the hands of knightly monks?"

"That's an easy event to surmise. But, again, my theories cannot be proven. The simple answer is through carnage and pain, blood and tears. You see, gentlemen, both the Templars and the Hospitallers were founded to assist European pilgrims in Jerusalem, the former by the establishment of a religious order of warrior monks to protect pilgrims from marauding groups of cutthroats intent upon wreaking havoc on the infidels flocking to their city."

"The point being?"

"Few people understand that for the first two decades of

the campaign, the Crusaders had full control over only a small number of strongholds within the Kingdom of Jerusalem. Christian pilgrims were clearly vulnerable in many areas. As France was the greatest supporter of the First Crusade, it's not surprising that it was some eight or more French knights under the leadership of Hugues de Payens who initially took a vow to establish a religious order and devote their lives to the protection of the pilgrims, under the patronage of King Baldwin II of Jerusalem. They were billeted in part of the palace that had formerly been the Jewish Temple, hence the name Templars.

"And the Hospitallers?" enquired Fairbourne.

"Conversely, the Hospitallers were founded to look after sick pilgrims at a hospital near the Church of St John the Baptist in Jerusalem. Yet, despite this philanthropic ideal, they too were a religious military order. The Hospitallers gained for themselves several different names, the best remembered being the Order of the Hospital of Saint John of Jerusalem, and the Sovereign and Military Order of the Knights Hospitaller of Saint John of Jerusalem."

"So, the Hospitallers weren't fighting monks, like the Templars?"

"Not to start with, but they became so. Soon after the Hospitallers founded a hospital in Jerusalem, the Crusaders finally conquered the city, in 1099. Thus freed to expand the calling, the religious superior of the Hospitallers, a monk by the name of Gerard, increased his areas of influence in the city, while also taking the decision to help pilgrims and knights on their travels to the Holy Land by offering them assistance during the dangerous journey itself. To do this, which was no mean task for the time, he established sanctuaries that were on the pilgrimage route from Europe. Soon, knights saved from the clutches of death and healed of their sicknesses and battle scars conferred riches and land to the Order, while others swelled the ranks of knights and stayed on to do battle with the Moslems. This became the Hospitaller's more militant military arm, so to speak. All was well for a time, but then disaster struck."

"Please continue," begged Fairbourne.

"Wait a minute," interrupted Thackeray. "I still don't understand why western Christians were so interested in seizing the Holy Land."

"There is no simple answer to give. It was a combination of several factors, some noble and some far less so. Think upon the 11th century as a time of growing international trade, with new markets being opened and frontiers expanded. With growing wealth came the desire to take up even greater challenges, while many young nobles sought adventure. It was a volatile mixture. An important trigger on events was the growing influence of Islam in the east."

"Go on."

"It was widely believed that the end of the world would happen at the first millennium. You must understand that the date would have been extremely flexible by the lack of science. Thus, the end of the world would be seen as anytime in that century. Popular belief was that the King of the Franks would lead the faithful to conquer Jerusalem and thereby prepare for what Christians believed would be the Second Coming of their Christ. When, in 1095, Pope Urban II, who himself was French, urged for a crusade to assist the plight of eastern Christians and put a halt to the attacks on western pilgrims and the desecration of holy sites, it fell on extremely responsive ears. With western coffers full of gold, the campaign begun with thousands of mounted knights and tens of thousands of infantry first converging on Constantinople. The siege of Antioch was completed by June 1097."

"Where the lance was discovered?"

"Yes. Then, moving on with a force half the strength of that previously assembled, the Crusaders successfully attacked Jerusalem in July 1099, using siege towers and scaling ladders to breach the walls. Problems began when a large element of the army then just got up and left, having fulfilled their Crusader vow and pilgrimage, and headed home. When Baldwin of Edessa took the title of king, Jerusalem became a feudal kingdom, opposed to the Christian church state that had been anticipated."

"What happened to end it all?"

"Jerusalem was eventually lost to Saladin and his Moslem armies in 1187. It was a huge outrage that sent shockwaves throughout crusading Europe. Dismay reigned unchecked. This was followed by the failure of the Third Crusade in 1192 to recapture Jerusalem and restore the Christian kingdom. It ended in tatters. Notwithstanding this setback, a treaty was later arranged that allowed Christian control of some coastal land, plus it permitted pilgrims to enter Jerusalem. All things considered, it was a very magnanimous gesture on the part of the Moslems, although pilgrim Moslems themselves had been similarly well treated by the Crusaders. It's amazing how well everyone could get on, even in those ancient times, if they had the will to be reasonable and forgiving."

"What happened to the fighting monks?"

"The loss of Jerusalem didn't spell the end of the Hospitallers. Far from it. No, it wasn't until between 1289 and 1291, when the Crusaders finally lost Tripoli and then Acre in Palestine and thereby fled their last mainland strongholds, that the Hospitallers themselves were forced to seek an island retreat, although always anticipating a return to the Holy Land in better times. Acre had been heroically defended, but fell to the Maml_ks after the most terrible carnage, those inhabitants left alive after the slaughter being enslaved by the victors. It was all a sickening blow to the heads of Europe, almost as great as the fall of Jerusalem itself a hundred years before. Anyway, retrenching in Cyprus, the Hospitallers re-established themselves to continue their support of the sick, while still assisting pilgrims seeking the Holy Land."

"And then?"

"Using their great wealth, the Hospitallers founded a new hospital on Rhodes, which became a Hospitaller independent territorial state from 1308 with its own impressive navy. This lasted over two hundred years, before the Ottoman Turks attacked and drove the Hospitallers away. This is one Turkish connection, others being that the ancient city of Antioch itself is in what we now call south-eastern Turkey, nestling by the river Orontes. Saint Paul preached there and, significantly, Antioch is where followers were first called 'Christians'. Anyway, to end the story, eventually the Hospitallers fled to Malta, where they founded a new and highly efficient hospital as the Knights of Malta. Finally, the island was conquered by Napoleon in 1798."

"The Bogeyman."

"Yes."

"And now?" asked Thackeray, at last fully fascinated.

"Nowadays, the Hospitallers have no state of their own, but their humanitarian work continues under various guises. In this respect, the knights live on."

"But the Templars don't?"

"That's correct. From small beginnings, expansion of the Templars' ranks was extremely rapid. Indeed, an entire army gradually formed, still acting as bodyguards to protect pilgrims, but also later taking the fight directly to the non-Christians. Like the Hospitallers, the Templars amassed huge wealth, owning land across Europe. In fact, so great became their military power and treasure, cloaked in total secrecy of action, that King Philip IV of France, ironically known as Philip the Fair, sought their destruction in order to plunder their pickings, knowing that the backbone of their military prowess had been broken years before."

"And their usefulness to their country of origin was over, I suppose."

"Just so. Typical politics, Russell. Anyway, it's well documented that Philip accused the Templars of heresy, sprinkled liberally with allegations of grave immorality. Leaving no stone unturned to get his way, Philip was not above abusing his position to get what he wanted through all means at his disposal, and in a brilliantly executed masterstroke he managed to manipulate a Frenchman into being elected as the next pope, by creating a majority of French cardinals. You see, even then corruption reigned in high places. In essence, Philip wanted France to be more politically important than Italy. This created Pope Clement V and put the papacy in a position of submission to the French king."

"Allowing Philip's accusations against the Templars to be forced upon the Pope, I suppose?"

"You have it in one. Clement V was pontiff from 1305 until 1314. As for Philip, he wanted to distance himself from the final destruction of the Templars, to save his reputation and mask his real intentions. What better way of achieving this than by forcing Clement to do his bidding. Philip also ensured the papal registers were cleansed of any documents from foreign representatives of the Pope that denounced Philip and his army of secret agents. In consequence, Clement ordered the final suppression of the Templars in March 1312, after many years of French Templar arrests. In 1314, the grand master of the Templars, Jacques de Molay, was tied to a wooden stake and burned alive."

"Knightly monks, blessed equally it seems with compassion and wealth, are all very interesting, but where does this lead us?"

"To the Teutonic Knights, a third order of charitable crusading knights."

"Oh, good grief!" cried Thackeray in dismay.

"Germanic?"

"Just so, Wendell. Like the Hospitallers before them, the Knights of the Teutonic Order were initially affiliated to a hospital, this time in Acre in 1190, later becoming extremely militaristic and subsequently moving their operations to Europe. The last remaining branch of the Order was itself brushed aside by Napoleon, in 1809."

"And the point of knowing this was?" enquired Thackeray, finding it hard to take in.

"Knowledge is power, Russell. Power comes from knowledge."

"Returning to the lance," said Fairbourne, gesturing towards the weapon on the desk, "tell me, have you missed out something from the story?"

"Oh, yes, the lance. I wouldn't want you to die ignorant."

For the third time Burgerhout had mentioned death. This time he had no smile on his face. The change of expression didn't go unnoticed. Thackeray felt distinctly uncomfortable, slightly threatened, Fairbourne less so. Burgerhout stood. As he pulled the cloth towards himself, he suddenly lunged for the weapon and in a split second thrust the tip at Thackeray's throat, forcing him to stand and making a small indentation in his ageing skin.

"The interesting thing about a lance, spear, sword or dagger, gentlemen, is that they're just as dangerous now as when they were first put into a Roman's hand nearly two thousand years ago."

Thackeray shook nervously. "For goodness sake, man, put it down before you hurt me. The joke's over!"

"*The wicked man is doomed by his own sins; they are ropes that catch and hold him*. Proverbs 6." Then, through a sick laugh, he just as suddenly withdrew the weapon and placed it back on the desk. Thackeray dropped to his seat, clutching his throat.

Instinctively, Fairbourne snatched the lance, grasping it firmly with both sweating hands before jumping back one pace to give himself room to think. He aimed the point towards Burgerhout.

"Keep back, you bloody stupid idiot. What the hell was that about?"

Burgerhout stood perfectly still, his features calm.

"Put it down, Wendell," he said in chilling monotone. "Take your time, lad. I'll give you to the count of three!"

Fairbourne glanced sideways to Thackeray.

"I said, put it down! One . . ."

Fairbourne shook with fear. Burgerhout's stare remained fixed, his eyes wide and cold. He showed no compromise, no reluctance to see the threat to its conclusion.

"Look into the jaws of Hades, Wendell, to the damnation of a murderer. Two!"

Fairbourne, imagining the hangman's noose, released the lance from his fingers. The tip resounded metallically as it struck the stone floor.

"And . . . three," taunted Burgerhout, stepping around his desk and past Fairbourne's frozen body to recover the lance. He walked back, placing it on top of the cloth and carefully folding the material into a parcel. With the final fold he burst into a roar of laughter.

"What do you think would've happened if you hadn't dropped it, Wendell?"

"Someone would be composing my eulogy?"

"Oh, come now you two! You know full well I meant you no harm. It was a joke for goodness sake, Russell, a lesson in history. You can see that, can't you Wendell?"

As he spoke, his hand slipped discreetly into the open desk drawer. His fingers closed around the cold handle of a revolver.

"You would not have wanted to write my name into

history, would you Wendell, as the first man to die from the blade that wounded Jesus? Would you sacrifice me to ignorance?"

"Stop it. You're playing with my mind."

"Wrong answer!" he shouted, whipping out the gun and pointing it straight at Fairbourne's forehead with a steady hand. He pulled the trigger. Fairbourne grimaced at the click, expecting a searing pain to explode in his skull. Nothing! Then, just as quickly, Burgerhout grabbed the barrel with his other hand and thrust the handle submissively towards Thackeray, who snatched it.

"There. You see," he said, "I meant you no harm and now I prove it. Shall we have dinner?" He turned for the door, but stopped after a pace. "By the way, where was your famous British stiff upper lip?"

He grinned and left.

After Burgerhout had walked briskly from the room, Fairbourne shrank nervously towards Thackeray and flopped down on his knees beside him. His hands still shook.

"That man's deranged. I thought we were goners. What shall we do?"

"Change for dinner, I suppose," said Thackeray, mopping his brow with a handkerchief.

CHAPTER 10

Inquisition

Burgerhout entered the kitchen. It was the cook's night off. Helen stood at the range stirring thick vegetable soup. She wiped her hands on an apron.

"Did you tell them *all* your ideas?"

"Of course not. But I did whet their appetite with the monk knights. It hadn't been my intention to tell them of the Hospitallers, but on reflection it can do no harm. After all is said and done, knowing about the Crusades hasn't done me much good in my search for the cup, and I know far more than they will ever discover for themselves. No, it'll merely lead them into more confusion, which will keep them away from me. Cleverly, I don't suppose they think I answered anything they wanted to know. I told them stuff that was beyond their comprehension."

"Intentionally?"

"Of course."

"What *did* they want to know?"

"To be honest, I don't think they know that themselves. I

still can't make up my mind if they seek Jesus' cup, their 'Grail', or not. It would be a wonderful prize for any government, but I have a feeling the interest just isn't there. On the other hand, I cannot believe how much they continue to bang on about Arthur's nine maidens. Part of me says Arthurian legend has to be a front to cover their real investigations, yet they show no sign of getting down to the nitty-gritty over anything else. They haven't pressed me for more information on Joseph of Arimathea, which would be the logical starting point if they sought the cup. I'm confused."

"Could there be something else they're covering?"

"I've wondered that, too. You do realise, Helen, that there has been a search lasting millennia for another fabled object every bit as renowned as the Christian 'Grail', and possibly of breathtaking material reward?"

"You mean Philosopher's Stone, don't you?"

"Of course. I've found plenty of evidence that the Crusaders brought back Jewish, Moslem and other manuscripts concerning this lionized phenomenon, the search for which has been as long lasting and possibly more widespread than for the 'Grail' itself."

"The legendary stone capable of turning base metals into gold, and giving the owner of the secret immortality."

"Except that it isn't a stone at all. According to ancient accounts, it's a red or yellow powder, or perhaps a liquid. Imagine, it would be the fountain of unlimited wealth."

"Yet, nobody has succeeded."

"No, because the secret demands the formula to be created, instead of an existing substance to be found. Many medieval alchemists tried. It's a thought!"

"Will you test your theory on them?"

"Not likely! It doesn't concern me and, anyway, they would only deny it."

"What do we do now?"

"Give them a good meal and send them packing in the morning. I've frightened them into not asking any more silly questions. They won't stay a moment longer than they have to."

She kissed his cheek. "Does it remain safe for you to continue your work, here I mean, in England?"

"Of course. But, maybe, now *I've* done with the place. Cornwall and Wessex hold nothing more for me. I think I'll continue my search in three new places, starting with France. The Cathari still fascinate me."

"But, Father, you told me the Cathari were a heretical Christian sect who didn't believe anything written in the Old Testament and renounced the incarnation. Surely, if they believed Jesus was not a real man, but an angel, how could they have any connection to a real artefact, Jesus' cup?"

"You miss the point, Helen. Sometimes it's necessary to know a lot to get at a single, simple truth, even if it's a diversion. The Cathari were closely linked to sects in the Near East and Balkans. That could be important in itself. A resurgence of Cathari dualism, believing in the outright authorities of good and evil, happened at the time of the Second Crusade. To them, Satan wasn't a fallen angel at all, but a completely separate deity. Hence, God represented all that was good and Satan all that was evil. That is why the enemies of the sect proclaimed their immorality and heresy. Persecution by Louis IX, using the emerging powers of the Inquisition, finally destroyed their hold."

"You've now lost me, Father. Where's your reasoning? From what you say, nothing about them could possibly help your chivalrous quest."

"I have a mind to know more for two reasons. The first is that under the Inquisition, the Cathari were asked to repent their beliefs. Similarly, under the Inquisition some Jews were asked to convert to Christianity or suffer the consequences. Convert or die! I want to discover how each religion coped with the threat."

"But, Father, we might be Jews by birth, but nobody could say you and I are devout. As a scholar you are happy to look into the beliefs of all religions, but fully embrace none."

"No, darling, you are wrong. I keep the faith in my own way, and leave you to decide yours. If I have learned one thing through the years, that single wisdom is that much suffering to the human race has been brought about under the banner of religion. In my opinion, faith should be a matter of personal conviction. It's not wrong to talk of faith, or even suggest its particular virtues to others, but history provides sufficient evidence of what happens when it's used as a means of domination and suppression. Should I promote one religion or another to others? Absolutely not. I actually believe most religions are like languages, all different in sound but with a foundation built upon similar virtues. Just like the Moslems and Christians in the Holy Land, when fighting gave way to co-operation and tolerance. By all that is true and honest, the world needs such peace as never before and it's the burden of the humble to make it happen. I'm sure that is what's meant by the meek inheriting the earth!"

"Be liberal minded?"

"To be a free thinker."

"And the second reason?"

"I want to see if I can discover how the Cathari viewed contempory events. During ancient times, books and records were almost entirely the domain of religious bodies and regarded as hugely important. Often it's only amongst such documents that answers can be found."

"Is that why the church tried so hard to stop general book printing and distribution?"

"Exactly right, in the 15th and 16th centuries. Before that time, books had been fantastically expensive to produce by hand and could never be owned by ordinary people. With the eventual coming of a simple printing process, books at last could be produced on mass and at a fraction of the cost. The printed word held the key to the spread of free thinking, affiliated to the church or not. For these who wanted to suppress free thought and radical questioning, readily available books were viewed as heresy."

"Unstoppable, though."

"As it proved. One of the greatest opponents to the phenomena in publishing was Italian Pope Paul IV, who many believe was an absolute disaster from the start of his pontificate in 1555. His excessive violence in the pursuit of orthodoxy and reform spelt real trouble. He dealt ruthlessly with any opponents of his doctrine, using the Roman Inquisition to launch a reign of unique terror, in which printing, distribution or ownership of books of a questioning nature became embroiled. People lost their lives for the printed word, but distribution continued, often by smuggling. For me, personally, I abhor his time for what he did to the Jews."

"To the Jews, Father?"

"Oh yes! Before he came along, on the whole Jews enjoyed an era of guarded tolerance in Europe. They remained stateless, but were in honourable and professional occupations. Under Paul IV, a new hatred was launched, demanding their separation from Christians. In Rome, Jews were made to wear identification, so that they could be shunned. Vast quantities of Hebrew books and records were lost to Inquisition bonfires."

"But it was all such a long time ago."

"I wish you were right, Helen. It actually continued even into our present century."

"No!"

"Sadly, yes! The Papal States and the doctrine that flowed from them held much of Europe in fear for centuries. Life, then, was utterly dominated by religion. Much later, in 1808, in your grandparent's time no less, Napoleon finally freed Spain from papal domination and vowed to destroy the Inquisition. But when Napoleon himself was defeated, papal influence returned to prominence. Documents seized by Napoleon had shown, conclusively, that the Inquisition had burned over twelve thousand men, women and children. Naturally, the Pope insisted on the return of all documents, to guard their secrets. In the event, the number actually returned was fairly small. Unbelievably, apart from many documents already sold off in France to private buyers, some had been handed out to wrap fish and vegetables! It's my hope, my dream, that even now there might still be some of these papers to be found that survived in private hands. If so, there's no knowing what they could reveal. There'll be the only ones I'll ever see."

"I had no idea the Inquisition was still around in our 19th century. It's a frightening thought."

"Under one name or another, I doubt it will ever properly go away. And there's more, daughter, which affected our race. The Inquisition, at a less bloodthirsty time of course, sometimes even kidnapped Jewish boys to be converted to Catholicism. It was only thirteen years ago that Italy finally unified from a series of Papal States into a single country under the Piedmontese Royal Family. Unsurprisingly, the Pope and his advisors fought against it."

"Mercy!"

"Don't be frightened. The role of pope has changed in modern times and it's now a truly honourable institution. Remember, many leaders of different faith groups had been similarly abhorrent in centuries past. It was a sign of the violent times, when life held little value."

"Honour and obedience above life?"

"Once, yes. Still, happily, no longer are Jews singled out by the wearing of special yellow hats, as once ordered by their papal masters."

"Just as well. I hate yellow. It looks so bad against my complexion."

"It's not a subject for joking about, darling. I hope history will never again see Jews being 'badged' in such a way. It was inhuman and wrong, and must never happen again in our modern world. But who knows what new horrors may await our race. Institutionalised intolerance is the most dangerous, and always will be. That's why I dedicate myself to understanding the past, in the hope of influencing the future."

She took his trembling head and kissed it, slowing his pounding heart.

"I still think the Cathari will prove to be a waste of time. But, I like France and will happily spend your money there in the shops and cafés. The sunshine will do us good too."

Burgerhout allowed his mind to free itself from torment. He looked at her face in admiration, showing through his kind expression that she was too young and inexperienced to fully appreciate the terror of the past.

"Spoken like a true woman! You do realise, Helen, that if I strike a blank there, then we must travel to Rhodes. After all, anyone who managed to gain possession of the lance that struck Jesus could just as easily have gained possession of his cup. The events were only days apart. If not there, then Cyprus will be our next destination. Do you mind so many moves?"

"Not in the least, Father, if we can afford it."

"But, what about a life of your own? Meeting the right man, I mean?"

"I don't see why moving from pillar to post will stop me from gaining a husband. I absolutely insist on having a child to hold in my arms, who relies on me, before I shrivel up and die."

"And you shall, I'm sure." He kissed her forehead.

"After all, Father, Jews remain stateless. Home is where we lay our heads. Isn't that true?"

"I'm blessed with you, Helen. As for money, don't worry. I still draw a good income from my share of the plantation in the Dutch East Indies. That will continue to provide everything we need. Indeed, now I think on it, it might be sensible to go there first, see how my investments are doing. I might even sell the shares if I can find a high bidder, so that I can concentrate on my research. However, make no mistake, dear. I'm still not completely convinced the cup ever left Palestine when the Christians fled. We may trek from place to place for the rest of my life. What I'm fairly sure of, though, is that Joseph of Arimathea carried only the two bottles to Glastonbury. Everything points to it. I must learn to rely even more on the knowledge of others of centuries past. Yes, we will leave this place and waste not a moment more.

"Why not tell your friends about the Cathari over dinner? That would confuse them even more."

He deliberated for a moment, smiling at the sport to be had.

"Not a bad idea, but perhaps 'no'. I don't know what might be out there to discover, and I certainly don't want to run the risk that they might blunder into anything worthwhile by fluke."

"Then, Thackeray is of no further use to you?"

"None at all. If he'd discovered anything I had missed in Glastonbury, he would've said so by now. As it is, he's totally bewildered, as is that popinjay he brought with him."

He walked to the door, looking gingerly through the gap. Helen followed, careful to be hidden behind. She could see them without risk of being seen. They giggled, watching the two console each other as they recovered from their ordeal.

"I think you scared them a lot."

"It was so easy."

"Men or mice?"

"Oh, definitely rodents. After all, I ask you Helen, what kind of man is named Wendell?"

CHAPTER 11

A vision of society

The short journey by foot from church to 'Little Thatch' gave Sally no opportunity to explain why she had been late. The Browning family walked hurriedly in front, kept tightly grouped by Ella who talked grimly to her husband. When they reached the uppermost step of their entrance, Ernest unlocked the door and Ella and the children entered, leaving Sally at the bottom, unsure whether or not to follow. Ernest stepped down to her.

"You'd better come into the lion's den," he said quietly, leaning towards her ear. "I'm aware of the trouble Douglas caused you." Sally winced at the news. "It was rotten bad luck. I spoke to Ella as we walked along and told her Douglas was the cause of your delay. She has accepted it."

Sally showed no relief. "What did you tell her, exactly?"

"Nothing, really. When I finished, she merely said that you were obviously *that* kind of woman and that I should be wary of you at all times if left alone together."

"You mean, Mrs Browning thinks Mr Cox and I spent the night together?"

"I didn't say that, well, not in so many words. However, better she thinks that, than be told you were arrested for prostitution."

"For goodness sake, I wasn't arrested. I was picked up for no reason. I'm innocent in all matters."

"I know, I know."

"So, I'm disgraced in her eyes. And I can offer no defence to protect my reputation?"

"That's about the score of it! When Douglas came to speak to me early this morning and confessed all, before church that is, I knew your head was on the chopping block either way."

"So you chose to lie."

"Stick to what you're good at, that's what I say. Anyway, there was no way Ella would have believed in smoke without fire. Look at it this way. By matching you with Douglas, Ella has only had confirmed exactly what she already believed. So, what's the odds?"

"Which was?"

"That you are a scandalous, unmarried woman, with an illegitimate child. You could hardly sink lower in her estimation. Still, the choice is yours. You're free to enter my home and work, or you may go now and face whatever uncertainties lay ahead. Which is it to be?"

Humbled and resigned, Sally entered.

Within a short stroll of 'Little Thatch' lived the last surviving member of a once eminent family, with whom Ella had established quite a friendship. Lady Trafford was a widow in her late fifties, lean and elegant, whose former country estate had been lost when her husband had passed away owing a goodly sum to various investment banks. He was, nevertheless, remembered kindly by her in all ways excepting his financial perspicacity. Before he died, she had been asked by a close friend how as a couple they got on. Her answer had been "tolerably well." The same person repeated the same question at the funeral, her reply then being "Much better now, thank you!".

Lady Trafford's misfortune at having to leave the family home, a surprise which she bore with all grace, had not been allowed to crush her spirit. For, although titled, she had not once used it to gain advantage over others. Indeed, she held herself no higher in status to those commoners she regularly attended socially. By nature she was caring, courteous and affable, everything at a stroke that made her the first choice for company.

The day of Sally's entry into the Browning's home was marked by Ella's hosting of a Sunday dinner party, which kept her busy overseeing preparations. This left Sally with a much appreciated breathing space. Her duty was to play with Esme and Edward, keeping them amused and away from the adults as they ate. The day was warm and the children played happily in the extensive garden, running between oak trees that dotted the lawn which gradually fell away to a large pond at the bottom.

In the house, Ella greeted her first guests.

"Good afternoon, Florence dear. I see you've brought your friend. How do you do Mrs Campbell."

She acknowledged with a smile and a slight nod. "What a most charming little house you have. Is it yours, or rented?"

Ella was taken aback. "Ah, ours!"

"I thought as much. If you were to rent, you would surely have looked for something larger and more fashionable. As it is, it is charming, and your own!"

"Thank you," was all Ella could think of saying in reply.

At a further knock, the remainder of the guests entered together, the last across the threshold being Hubert, who sidled up to Ernest.

"Where is she?"

"Sally Ayres?"

"Of course. I've heard what happened."

"In the garden, with This and That. If you want to see her, I suggest you wait until after dinner, when Ella is otherwise distracted."

"What do you make of it? Is she involved with that blighter Douglas?"

"Probably," replied Ernest, enjoying scandal.

"I thought you would say 'no'. I thought Douglas confessed it was a mistake brought about by the amount he had to drink?"

"Believe whatever you like, old boy. All I can add is that she arrived late to church and looked in need of a good night's sleep and a press for her clothes."

"Oh! Well, maybe I'll leave seeing her for another time."

A gong sounded and the guests were summoned to the dining room.

"Now, Mrs Campbell, you should sit by Lady Trafford. Hubert, please move away from Ernest. You're a bad influence. We don't want too much men's talk at dinner.

Florence, take Hubert to the corner, where you can keep an eye on him. Maximillian, put yourself between Beatrix and Mrs Campbell. That only leaves you, Bishop. I want you by me. Are we all settled?"

"That places me next to you, dear," entreated Ernest.

"She wants to keep an eye on you," laughed Maximillian. "Ella?"

"Just park yourself, husband."

"I love Sunday dinner in society," said the Bishop, tucking his napkin under his chin. "It is the only place where the great and the good, the boobies and the halfwits can mingle without the slightest fear of being found out." He giggled heartily, inviting others to join in.

"And which are you?" enquired Mrs Campbell.

"My dear lady, that is for me to know and you to find out over five courses." His merriment increased in bounds.

"Well, I would put the Bishop in a position of his own, for none of the headings suit," said Hubert, attempting to keep the atmosphere light. "He is, to my mind, a man of singular importance. Let me put it this way, by way of a rhyme I shall make up.

> *It is simple for sinners being rich and lazy,*
> *to call on his words on Sundays and say,*
> *when we fail to live up to his expectations,*
> *take two-pence collection and please go away.*
> *But the lure of forgiveness is all that we seek,*
> *and our pennies and silver we place on his tray,*
> *in the hope of salvation and peace for a week,*
> *but seven days later he hasn't gone away."*

"Bravo, Hubert. But what's the moral of your story?" asked Ernest from across the table.

"The moral? Does there have to have one?"

"Of course."

"The moral is that the church grows fat on our sins," interrupted Mrs Campbell. "Is that not so, Bishop? Is that not why the Abbey here was made derelict?"

The room fell into momentary silence.

"By-the-by, Beatrix, did I hear say you had been invited to Miss Elizabeth Makeshift's coming of age party last month?" Ella asked in panic.

She answered that she had, but had found it the least enjoyable gathering of the new year.

"Why so, pray?"

"Because the guests were only invited to hear her father recall every small trifle of her life in intricate detail. I was not there for my education, but to enjoy myself."

"Was there dancing?"

"Alas, if it was planned, it never happened. By the time the back-slapping had ended, the tired look on everyone's faces gave little hope for renewed merriment. I found myself talking to a salesman from Tiverton. He was the worst kind of man, a new father. He cared nothing for anything I said, but brought his *little Harold* into every conversation. As far as I can tell, the boy eats and passes wind, with only the slightest pause to draw breath or sick up milk over his father's shoulder, if the smell on his jacket was any indication."

"And you, Maximillian, I see you have come without your wife. Why is that?" enquired the Bishop.

"She's heavy with our first child! We're hoping for a boy. If so, he will be named after her grandfather. He was . . ."

". . . Harold, by any chance?" enquired Mrs Campbell.

"William, actually."

The grave look on Beatrix's face as the name passed Maximillian's lips caused great hilarity.

The soup plates were cleared and fresh plates arranged for the beef, oozing with red juices and ready to carve. Lady Trafford's glass was refreshed with a fine claret. She raised the vessel.

"To my good friends and hosts, Ella and Ernest."

"Ella and Ernest," rang around the table.

"Do you have a family, Mrs Campbell?"

"I do indeed, Lady Trafford. My son is of that age when he is little at home. He sleeps in the morning, rides in the afternoon, attends the theatre in the evening, and gambles and drinks the night away. I am a fortunate mother."

"Sounds like an indulgent lifestyle, if I may say so."

"My dear Bishop, he is young and being young has energies to expel. Better that than change his clothes four times a day as some fop, lusting around girls who are all too eager to catch a good husband."

"And when, pray, does he find time to eat?"

"He doesn't take meals. He merely grazes, eating little and often as the pleasure takes him. As a result, he is never in the least bilious and will avoid those flabby cheeks that so many young men get as the years pass and waists expand."

"I should have a word with the boy," suggested Mrs Campbell.

Beatrix turned discreetly to Hubert, covering her mouth

with her napkin. "I beg that would not happen. For, to be disliked by her would be greatly more pleasant than to be admired and receive her company on a regular basis. It would indeed be a grave misfortune to be her friend."

"Did you speak?" enquired Ella for the opposite end of the table.

"Not in the least, dear, other than to pass a mere nothing with Hubert."

"Then, let us all enjoy the nothing."

"If you're sure you wish to hear. I said . . ."

". . . that modern society should tolerate all and should pass no judgement on any individual," cut in Hubert, red in face. "It was a wise expression; I hope you agree as I do."

"But impracticable," said the Bishop. "No man is an island and good society demands the best efforts from us all. No, I object to no man, or woman for that matter, save those who try to break down the natural barriers of life. I am thinking that our nation works so well because of the natural order of things, born of generations. We, the privileged ones, should have no objection whatsoever to sit to dinner with our butcher or baker or candlestick maker, although I would object to my tailor, for he is always making my clothes so tight as not to allow inside a good second helping of Sunday dinner." Again he laughed heartily.

"My son is the fruit of my third marriage. My first two husbands failed me on that score."

"How sad for you, Mrs Campbell, to have lost two husbands."

"I too am perplexed by the quick leap from one to three, Bishop. It all happened so rapidly. One moment Oscar was walking with me admiring the view from the cliffs, and the next he had stepped away and fallen to his death. I'd been talking so much of interest, I can only assume it took me a few moments before I realised he had gone!"

"What are you chuckling at, Hubert?"

He wiped his mouth on his napkin. "Nothing at all, Ella. You mistake my choking for amusement. A small morsel of gristle, nothing more. There is an irritation."

"As to my second husband, he died bell ringing."

Hubert couldn't control his laughter and let out an unstoppable burst, ended only when Florence slapped his back in the way of first aid. "How so?" he eventually asked between rapturous giggles.

"He hanged himself, by accident."

That was all Hubert could stand and he rushed from the room, chortling into his napkin.

"What's so funny?" asked Mrs Campbell, looking around the guests. "I see no levity in it. He had asked to see the bells in the church tower. As it was the evening for bell-ringing practice, he was given a rope to hold and try. After, when ringing ended, he played with the rope by holding it loosely around neck, pretending to be hanged. Then, as I was told, the 'stay' that stops the bell swinging too far snapped and the rope flew upwards. He only stopped when he hit the ceiling that separated the ringers from the belfry, knocking him out. Nobody could get him down in time. He swung to the Treble 2."

"Tragic," said the Bishop.

"Tragic," said Maximillian.

They all agreed it was tragic.

"Mrs Campbell, I hear from Florence that your present husband is in jute."

"You are well informed, Lady Trafford. He is, as we speak, away on jute business."

"Counting his profits, no doubt."

"I will ignore that, Maximillian. Every owner and worker seeks to profit from his labours."

"He couldn't come today? Is he not working in these parts?"

"No, dear Beatrix, not here, alas. He is a small investor in a Dundee enterprise, which yields much. He was persuaded to invest in the early 1850s, when the business was quite localised. When the war in the Crimea broke out, followed by the Civil War in America, the need for cheap sacking and canvas multiplied relentlessly. The city is now five times the size that it was at the start of the century. He is much pleased with the investment."

"And how are the workers in this grand scheme?"

"They are housed and fed."

"And supplement their meagre existence by crime and vice, no doubt."

"That, my diffident Maximillian, I care not to know. All I can say in my husband's defence is that jute also helps keep the whale fishing industry in labour."

"How so?"

"Why, whale oil is used to soften the jute fibres. I know he, himself, intends to invest in a whaling ship. He sees no risk attached and the money he makes will come *south* of the border in pail loads."

"Then, Mrs Campbell, he should think again. Many of us

are lobbying for the restoration of the position of Secretary of State for Scotland, with its own Scottish Office in London to preside over such Scottish matters as local government, health, education and so on. The Scots have been punished enough for the 1745 rebellion. It's time for a Scottish Office to look after Scottish affairs and keep its wealth *north* of the border."

"I will pass on your advice to him. I'm sure he will know what to do with it!"

Florence left the table to check on Hubert. Presently, she re-entered and sat.

"He's taking a little air, for his cough, you understand. He gives his apologies and will return shortly.

"I see from the window that he watches my children playing," said Ella, trying to recover her party.

"He doesn't watch *them*, my dear wife. He looks for Miss Ayres."

"Is that true, Florence?" asked Ella in annoyance.

"I think he may be watching Esme getting into the rowing boat. Edward seems to be rocking it."

Outside in the garden, Sally had ended a period of vigorous play. Feeling weak and slightly light-headed from not eating since the previous day, she had retired to a nearby seat, where she could watch the children in comfort and rest. The air was still and warm and, bit by bit, she had closed her eyes, the laughter of the children ringing in her ears for assurance. To Sally, the sound of children playing was as familiar as a clock ticking. But, as Esme and Edward had worked their way down the length of the garden, their voices had only gradually faded, creating such a slight change at first as to provide no alarm to their carer.

At the water's edge, Edward had pushed over a small section of the picket fence that surrounded the pond, allowing the children to pull on the rope that tethered a small rowing boat. Edward had removed his shoes and had been first to climb on board. Using the oars, he now tried to get the boat even closer to the water's edge, but the mud held the bow in a firm grip.

Reluctant to get too dirty, Esme cautiously picked her way forward with her shoes on, holding out her arms for Edward to grab. But, as she sank into the soft mud above her ankles, the suction made it extremely difficult for her to pull free. All at once she panicked. Edward led go of the oars and jumped up, leaning over the edge to help her. She screamed.

Edward stretched as far as he could. He shouted that she should do the same. Losing her balance, she fell forward, grabbing the tethering rope for support. This caused the little boat to pitch violently. With her feet cemented and with just one hand pulling on the rope, she flapped violently to keep her face above the water. Edward gave out a piercing cry, as he fought to push the boat well away from the edge with a recovered oar, to keep the rope in tension and her head from submerging.

The scream instantly roused Sally, and so alarmed Hubert that he tore off his jacket as he sprinted down the lawn towards the pond. They met as one at the edge, where deep footprints crossed the broken fence and disappeared into the water.

Hurriedly kicking off her shoes, Sally took a step into the pond, but stopped rigidly and froze.

"I can't do it. I can't enter the water. I'm afraid of it! I'll drown again."

Hubert pushed her out of his way with considerable force and waded straight in, shouting for her to get a grip as he splashed through. With feet stuck, Sally fell sideways into the pond, instantly bringing her to her senses, driven by Esme's shrill cries for help. She fought to stand, her long dress soaked and holding her back like an anchor.

Struggling against the weight, she lunged at Esme, placing her own body beneath the girl's to cradle her, allowing Hubert to trace the line of Esme's legs into the muddy bed, where he dug his fingers into the slime to free her feet from her shoes without asserting too much strain on her fragile bones.

Once free, and with her arms holding Sally tightly around her neck, Esme was carried to the grass. Hubert turned and plunged straight back into the water to steady the stern of the little boat, which rocked with Edward's sobbing and the ripples caused by all the splashing about. Treading water, Hubert spoke softly to the boy, comparing him to the bravest of the pirates in the Caribbean. Bit by bit, Edward recovered his composure. Once the boat was entirely steady, Hubert pulled it forward and out of the deeper water, where he took Edward in his arms and carried him to Esme.

As Ella and Ernest flew from the house, with the bishop some distance behind the other guests panting with every hurried step and waving his napkin, the four were already away from the water's edge and laying on the grass, gasping. None was hurt, but all were in shock.

"Thank you," cried Sally, lifting her head towards Hubert. "You're a hero."

He smiled weakly. "We both, I think."

They looked at the others approaching quickly in various states of anxiety.

"Now you're for it, Miss Ayres!"

CHAPTER 12

A humane woman

A horrible conviction struck Sally as Esme and Edward were cosseted back into the house, leaving her alone to follow at the rear. Even Hubert had left her, although against his wish and with much protest, as the other guests surrounded him with praise for his bold actions and herded him inside.

As Sally reached the door, Mrs Campbell alone appeared to greet her, blocking the way forward. She held three towels and a long coat, barking an order to clean off the worst of the mud before entering, using the pump and trough in an outbuilding. She was not to drip any wet clothes over the rugs.

Submissively, Sally took them, agreeing that the smell of the mud from deep below the surface of the pond floor was, indeed, quite nauseating. Her attempt to trivialise the embarrassment she felt fell entirely on deaf ears. As the door was closing in her face, she quickly looked past and noticed many black footprints and wet patches already on the floor, but these were clearly heroically tolerated for having been left by Hubert and This and That.

As she removed her stockings to run cold water over her feet, Sally felt abused. She was a passionately humane woman that life, she felt, had taken advantage of. Before leaving her family home, she had cared for her siblings as a teenage surrogate mother without serious incident, and had later spent most of her wages as a novice teacher in Westkings purchasing additional books for the children in her care, in the hope of providing those little minds with a wider appreciation of life. Now, it seemed, she was not to be trusted among children.

Once ruminating self reproach, with the water tingling around her toes, more of life's little injustices just kept popping into her head. And, there were so many to choose from. Her recent experiences had left her well stocked. Shipwrecked while travelling to spread the gospel in Africa, she mused, would have been tragedy enough if isolated, but, of course, it wasn't. She had been hit by the aftershock of hearing her husband pathetically call to her as he had been dragged helplessly under the sea, still grasping part of the doomed ship. And now, she reflected, she was approaching middle age, outcast and disregarded. Her world was upside down, with only the spectre of long-term loneliness in view, with nobody to share the comforts and burdens of old age.

Yes, loneliness was indeed her greatest fear. As she dried her legs, rubbing the rough towelling over her still curvaceous limbs, she reflected on what might have been. Had she been too benevolent all those years before in giving up her only child to James Elvington, when such a son as Edmond had become would never have allowed her to be so ill used by strangers? It was a curious thought. And for what, she wondered? To now be treated like an outsider even by him, the very person who could have enriched her world; her own flesh and blood. Edmond could have been the most important thing in her life, as she would have been in his. Even denied James' wealth, she would not have failed him.

After donning the coat, she wrung-out and folded her wet clothes. Both wet towels were placed within the last dry towel and knotted into a bundle. She turned, ready for the house and all that awaited her therein. Thoughts of horrors past faded with every anxious step, replaced by a dread for her immediate prospects. Today, she considered, had not been entirely successful! She laughed hysterically for thinking of the phrase 'entirely successful'. The last twenty-four hours had actually been another pig of a day to join all the rest. Life was so unfair, so ironic. And now, having fought against her own fear of water to help save This and That, she could expect only censure, when hunger had been the enemy of her attentiveness.

She entered the house, careful not to step into the mud with her clean feet. Leaving the bundle of towels in the corner where other abandoned clothes leaked into a small puddle weeping on the floor, she climbed the stairs to her bedroom. And there, just as she feared, a letter lay propped against the mirror of the dressing table. The writing showed it to be hurriedly written. She opened it anxiously.

Dear Miss Ayres

I am called upon to look at your ability to care for my children in the light of what has passed, both today and before. It makes not for a happy picture.

You might come recommended by my true friend, James Elvington, but I have responsibility to my family and I now believe his trust in you to be misguided. It is clearly influenced by your former relationship, the progeny of which I hold you entirely responsible for, as it is nature for a man to be beguiled by a pretty face, and, alas, all too frequent for some women to get her hooks into another woman's husband. Thus, I hold James blameless in your affair. He has my complete admiration for the way Edmond has turned out under his tutelage, and his alone. I am bound to say that, having experienced your deficiencies myself, Edmond might have become quite different if left in your keeping.

Please pack your bags at once and leave in the morning. I will see to it that you are paid for the week, plus another week's wages for the time you waited to begin your employment. That, you must agree, is generosity itself on my part for one day's effort. In exchange, I insist that you do not approach my husband on this or any other matter. I will inform him of my decision only after you have left.

A meal will be sent up to your room shortly, followed by another before you retire, and breakfast tomorrow. I will tell my husband that you are fatigued and that I have given you leave to stay in your room. In this manner, you may keep yourself to yourself.

Yours truly

Ella Browning, Mrs

PS. Mrs Campbell suggests, and I agree, that you should not enquire after the children. On that, I can assure you they are in recovery.

When Ella knocked at Sally's door the next morning, there was no reply. The room was vacant and tidy, the note of the previous day torn in half and lying on the dressing table. Two food trays were neatly stacked, covered by a cloth to prevent flies.

The occupant had not waited for her wages, but had slipped away in the early hours and was now to be found sitting on her bag at Market Place, looking for a public coach to carry her out of town. At this early hour, the town was as quiet as a graveyard, completely empty of other sounds beyond the slow footsteps of the man from the gasworks, who walked the streets in succession at the advent of dawn.

Sally felt mixed emotions, part anger and part foreboding. Anger was uppermost, caused by her recollection of the conversation she had had with Ella when they first met, when Ella had confessed to having been another of James' female conquests. Why had she so turned against her now, citing perfidy in her letter as one reason for her displeasure? She could only think Ella had forgotten that she had shared her own deep secret with her. "There is no-one more virtuous than a bad woman turned righteous," she said to herself, smiling at the thought of what damage she could do to Ella in return by informing Ernest of his wife's infidelity. But, then, what good would it do either? She recalled a short biblical text from St Mathew, stitched in canvas and framed by her late mother, which had adorned the parlour wall:

I am not come to call the righteous,
but sinners to repentance

"Perhaps Ella and I shall be saved," she said out loud.

"Saved," said the man from the gasworks as he walked by, struggling with his long pole. "Tis an awkward thing to play with souls, and matter enough to save one's own."

Sally looked up in disbelief. "Sir, you have quoted Robert Browning."

"Is that so, Missy? I just like the words. Don't you?"

"I hate all Brownings, but it will pass!"

CHAPTER 13

The truth revealed

For several days, Hubert enquired about Sally in vain. His concern for her had grown out of three innocuous visits to the Browning home, each time being met at the door by Ella, who appeared to be in an agitated state. She had made vague excuses why his welcome into their house at that moment was impossible. On each occasion he had tried to explain that it was Miss Ayres he wanted to see, but the very mention of her name only made Ella more determined not to let him pass.

Puzzled by her reaction, Hubert had at first been concerned for the well-being of the children, thinking that Ella's strange behaviour could only be caused by some grave concern for their health, perhaps resulting from the incident at the pond, where they might have picked up an illness from the water. But, prior to his last visit, he had seen them playing with a hoop in the street just before being called back into the house.

* * *

The following Saturday saw a much awaited cricket match between the Glastonbury eleven and a visiting team from the village of Midsomer Norton. As both Ernest and he were down as team members for the match, he saw it as an opportunity to get to the bottom of the problem, away from Ella. Unexpectedly, though, Ernest hadn't turned up until the game was over, his place filled at the last minute by Rufus Marsh, a baker's apprentice from Sturminster Newton who was temporarily renting a room in Northload Street and so qualified to be a Glastonbury player.

Despite Midsomer having a strong reputation, the team had only managed twenty-seven runs in their first innings, which included ten 'byes' and 'wides' that required no effort on the part of the batsmen. The Glastonbury captain had cut through the opposition like butter, taking five of the wickets for only six runs made by Midsomer's finest. In reply, Glastonbury had amassed thirty-three runs, with the captain and his partner making nineteen before being bowled out. The second innings scored little more, but Glastonbury ended in high spirits, winning with six wickets in hand.

It was a jubilant Hubert, therefore, who emerged from the pavilion to see Ernest propping up the bar, several empty beer glasses forming a guard around his elbows.

"I know you called," he answered to Hubert's first enquiry, a slur in his voice. "What I didn't know was how to face you, or anyone else for that matter, sober that is."

Hubert said that he remained in the dark.

"Why should you understand, my old ginger friend. I don't either! You know I've often joked that in modern society people are free to marry often. I've always thought it was a bloody good idea, borrowed from the French. It's quite fashionable, too. That Mrs Campbell seems to be well versed in the sport." He slurped from a refreshed glass. "Well, I no longer hold that view. Of course, with divorce so devilishly hard, the circumstances of repeated marriage should more usually be occasioned by the death of a spouse, anyway, as with that dreadful woman."

"What *are* you saying, Ernest? Has Ella died suddenly? Tell me, man! I only saw her a couple of days ago. She looked fine then."

"Not dead, although she might as well be to me." He took another gulp, burping with the intake of air. "As the death of a spouse is rare in couples of a young to middling age, one has to suppose, I suppose, that any fashion requiring several bedroom partners doesn't dictate the need for actual bodily or legal separation at all! Not at all! I find that useful to know, don't you? Wish I'd known it years ago. Separated not by death or divorce, it leaves but one route to multiple copulation, carnal knowledge, love-making, mating, intercourse, or even buggery as Douglas would say if you're of that persuasion. Now you understand?"

"No, not a word, other than I can see you're drunk out of your mind."

"Out of my mind? Yes, that's the most sensible thing either of us has said in the past five minutes. Get me another drink, my little money pit!"

"For pity's sake, Ernest, how long have we known each other?"

"Years upon years. An age. An eternity. Infinity!"

"Exactly, we were at school together."

"Were we? Yes, I suppose we were. I have a slight recollection that it was loathsome."

"So, you can unburden yourself on me, if you wish. Please, is there anything you want to tell me, before I ask you a question of my own? I'm worried out of my mind."

"You too, old carrot top? Join the club, mate."

"Mine is regarding Miss Ayres."

Ernest's expressed changed in an instant. He banged his glass hard on the bar, spilling more of its content.

"Sally . . . bloody . . . Ayres, the woman who has wrecked my life. If you want to see her, then go to the devil." He turned away, taking a full glass with him in each hand. Hubert was shocked. "That woman has caused a proper upset in my house. And there was I thinking she was good and kind, when all along she was spiteful," he said to the wall.

Hubert took Ernest's shoulders and turned him back. "Explain, for my sake as much as yours."

"Explain, what? How can a mere man explain the thinking of women? They're irrational as a species. Am I not right, my old ginger biscuit?"

"Well . . ."

"What am I thinking of, asking you? How would you know?"

"Ernest . . ."

"Alright, alright, I'll tell you, my little short-house, and save you thinking for yourself. Now, where was I?"

"You were going to tell me about Ella."

"Was I? I don't remember that! No, yes, I remember now. I was telling you about the difference between men and the other gender. What do you want to know?

"For heaven sake, Ernest, stop drinking that stuff for a moment and concentrate."

"Procreation, now, that's a pretty big subject. You see . . . is that what we were discussing?"

Hubert was becoming angry. "Ernest, stop drinking! You were telling me the difference between men and women."

"Was I? At your age, my old ginger beer, you should know that for yourself. Didn't your father . . . no, I don't suppose he thought you would need to know. Well, let me be your daddy." He swung his arm over Hubert's shoulder, pulling himself closer to Hubert's face. His breath was bad. "Whereas a man's actions are predictable, reasonable and judged on merit, a woman wishes only to be admired. You see the difference, old love? They don't care if they're illogical, scatterbrain and, and . . . give me another word."

"Considerate."

"Yes, contrary. Despite anything said, they merely want attention. Pretty this, pretty that . . . pretty damned silly." He laughed into his glass.

"All women?"

Ernest looked askance at the question. "Of course, you bloody idiot. But, then, what do I know. I only know women of a certain type. Maybe, the more lowly the female, the greater would be her ability to reason. It's a matter of natural selection, in reverse. The higher up the social scale they climb, the less they need to be rational. Conversely, old dear, the lower in the pecking order they plummet, the more they need their wits to survive."

"It's that simple?"

"Absolutely. Tell me you believe it isn't! However, old

fruit, I expect women see the whole riddle in reverse. Ella is always telling me I'm shallow. Me . . . shallow!"

"And, now, if I ask again what has happened, would you consider me imprudent?"

"Your asking wouldn't be, Hubert, but my answer might be."

"Then I ask that question."

At last Ernest's attention was caught. After looking into his glass for a few moments of reflection, he pushed it to one side and pulled himself up, regaining dignity as if measured by the inch.

"I first met Ella when she was a girl. She was my sister's best friend as it happens. She would often be at my home, where I avoided her with all the guile of a boy. When she was ten she told me that she loved me. I can still remember her smile showing a row of little white teeth that were framed in a mouth of developing shapeliness. That moment, for a split second, I felt something new, something which warmed inside of me. Of course, I told her she should go away and play with her dolls, and I quickly climbed the highest elm tree. Soon after, she was packed off to some school or other, and that was the last I saw of her for many years. She became forgotten to me, as I was to her. Then, one November morning, when I rode out over Dukes Wood, I came across a young woman walking beside her pony, which had pulled up lame. I stopped to help and looked on the face of a stranger, but with familiar features hidden within the fairest skin. It was her, and that very instant that same feeling in the pit of my stomach returned. I fell in love, well, that or my breakfast was playing up."

"You're telling me that woman was Ella?"

"Yes. We met over and over again, sometimes by accident but more often by contrivance, until one sunny morning we sat by a brook, where we picked buttercups and she watched them float away in the stream like little yellow fairy boats, and I watched her make necklaces from daisies. We dangled our feet in the water, which bubbled over small rocks and tickled our toes."

"How romantic."

"Get out of it! I'm no romantic, you should know that. Anyhow, at that moment I felt the strength of the world's greatest poets trip words from my lips that startled even me by their grace, as if I now noticed things in nature that I hadn't before. Presently I proposed, but she was too young to accept. I apologised for my recklessness. She told me that I hurt her by saying I had asked for her hand in recklessness."

"What happened?"

"I waited another year before asking again, and this time she accepted. We were married within the month."

"But? I just know there's a 'but'."

"But, it wasn't to last. We moved from Winchester to Glastonbury when we were both still in our twenties, way before This and That arrived on the scene. It was a happy move, or so I thought. I was then in modest employment at a bank, working my way up the ladder of success at a painfully slow rate. Ella, I think, expected more of me, but never said as much. She was used to having things I couldn't afford, and as the years passed the gap between her expectations and the reality of her life widened. I see that now."

"I'm sorry."

"Then, one day, I found out that Ella was seeing another man. It tore me apart. I had formed suspicions, of course, but had dismissed them as jealousy. One day I followed her. She journeyed only a short distance to the edge of town, where she met a man I recognised in a cottage he rented under an assumed name. It was so remote in its location that there was little chance of them being seen, or of their meeting being merely coincidental. He was considerably older than her and of greatly improved position over me."

"What happened?"

"I didn't have the wit about me at that time to confront them, needing more evidence of wrong doing before destroying our marriage. I played a watch and wait game. Each time she arrived back home, she was so bright and caring that I doubted my own reasoning. But, it happened time after time, without scheduled regularity, but often. I was beside myself with indecision, which allowed the situation to get out of control. Then, after I had finally prepared myself for confrontation at the cottage, I watched as a messenger handed Ella a note and she turned away, crying. I stayed hidden, almost feeling sorry for her and hateful of his treatment. How daft is that? By the time she returned home, she had complete composure again and life continued as before. Sometimes she cried, but while hiding in secret little places. Twice more she left for the cottage and twice more she returned only with a message. She never went again after that and the cottage was let to elderly sisters. As the weeks passed, I felt less and less inclined to ruin any happiness we had left. Of course, I never told her I knew about the affair, and when the children eventually arrived she became totally absorbed in them.

Everything had returned to the status quo, helped by an inheritance which allowed me to pursue the occupation of a gentleman, until Miss Ayres put in her tuppence worth, that is."

"Miss Ayres? How does she fit into things? Tell me, so that I may judge."

"She gave me a note which said '*I am not come to call the righteous, but sinners to repentance*'. It was signed by her."

"That's all?"

"Yes."

"Nothing else?"

"No."

"Do you think it was by way of an apology?"

"Maybe."

"And that trifle was harmful in your eyes?"

"Not mine. I was careless and left the letter in my study. Ella picked it up. She obviously thought Miss Ayres had said something to me and duly confessed her affair in atonement. I told her afterwards that I had known nothing of it. It seemed easier than explaining how I had followed her all those years before and hadn't intervened. That's when she ran screaming from the room and hasn't properly spoken to me since. What should I do?"

"Was it given or sent? It makes a difference."

"Sent."

"That's not what you said before. It tells a different story. As to what you should do, I can't think. All I can say is that you blame the wrong person. You should hold Ella to account and the man for abusing your trust, or even yourself for standing on the sidelines letting it happened, but I fail to see that Miss Ayres or her words can be condemned in any way as the cause of your present situation. Truly, I can't. If you don't mind me saying, it seems to me that you hide your deeper thoughts under a mask of temerity, but it's this impulsiveness that most frequently heralds your actions. Go back to her. Tell her the truth and offer forgiveness. I'm sure it will work wonders."

He nodded.

"But, what of Miss Ayres? You don't tell me."

"She was fired by Ella the afternoon of the boating accident. She left our home before we awoke the next morning. We have absolutely no idea where she has gone."

After Hubert left, vowing to find her, Ernest ordered another drink, mumbling into his glass, "but I bet I can guess to whom, the bastard."

CHAPTER 14

Return of the Rose Month

Ask me why my heart bestows, joyful lift from seeing
the country rose

It was June, that glorious and incandescent month, when the leafy countryside was dedicated to renewal in its many forms. Deep in the lush undergrowth scurried reclusive rodents, among them tiny newly born shrews keeping close to their mother by nipping at her tail. Squirrels danced among the trees above, and little girls sat cross-legged in the sunshine picking wild flowers to decorate their bonnets.

Elsewhere, buttery-white petals of the stunted burnet rose bloomed in patches, and the pink sweetbriar with its prickly stems and apple-scented leaves produced a fragrance that wafted lightly through the air. At the forest edges, butterflies flitted erratically in brightly lit glades, while tortoiseshell caterpillars fed on nettles and the caterpillars of cabbage whites began their relentless attack on vegetable crops.

At the edge of ponds and lakes, willow grew and hoverflies

sought the yellow flag and iris. Below the shimmering water's surface, the tadpole larva of frogs, toads and newts began their hazardous existence, and water-boatmen scampered across floating vegetation. Elsewhere, bramble threw out its prickly shoots, and honeysuckle, corn poppy and a rich variety of other flowers hosted hard-working bumblebees, while honeybees gathered pollen and nectar, inadvertently pollinating as they went. Even lime trees produced nectar at this time of year, their leaves glistening with honeydew, that sweet and sticky substance excreted by aphids that infested their host.

Swooping in the clear, radiant sky were swallows and swifts, watching their fledglings take flight or master the art of catching a meal on the wing. Then, the day over, it became the time of the less exotic moths, whose caterpillar larva, like those of their more-beautiful daylight relatives, had been harvested by breeding thrush, nuthatch and other birds intent on nurturing a new generation. It was, in celebrated multi-colour, the start of Summer, the Rose Month.

Ernest's private thoughts regarding Sally's intended destination had been wildly wrong, but he cared nothing more either way and wasn't in the least troubled to discover the truth. Hubert, on the other hand, did care, but with other pressing business coming up, he had allowed himself only a short time to find her. In his anxiety to fulfil the mission in haste, he too had followed a similar hunch that one day led him by horse to Westkings, where James and Edmond Elvington expressed their own genuine concern for Sally's welfare.

"I just thought that she might have come here to ask for your help, since it was you who introduced her to the Brownings. She probably knows few other places of refuge. I was at Ernest's home, at a party, you understand, when she first arrived. We struck up a bit of an acquaintance. Unfortunately, it appears that I was mistaken to come here."

"We must help find her, Father," interrupted Edmond, careful not to reveal his own agenda. "I had hoped she would stay in Glastonbury."

"You had hoped that, Edmond?" said James, puzzled. "What can she be to you that you should care one way or the other?"

"Don't make yourself ill over it, Father. You're beginning to look red about the face. It really is of no importance. Trust me in this."

James stared at his son, concerned for matters best left long buried. When Edmond shrugged and walked away, he turned back to Hubert, raising his one good arm to Hubert's shoulder.

"Sally is a friend from long ago, no more. I owed her a favour, so I helped. We are now full-square even and I very much doubt if our paths will ever cross again. But, if they do, I would make her welcome, you can be comforted by that."

"I feel she has been ill-used. Without finding her, I can't help."

James relinquished his hold and reached to the mantelpiece, where he took his favourite pipe from its rack and placed it between his teeth. The matches were held in a small metal container, once one of a pair of snuff boxes. He lifted it, looking at its gilding and remembering how his wife had given the other away on the day Christabel had been taken from their manor as a baby. It still hurt him to think of the pain he had caused to both the child and his wife, incidents that were now beyond any human alteration. He replaced the box on the mantel, then the pipe without lighting it, each of his eyes glistening with a single tear of remorse.

"Events of the past and events of the present will, I can assure you, be looked upon as one single event in the future, my dear Hubert. The past is a foreign land we cannot revisit, the future a land we will never reach. Maybe she has been ill-used, as you profess, but only what happens after today is of any importance now. Find her if you can and change her destiny, for life is mere flotsam that floats where the waves take it, each point of the compass guaranteeing a different outcome. For my part, I can offer no further assistance."

In reality, Sally was already a long way to the east, taking an almost opposite route. She walked slowly from village to village, never taking any permanent work but merely drifting as the mood took her, often undertaking small sewing or cleaning jobs for nothing more than a bed for a night or two and several good meals. The countryside here was best described as rolling, neither with high peaks or low valleys, but offering a gentle undulation, making the walk a pleasant experience.

She had heard much about that mystical place known as Stonehenge, a little further on from Winterbourne Stoke, but not quite as far as Woodhenge and Larkhill. It was a place she wanted to see for herself. What better time to reach it than the 23rd of the month, she had thought, St John's Eve, when a chain of bonfires would be lit across the countryside, from east to west, their blaze symbolically challenging the sun not to fade after Midsummer Day, when daylight began its slow but relentless retreat towards longer nights. She had also heard of the Salisbury Giant, a fourteen-foot wood framed figure that had once been paraded by the Tailor's Guild in a midsummer torchlight procession, but was now housed in a local museum. It all sounded a great deal of fun and a panacea for her present moods.

One afternoon, on reaching the outskirts of Salisbury Plain, Sally took early shelter at a cottage in Puctonbury Ash, close to Tytherington Hill, which offered a room to travellers. She still had four days before St John's Eve and saw little point in unnecessary exertion, particularly as the route ahead became sparsely populated and there was no guarantee of accommodation.

The cottage was small and dark, with cob walls of mud and tiny low windows, kept darker still by trees on all sides that formed a barrier to any natural sunlight. Inside, her bedroom was not plastered or finished in any way, a dreary little space with a bare thatch ceiling.

She had been given a Benzoline oil lamp for light, although it was still bright outside. Sally knew of these dangerous little lamps, but had never used one, having generally been replaced by safer paraffin lamps with glass globes. The Benzoline lamp was the size of an apple, with a central pipe and a wick. Other than the addition of a regulator for the wick and the refinement of the oil, the concept had not altered much since biblical times, although for most poor homes in Wessex candles had preceded the coming of the brighter paraffin lamp. Knowing she had been warned that if the wick was set too high the lamp was likely to get very hot and suddenly catch fire, she arrested her curiosity to use it.

The landlady was middle-aged, but hard living had made her a shrivelled-looking figure wrapped in several layers of rags that were abundant with tears and holes. She had no better clothes, but these garments were regularly washed. Additional layers were added as the weather cooled, or removed as warmth allowed.

In truth, she was probably no more than ten years older than Sally herself, but looked another generation. It was not that she had to live so meagrely. Far from it. Remaining a spinster after her father died, having been fully occupied as his carer and housekeeper all her adult life, she had inherited the place plus four other cottages in good repair. The others were all close by and all were a great deal better than hers. But, she had been taught to live sparingly and now could imagine no other way. The decision to continue occupying the same draughty cottage at been an easy choice, the others yielding greater rental profit.

The downstairs being a single room, Sally took a seat by the range, where she was given a bowl of thick broth, containing only a few strands of meat but heavy with chopped swede, potatoes and horse beans. It was warming and she was grateful for having her stomach filled.

"Try my bread, dearie," said the woman, breaking a small corner from a loaf.

It tasted strange.

"Barley bread. It was my mother who showed me how to

save money by baking without wheat flour. Get it down you and have a mug of my tea to wash it away. Waste not, want not."

As she sat with her tea, Sally expressed her gratitude for the oil lamp but said that she didn't want to use it, particularly as her bed was directly under thatch.

"So be it. I don't mind. I just thought you might like the extra light it gives out, as you have books. Here, have two candles."

"One will be sufficient," she replied, smiling.

"No, dearie, you take two. They don't burn bright and you'll need one to see the other! My old dad bought the 'rats-tails', that's candles that were twenty to a pound weight. He wouldn't buy the larger ones that were sixteen to the pound. But he did stock enough while they were cheap, so I'll never be without light while I live."

"Did he farm?"

"Bless you, no. He produced a bottled hair tonic that was sold in all the main towns around these parts. He made it of glycerine and lime juice. Of course, he only made it. He didn't retail it, as he was a bald as an egg and seeing him would've killed off his business at a stroke. For a long time he had several men working for him, but they all remained his apprentices, no matter how old they were."

"Why?"

"Because, by keeping them apprentices he could legally pay them less than the going rate. By the way, as we're talking of candles, if you see any blue ones lying about, don't touch 'em. My father would put up with the rats and mice eating the white tallow, being made from rendered fat from the carcasses of sheep, cattle and horses, but he wouldn't forgive any of his men pinching them to snack on. So, he had them laced with poison and coloured. '*Put an end to both types of rat*', I remember him saying to my mother." She smiled at the memory. "The old sod."

"Blue?" checked Sally.

"Blue," replied the woman, "sometime found dragged into a corner and with the skeleton of a rat attached.

By eight o'clock, the woman was in bed. The range had been allowed to burn to ash and the temperature dropped quickly. Despite the early hour, Sally followed her example and climbed the stairs to her room. There was coldness about the place beyond the lack of fire and sunlight. Noticing the walls were infested with tiny flies, she pulled the bed slightly into the middle. A black spider that had marched across the inner thatch, now hurriedly tried to bury itself amongst the straw.

Sally tried to ignore the strangeness of the evening, snuggling beneath the blankets by pulling them high up around her neck.

Soon after midnight, she was disturbed by tapping near the window. The trees being so close, she thought nothing more of it. But it persisted, an annoying sound that once heard could not be ignored. Further sleep would be impossible without doing something about it. With some reluctance, she threw back the warm covers and walked trance-like to the window.

There she stood motionless, looking at the moon through the branches. It appeared almost phosphorescent, yet made the fields below look shadowy in their tincture of greys and browns. There was at atmosphere about the night that seemed different, something that she could not quite put her finger on. Perhaps it was the isolation of the place.

She looked down. The fields, previously full of sheep, now appeared empty. Maybe they had gathered under the far side of the wall, she thought. She opened the window. To her surprise, outside there were no sounds to be heard, nothing at all to disturb the night. Not a single animal or bird broke the silence. Then, something caught the corner of her eye. To her right an owl sat on the ledge, motionless. Slowly, she stretched out her hand towards it, but it did not move, its head fixed and occupied. When her fingers were within a span of its feathers, she pulled back, amazed how it ignored her.

Slipping on her coat and shoes, she made her way downstairs, careful not to let the creaking floorboards wake the woman. She crept outside and over to the nearest dry stone wall where, as predicted, the sheep were huddled around some prickly gorse, tightly packed and facing in one direction. She looked up to her window, where the owl still perched motionless.

Her eyes moved to the next curtained window along, occupied by the owner. An oil lamp recently lit showed the woman to be awake, pacing backwards and forwards like a shadow puppet, with her hands over her ears. This was strange behaviour, Sally considered, as the night was deadly silent.

As she turned her back to the fields, an unexpected flash tore across the sky and startled her, followed by the rumble of great power. A huge lightning fork from the heavens stabbed the earth, quickly followed by a shrill crack of an intensity she had never experienced before. The storm was nearly overhead.

Another followed, then again. It got closer by the second, a deafening noise that became hard to bear. She ran inside and slammed the door shut, placing her back against the slatted wood panels. The windows rattled. The range whistled as the wind forced its way down the crooked chimney. Suddenly, brutally and in darkness, the stairs pounded to heavy steps and she was pushed aside by the woman she thought to be in her room, who dashed from the house screaming.

"What's happening?" Sally shouted after her, while straining to hold the door slightly open against the low wind, her voice lost to the night. Then, just as dramatically, it stopped. She led go and the door swung easily on its old hinges. The woman was gone.

Unsure what to do, Sally pulled the range door open and laid a fire for the woman's return. She filled a pan with water from a pail, ready to take away the night chill with hot tea. The owl now swooped low over the field.

As the fire caught, the flames danced on her face, spitting embers from the slightly damp logs. She arranged more logs on top of the range, wanting the heat to dry them. Then, as she piled further logs in front of the fire, the windows began to rattle once more. She looked up. The owl now perched on the lower sill, its head turning one way and then the other, as if a lookout. There was a bang and then another as the door again pulled on its hinges, not as a constant pressure but as bursts that caused it to clatter.

Sally took a candle to the window, but was unable to see out. She snubbed the wick and at once the panorama showed itself.

The tapping sound began again, this time more distinguishable as if a hammer striking wood. There was another vertical flash, this time momentarily illuminating what looked like a figure in the distance holding boots. It had to be the woman returning. The rain was now falling hard and constant.

With thoughts only for the woman's safety, Sally grabbed a tattered shawl that lay across the back of a chair and ran out to her, but within a few yards she pulled up hard with an almighty scream of terror. It was not the woman at all, but a man with a rope around his neck, hanging.

When the older woman arrived back in the house some minutes later, she found Sally lying on the floor in a faint, soaking wet and dripping. She hurriedly placed a folded sack under her head and covered her with a blanket, talking to her gently and reviving her with smelling salts wafted backwards and forwards under her nose. The pail lay on its side. Slowly, Sally's eyes began to show movement.

"Come on, dearie, that's right. Take another sniff. You'll soon feel better."

As Sally revived, she grabbed the woman's wrist in a fierce vice-like grip. "What in God's name was out there?"

"What have you done to get so wet, dear?"

"What? There was a storm. You know there was. I saw you go out in it."

"There was no such thing, I can assure you. I was out checking my hens. I heard a fox."

"No! No! There was rain and lightning and thunder, yet, before it struck, the night was as silent as a graveyard. I know it was."

"Do *I* look wet?"

Sally looked at her. She ran her fingers over the woman's sleeve. It was dry.

"How can that be? I don't understand."

"This is a strange place to those who don't live here. What did you see?"

"A man, hanging."

The woman shuddered visibly. "You saw that?"

Sally nodded.

"Then I'll tell you straight. You're blessed with a sixth sense. Did you not know that?"

"I don't want to be. I want to be ordinary."

"That really isn't up to us to decide, dearie. I, too, had it once, but it's left me now. I'm not sorry, either. My guess is that you've had other experiences, elsewhere and at other times. Am I right?"

"Possibly!"

"I thought as much. Don't hide it. Now I know, I can explain one or two things held secret from others. What you saw was the Bulford cobbler."

"Who, God forbid, is that?"

"Not *is*, but *was*. Sit over here." She helped Sally to a window seat, where the younger sat on her feet and embraced her legs in a foetal position, warmed by the heat of the embers that were glowing around the logs. The fire was poked into life after a few of the logs from above the range were tossed inside.

"Long, long ago, generations back to be sure, a cobbler living in Bulford became the focus of anger throughout the village. Folklore says that he had an apprentice, a nice young fellow, who he treated so badly that everyone began to hate the cobbler. Their anger became so intense that, one day, some of the folk made an effigy of him and carried it around the village, finally hanging it from the gallows. This happened day after day, in the hope that the message would get through. But, things really got out of hand. Feeling threatened, desperate and hated, the cobbler asked a friend what he could do to stop it. '*Do what the villagers want you to do*,' replied the friend, no doubt suggesting that he should start treating the apprentice with kindness. Taking the advice the wrong way, and in desperate state, the cobbler hanged himself. Bulford is but a stone's throw from here. His spirit used to visit me, quite often as it happens, but I haven't seen him for years."

"I can't believe any of that. I won't believe in ghosts."

"Oh, did I say it was in the middle of a storm when the rope bit hard around his neck?"

"I saw you at the window, covering your ears."

"I didn't say that I don't know when he's coming, did I? I merely said I can't see him anymore. He always frightened me to death! I'm thankful to be left alone."

"Am I to believe any of this?"

"You must believe what your eyes tell you is real, not what your heart makes you think is possible. What powers have the dead over the living, I cannot say. Can a life so rich in love one moment, or so ruined by hate, be laid to rest at a stroke, when the mortal body draws its final breath? If so, then what point is there in life itself? If love is life, then life is love. Tell me a person who can physically touch love, yet it's all about us?"

Sally shuddered involuntarily, taking the woman's hand

and holding it closely to her breast. "I'm of the belief that there's a heaven and a hell. Only, heaven is where the soul goes for eternity after a good life has been lived, to share in a heavenly body of love and understanding. Hell is not a fiery inferno at all, not place of fire, brimstone and damnation as passionately told by vicars from the pulpit. It is, instead, our own world where a soul is sent back to live a life again and try once more to aspire to God's grace, to begin as a child and then suffer all the anguishes of three score years and ten. That is hell, a living hell."

The woman smiled gently. "You are of our type, I am sure of it."

"Will I ever see this cobbler again? I don't want to."

"If you stay here, but not if you don't. I always knew when the cobbler was likely to appear. I used to hate walking back to my lonely home on those particular stormy nights, when the raw wind of twilight abraded my hands and feet and caused my humble heart to sink at what dreadful images might lay ahead. When frightened by the cobbler, or other appearances reason could not explain, I used to shout 'why me, why me', all the time hoping for no answer to encourage the spirit to come closer. I could hear in my head a reply, or my mind played tricks on me."

"The woman in the water," Sally said. "She called to me. At last I remember what she said. Like your experience, there were no audible sounds, but she whispered the words gently in the sea and I heard them in my head. I answered, 'Where am I?' Only then was I shown my escape by her outstretched hand. Yet, strangest of all, after helping me she then seemed to shun me, as if I was not worthy. I thank God that in my time of gravest peril, when the Day of Judgement was upon me, I was visited with mercy."

"You see?" said the woman. "There was a point in the cobbler coming to you tonight. I won't ask about your experience. In truth, I don't want to know. I'm content merely in thinking that you have been enlightened in some way. Do you have a plan?"

"Will anything be of my planning anymore, or am I merely a plaything for fate to do whatever it wants with me?" she replied diffidently.

CHAPTER 15

The Stones

The night did not pass well. Both women were disturbed in mind and body. Sally's request to pass the remainder of the dark hours in the woman's company, by resting at the foot of her bed, had not been welcomed. By the morning they felt low in demeanour and bleary eyed. The more fragile was Sally, who held onto the rail as she descended the tight stairs to breakfast. The older woman was already down. Sally found her at the table with her arms folded in apparent fury.

"You talked in your sleep!" she said abruptly, pointing to a place where she should sit. "I was much displeased."

Sally thought she had not slept at all and said so.

"Well you did!"

She apologised. "Did I say anything to upset you?"

The woman replied that she hadn't, as such. However, she added: "I thought you understood the need for folk like us to live a simple life. Yet, you talked in your dreams of wanting money. If you want my opinion, you should reconcile yourself to being humble. You'll get no relief from the rich, of that you can be sure. What little happiness a spinster can achieve in a world made for sharing couples will come only from prudence in her own actions."

Sally agreed. Compliance seemed to take the edge off the woman's temper.

"I'm aware you might find my remarks peculiar, even harsh, Miss Ayres, but I talk from grave experience. The mere thought of it still makes me angry. You see, I once relied on a man. He let me down and I never recovered. And now I'm left here, abandoned to my future." She sighed, turned, and opened the oven. A warm, sweet smell of new bread enveloped the room. "By and by, a man called for you earlier. I didn't like the look of him at all. I didn't say anything and he left here none the wiser. I let you sleep on. At least an hour has since passed."

"Did you get his name?" pleaded Sally.

"I didn't give him a chance to offer it. He was out of breath from much hard riding and as mad as a March hare when I shut the door in his face. He poked a calling card under the door, but I tossed that into the fire."

"I wish you hadn't!"

"You think he might've wanted to help you?"

"How can I tell, without knowing who he was? As to any dream I might have had regarding money, I can tell you straight that I only once asked for financial help. It was to be a small sum that I intended to repay, but it got me into terrible trouble that ruined my young life. I'm older and wiser now. I am now, as you say I should be, reliant only on myself."

* * *

The rider had been Fairbourne, who had begged a few days leave from his work in London to pursue a few of his own new ideas. Thackeray had accepted willingly, more than ever convinced that the entire quest for an answer to the riddle of the nine predicted maidens was utterly pointless. He had been thoroughly scared by his experience at Burgerhout's hands and no longer wanted to continue any inquiries. It was all a huge muddle of the first order.

For Fairbourne, there remained in the back of his mind the niggling thought that the nine maidens themselves, their starting point in all this, could just as easily be viewed as part of some larger conspiracy. Where to draw the line was a grey area. If the Government had taken the matter seriously enough to sanction an inquiry in the first place, then he too should give it his best shot, even if he had to do it alone.

It hadn't been hard to separate Arthur, the homeland defender, from those myths that had grown around the legend of King Arthur. The king stuff just wasn't real. But, that was only the start of associated complications. For such stories had also introduced Merlin, the legendary and, presumably, mythical wizard of Arthur's court. Yet, Merlin was said to have made his own predictions which later came true in the real world, some regarding the sea.

One such prophecy had declared '*There shall land on the Rock of Merlin, those who shall burn Paul, Penzance and Newlyn*'. Merlin's rock, he found, was at the quayside at Mousehole in Cornwall where, in 1595, a millennium after the prediction, a small number of Spanish ships had anchored and the town had been razed to the ground.

In reading about Merlin, Fairbourne had been struck by

other folklore surrounding this strange and magical figure. One such legend stated that the stones used to build an ancient monument in Wiltshire were magically moved there by Merlin, at the request of Ambrosius Aurelianus. Fairbourne knew Aurelianus to be a genuine Romano-Briton prince of the correct period. There was more. It was written that Aurelianus had wanted them erected to be a fitting tribute to Prince Vortigern and his followers, who had been treacherously slaughtered near Amesbury by Hengist, the Saxon invader.

Fairbourne harboured no delusions about Merlin's lack of authenticity. He was the least real of all the figures so far introduced into the puzzle, yet among the most charismatic. But, to be sure to leave no stone unturned, he had read academic papers on Stonehenge itself, written centuries before by the antiquarian and scholar John Aubrey, who had researched the site at the time of the English Civil War. These blew apart any chance of Merlin's hand in its construction. For, as he discovered, Stonehenge didn't date from the 5th and 6th centuries at all, but was completed long before the Egyptian pyramids, taking over half a millennium to reach its final form in 1400BC. That meant Merlin and Stonehenge were two thousand years out of kilter.

Strangely, the henge had not even been the realisation of a single plan. Far from it. It had been worked and reworked three times, developed from an original circular mud ditch and embankment, surrounded by small hollows into which the blood of sacrificed animals may have been poured as gateways to the underworld, to its final form with inner and outer trilithons, pairs of tall stones with a third laid horizontally. Stones marking the avenue, a pathway to the river Avon, had been part of phase two, when the river provided the main transport artery. All about the surrounding fields were raised mounds of mud and stones known as barrows, ancient Stone and Bronze Age burial chambers. Clearly, Merlin's mark was upon nothing.

It had been Aubrey who had made a tentative link between Stonehenge at midsummer and the Druids, an idea which had been subsequently appropriated and amplified by romantic writers. Strangely, new-generation Druids had taken up the notion, making the association real. As a fitting tribute, the hollows had been named Aubrey Holes for posterity.

Fairbourne, by then fascinated by Aubrey's writings, had also read extracts from his treatise on Oxford City itself, for personal amusement. A particular quotation tickled him and he stored it for future telling. It regarded the Earl of Oxford who, when bowing to Queen Elizabeth I, had 'farted'. So distressed by the incident, he left the city for seven years. Happily, on his return, the Queen commented 'My lord, we have forgot the fart!'

For Fairbourne, it had been a simple decision to visit Stonehenge and surrounding areas during this sojourn. After journeying by train to Glastonbury, where he had taken a room, he had arranged for the use of a good horse from the following morning. The present whereabouts of Sally Ayres was unknown to him, but he guessed that she might also visit the place after losing her job, having shown such interest in the mystical side of Glastonbury. It was a hunch that had a reasonable chance of success. Meeting her could be useful, he believed.

However, before leaving for Salisbury Plain, he had made a quick excursion to Westkings, where he had sought an urgent appointment with Edmond Elvington. Unbeknown to his father, Edmond had been the mole, keeping Thackeray informed of Sally's movements in Glastonbury, always one shady step behind and observing everything, that is until he lost track of her whereabouts. He held no allegiance to the woman, or so he thought, but had merely agreed to help after being approached.

"Why me?" Edmond had asked Thackeray those weeks before.

"A third party suggested your name," had been the reply. "I believe you are acquainted with a certain solicitor by the name of Sir Arthur Schofield. We told him of our little problem and he seemed ready to oblige with a suggestion. That suggestion was you. I have to confess to exaggerating a bit! We said our observations were for the medical welfare of Miss Ayres herself, given her mental state after the accident. He was all too willing to believe this, especially as he could suggest someone close to her to assist us. This made him very compliant, expressing that he felt very badly about all that had recently happened to her and wished to do anything in his power to atone. Such an honest man is easily manipulated."

"And the real reason why you want my help?" he had asked sincerely.

"She may be a threat to herself and others. Particularly others. I can say no more. Are you willing to oblige?"

"I don't know. Can I ask my father?"

"No, I'm afraid you can't."

"Then how do I know I, too, am not being manipulated?"

"You don't."

"I suppose I must agree, but you must assure me it's for the greater good."

He agreed that it was, and that he only wanted to protect Miss Ayres from further distress.

During the course of three days, Fairbourne had ridden wildly to cover as much area as possible, knocking at various boarding houses on his way and always in the general direction of Stonehenge and Woodhenge. He had left calling cards giving his whereabouts at places where nobody had answered, or where he had been snubbed. Each evening he had returned to his room, broken by a firm saddle and dejected by failure.

With the atmosphere freed of tension, the next few days at the cottage in Puctonbury were lived in harmony. On the 23rd, St John's Eve, Sally helped the older woman cut hazel wands, a tradition that went back centuries, although new to her.

"They have to be cut today or tomorrow or they won't work," said the older woman, brandishing a curved knife."

"Are they for divining water? I've heard of that."

"Not only that, dearie. The magic of the tree is good for finding buried treasure, or even discovering the hiding places of thieves."

"Thieves?"

"For shame you doubt me," cried the woman. "They piss

in their clothes with fear, don't they, allowing the wand to do its stuff. For love nor money, I can't think how else it would work." She grinned. "We must watch out tomorrow night for the fairies and sprites."

"Tush!" exclaimed Sally, "You've been reading *A Midsummer Night's Dream*."

"Whose Midsummer dream would you be referring to?"

"Why, William Shakespeare of course."

"Never heard of him. Is he from around these parts?"

Sally smiled, letting the remark go.

"I like your company," said the woman, placing more wands onto a growing bundle before tying them with well-worn string. "You say things I don't understand and make no joke of my stupidity."

"You know lots of things," added Sally, wrapping the blade in folded paper and placing it into a basket. "They are just different things. What I know comes from education, yours from life. Which is better depends upon the situation in which we find ourselves. Out here a volume of Shakespeare is only good for swatting flies!"

Their eyes met in merriment and they hugged. The woman took a bottle of ale from the basket and broke a loaf in half. She handed a piece to Sally.

"May I call you my friend? I would like to."

"I would be delighted if you would," came Sally's genuine reply, as she eagerly devoured the crust.

"Now that we're friends, I should apologise for being grumpy the other day. Living alone so much of the time, only going out to feed the animals or walk the forty yards to the water pump, I have far too much time on my hands to reflect on the past and what might have been. It's made me rather bitter."

"And for my part, I apologise for getting all hot and bothered about the cobbler. Delirium, I suppose. It must've been the shock of such a sudden change in the weather that brought it on. I've never seen such lightning before. It frightened me, caused me to see shapes in the branches of the trees that weren't there. Such a shock can cause the tremors, even hallucinations, you know."

"And soak you when it hasn't rained? No, dearie, it happened just as you saw".

"I don't want to believe that. It isn't modern thinking to believe in ghosts. Anyhow, I spilled the pail."

"Did you? Let me tell you about Matcham."

"Matcham?"

"Yes, Matcham. It was a night like no other, when a black aspect took hold of the sky, keeping the moonbeams from the earth and casting everywhere in sinister hue. Flashes of forked lightning pierced the air over Salisbury Plain. Caught out in all that weather was a sailor called Gervase Matcham and his naval companion. To his horror, he saw a drummer boy coming towards him, not walking on God's good soil as a man, but sort of gliding over the surface. Matcham was frozen with fear. Whether the apparition was seen by both sailors, I don't know. Matcham was so horrified at seeing the boy, he broke down and confessed to his friend that he had murdered the lad years before. He was arrested and hanged, accompanied to the gallows by the fearsome phantom of the drummer."

Sally shuddered. "Not real, though, of course?"

"Real enough," was the reply. "It happened in 1786, the year before the first flotilla of six convict ships left Britain bound for Botany Bay. They say the crew of one ship took great care in comforting the convicts while on board and in the choice of anchorage. Among them was a sailor who was particularly praised for his care of the youngest boys."

"I don't think I'll go to Stonehenge after all" replied Sally. "I'll pack my bags."

CHAPTER 16

Westkings revisited

One mid-morning in July, Hubert came across a small, stooped woman walking a crooked path near the top of Hop Hill, a local beauty spot a few miles south of Glastonbury that overlooked tiny villages nestling irregularly in the valley below. As she stopped to unburden her shoulders of a wooden yoke with pails suspended on rusty chains, Hubert noticed that she was not of old age at all, as he had first observed from a distance. Incredibly, she was someone no more than twenty, thin and disconsolate, her hair of rich young colour falling over her face where it had come loose from her floppy bonnet.

She stumbled to sit on a large rock on the edge of the drop, breathing hard and wiping her nose on her sleeve, looking with some pain at the distant meadows where a little house stood, one half of a labourer's double-dweller. She could just make out the tiny figures of children playing, poking sticks into the hedgerow to spook rats, their mother cradling a new baby.

It was there the young woman had rediscovered a reason for living after leaving Shalhurn, spending several months helping the pregnant mother with her seven children, two goats, a few hens and a drunkard husband. Food had been scarce, since most of the money he earned went at a tavern bar. But, between the two women they had managed the garden crops and provided the children with a regular dinner of at least a wedge of bread and a share of a penny's worth of sweet pickle or treacle and vegetable soup.

Now, with the warm weather of Summer had come the strength to move on, a far cry from her arrival at the place, when she had spent nights in a room that had been so cold that her breath had frozen on the blanket. Looking for better employment now suited her wanderlust spirit.

Hubert was concerned for the traveller's well-being and pulled to a stop, now under the woman's full gaze. But, as he began to dismount, she looked away with purpose. He rejoined his saddle and trotted away, without a backward glance.

As the woman stood to continue her journey, a pail tipped over on its side, spilling its contents. No water or milk poured from it, only a rag-tag collection of clothes rolled into small parcels. It was one-half of her worldly possessions.

Retrieving the clothes, she froze at touching a shawl, rubbing her fingers over the soft wool of the crocheted loops. She lifted it to her face, caressing her cheek with memories. Tears filled her eyes. Her hand instinctively felt for the ribbon tied around her neck, threaded through a gold ring that had once been given to her in friendship.

She remembered the day a few years back when John

Madden had ridden to Shalhurn especially to give her Christabel's shawl. He had found her at the church picking weeds from a grave that stood apart from the rest, under a watchful tower with one crooked and three straight pinnacles. He had been such a gentleman to the last, thinking of others when he, too, was hurting so badly from losing his life's love at the very moment of their reunion.

"It belonged to Christabel," he had told her at that time past. "You alone should have it. I need nothing to remember her. It's an unbearable thought that I shall never see her again. She was everything to me, my darling angel of Wessex. You know, Emmie, she now flies with the Herons!"

She had replied that she knew. "I have her ring, John. Should I keep it?"

He had nodded. "It's yours, Emmie, as it was her father's before her. There is no more fitting person to have it now. I'm sure she loved you like the sister she never had."

Emmie had wept at the thought of her friend, throwing her arms around John for strength, but feeling the throbbing of his chest as he too had cried in manly silence.

The passing few years had not dulled Emmie's memory of Christabel Mere. Time had simply begun to heal the feeling that she had to atone daily for her treatment of a gentle friend who she had abandoned when at her most vulnerable. She had taken the easy option of returning home to her parents, forsaking Christabel who was at her wit's end, leaving her sitting in a turnip field, penniless, falsely accused of betrayal and pregnant. But atonement no longer meant that she felt she had to sacrifice her own young life by tending the earthly remains of the Mere family, once of Shalhurn. She supposed Christabel wouldn't have wanted that, either. At least, she thought, Christabel would have understood that she wasn't likely to stay in any one place for long, however remorseful she felt.

Emmie folded the shawl, kissed it, and placed it carefully at the bottom of her pail.

It wasn't a new sensation for Emmie to feel totally alone. Since cutting herself adrift from her parents for the second time, she had experienced real loneliness, when the bitter-sweet sensation of adventure and new horizons had given way to the reality of the long distances to walk between menial work, cold weather and poverty. Early morning cheer at seeing the rising sun shining a resplendent glow over the earth, would quickly give way to the throb of fear in her heart as her load bit into her shoulders. Yet, she knew she could return home anytime, where a few words of censure would be followed by a comfortable lifestyle. This, alone, spurred her to seek her own life, which had already been punctuated with moments of extreme happiness and guilty misfortune.

In the hamlet of Westkings, where Emmie had once enjoyed a good life working on the estate before running away with a man she hardly knew, the daily routine was well in progress. Various large fields, enriched with dung from the farmyard that had been carried on two-wheel putts, ploughed and harrowed, already bore the signs of a cycle of newly sown crops. Pastures were being cut for hay, gathered by women working as a team behind the men, ready to be formed into ricks. Cows grazed the grassy meadows after yielding gloriously rich milk for the town and city markets, and the saw mill was working at high pitch, the steam engine driving huge saws which sliced quickly through the unseasoned trunks.

It was on such a day that two ladies approached the manor from opposite directions, walking separately through its high pillars and along the manicured lawn. At the door they stopped, deciding that the older should ring the bell. The door opened.

"Yes?" enquired the maid, before bursting into a smile at recognising the smaller of the two. "Why, it's our little Emmeline Sturry. You little rascal, causing us so much worry. And who is this with you?"

"I'm Miss Sally Ayres. I used to work at the school."

"Before my time, I expect."

"It was a very long time ago. I've come to see James Elvington. Is he available?"

"I'll enquire. Augustus, is the master at home?"

He replied that he was not, but felt sure he would return within the hour.

"Where can I wait for him?"

The maid hesitated. "Mr Fly, shall I take Miss Ayres to the conservatory."

"No," Sally shouted with unexpected abruptness, her tone shocking even herself. "Please, forgive me. I forget my manners. Is there anywhere else I can wait?"

"I'll ask Madam Charlotte if you can come in and wait in the drawing room."

"No! No," she added, only slightly calmer. "I'll go to the conservatory after all. I know the way."

"Madam wouldn't like me to leave you unattended."

"Best if Madam doesn't know. Trust me in this."

The maid hesitated, but Sally gave her no choice and headed across the lawn.

"And, as for you, my little Emmie, it's to the kitchen with you for a good square meal. You look three-quarters starved."

"Are any of the old gang still here, Mary, Louise and the others?"

"They are, but dear Mr Redmarsh died of his heart a few months back. Eating too many of his wife's fried breakfasts I shouldn't wonder."

"Golly, I remember those. Great pans filled to overflowing with bacon sizzling in the grease, eggs a-plenty and more. Nobody ever left the table hungry."

"It's not the same here without dear Redmarsh. Everyone loved that old man."

"Do you think I can get my old job back, milking and working in the fields I mean?"

"You'll have to ask Master Edmond. He's in charge of hiring and firing."

Emmie looked askance.

"Oh, of course, that could be a little bit difficult for you. But, like it or not, he's the man to ask."

"Then I shall face that after the meal you've offered. Lead the way. My belly rumbles!"

Sally reached the conservatory, opening the single door and taking a step inside. It was exactly how she remembered, hung with climbing vines and strewn with jardinières of all shapes and sizes, mostly white. Other plants sat in neat rows on shelves. The two chairs, separated by a wicker table, were still where they had been before, one now with a patched seat where James had put his foot through it while in a fit of temper.

She looked around in stunned silence, remembering all too well how the sunlit room had offered her no escape from Charlotte when the two had unexpectedly met that time before. Then, she had only wanted to see Edmond and James for the last time before leaving the country for good, not to introduce herself to the boy as his mother, but merely to capture his look in her heart before departing for Africa. As for James, it was to have been her final farewell. But James had been indisposed through drink and Charlotte had confronted the visitor instead, accusing her of wanting to confess all to Edmond and intending also to destroy her marriage. These had been false accusations, but such misapprehensions had startled Charlotte enough for her to seek a final solution to the problem of an unwanted third part in her marriage.

"Oh my goodness, I can't get rid of you."

Sally turned to see Charlotte straddling the door, lit up against the outside as an actor glowing in the limelight. She entered and pushed the door shut, trapping Sally as she had before.

"What must I do to end your interference in my life?"

"Calm down," begged Sally, taking a step backwards. "You misunderstand, as you did before. Listen to what I have to say."

"Listen to you? I don't think so. Now it's twice I've thwarted your plan to see James behind my back. You've suffered the consequence of the first time. Should it be different now?"

Sally heard a gruff, snarling sound approaching. She barely had the nerve to remove her eyes from Charlotte, yet managed a quick peek past. A lean man with a hollowed face was approaching fast, struggling to hold a large dog pulling against its leash. He knocked and entered at Charlotte's invitation, leaving the door open.

"This is Augustus Fly."

The man said nothing, acknowledging the introduction only by staring at her with vacant expression, his eyes dry and lips so thin as to be parallel red marks on a ghostly skin.

"He does my bidding. I saved him from prison and now he repays me as a loyal factotum. To me he's toothless, but on my command he bites as hard as his mad dog.

Sally remained still in breath and murmur.

"You have thirty seconds to tell me why you've come here again. I warn you, if it's to see Edmond or James, the dog will have your throat as quick as a flash!"

Fly took a threatening step forward.

"Still that bitch!" boomed a voice from outside, commanding and final. It was James, thrashing his tall leather boot with a riding crop. "I said take that bloody hound out of there, Fly, and you with it or you'll feel my strap."

Fly turned to Charlotte. She froze with indecision.

"Now, you bloody little earthworm!"

James entered, lifting his crop to shoulder level. The dog snarled wildly, frothing from the corners of its open mouth. It leapt up onto its hind legs, pulling so violently against the tether of the lead that Fly could hardly restrain it. Fly jerked the lead back, which tightened the leather around the dog's neck and caused the animal to snap backwards at its master.

Fly jumped, giving it its head. Infuriated, the beast leapt within an inch of James' stump arm.

James crashed the whip against the dog's nose. Its nostrils flared. A second harder blow followed the first. The dog dropped to the floor in painful submission.

"The next strike is for you, Fly, unless you get out of my sight at once!"

Hunched, Fly retreated into the garden, snatching at the dog's lead and mumbling revenge.

James turned to Sally. "Are you alright?"

She said that she was.

"As for you, Char, I'm lost for words."

She turned to leave, but he unexpectedly thrust his crop forward to block her path.

"No, I've changed my mind. I want you to stay. You can only want to know why Miss Ayres is here. So, stop and listen for yourself, and not accuse me later of lying."

James held no fear of what might be said, knowing their recent conversations had been guarded. Yet, whereas his demeanour showed no sign of impassibleness, he realised his inner defences were crumbling. He was, indeed, slowly becoming inflamed again in Sally's company.

Compared to Charlotte in her angry and tortured guilt, Sally was a gentle thing of broader wisdom, who, even now, blamed nobody other than herself for what had happened to her. Fearful of outward exposure, James took a firm grip on his thoughts, held ransom by a genuine belief that their time together had well and truly passed. If he was beginning to feel any renewed warmth towards Sally, it was as yet small and he would not expose it to the world for ridicule.

"Well," resumed James, throwing the crop onto the table, "if you find yourself choosing to come into the lion's cage, Miss Ayres, you must indeed be in need of our assistance or advice. Which is it?"

"Why should she?" broke in Charlotte, speaking as seriously as she ever had. "Edmond tells me she had employment in Glastonbury, but perfectly wasted the opportunity. Should we now take her in as our ward, with never-ending responsibility for her welfare?"

"I wouldn't want that," exclaimed Sally, taking the sting out of Charlotte's words.

"I dare say you would say that, Miss Ayres," cried Charlotte. "Any wilful person under your circumstances would."

"Shut up, Char!" bawled James. "I am often careless with your opinion and in dealing with your astonishing outbursts, but not today. I listen, I weigh and I regret. I find them wanting, and in so doing ask you, again, to be quiet!"

"You may object all you like, husband, but you will not force me away from my judgement. It is my persuasion that she didn't come here to see the roses."

"In truth," muttered Sally, asking no favours, "I don't know myself why I came."

"There we are then," exclaimed Charlotte. "There is no harm done and you may leave without reproach!"

"Is that what you want? To leave, I mean?" enquired James, softness in his tone.

"What else could she want?" demanded Charlotte.

"Be silent, damn it! Let the woman speak for herself."

Sally looked towards the gardens, where a stable-groom

held the bridles of a fine chestnut mare and a smaller dappled pony. Edmond emerged from the manor, arm in arm with a beauty of about eighteen, her fair hair roped and netted neatly beneath a tall black riding hat. She mounted, taking time to arrange her long skirt over legs which gripped in side saddle. Edmond mounted more casually, taking up the reins and tapping his heels, elegantly leading the way through the gates in a slow rising trot.

"Um, yes! Sorry. What did you say?"

"James asked you when you were going."

"No I didn't. I enquired only whether you might need any assistance or advice."

Charlotte gritted her teeth, adding coldly: "Do you know, I'm quite looking forward to the answer, myself! It would be quite a revelation to find that James of all people could dabble in emotional politics."

Sally understood the implied insult to both of them.

"Speaking as an outsider, I would say a man like James is deeply resented by many, but profoundly venerated by the few. It is the way of great men."

"And into which pond do *you* jump?" enquired Charlotte, sharply.

"Oh, very much the latter."

"You would," she replied, "being so much younger than myself and readily impressionable."

"Younger, be blowed," barked James, apologising to Sally after realising the unintended snub. "I only meant that you might look ten years younger than my wife, but you are in fact of very equal age."

Enraged, Charlotte swept up her dress and made for the

door, turning to say: "The more useful he tries to be, the greater harm he will cause. Take that bit of advice freely from me, Miss Ayres, as I alone know this much. Still, if he sees he has a duty to you above any duty to me, then you may flatter his wishes. The consequences are for you to bear, as before, if I'm not mistaken." She left, leaving a stunned silence in her wake.

In the stillness of the room, James began snigger, which became infectious to Sally.

"That was a dreadful thing to say to any woman, James. You should be ashamed."

"Be hanged if I am. I shall make it a new rule only to talk to beautiful people."

"Excepting me, of course?"

"Very much *including* you."

For the next hour, which easily stretched to three, James and Sally talked, quickly moving from serious matters to the more frivolous. It was the nature of Sally's company that made it hard to hold back from lighter conversation, her pleasant ways making talk on all matters, even the more grievous, an enjoyable experience. Light refreshments had been brought into the conservatory, forcing a slow pace by the spreading of jam and the pouring of endless cups of tea.

"I'm so sorry to burden you with my troubles, especially regarding those appalling men who seem to follow me everywhere. I'm probably just being a silly woman."

"Think nothing of it. As I said, I have a mind only to talk to beautiful people from now on."

"What about Edmond in this scheme of things? You must talk to him."

"Oh, my dear Sally, he is the most beautiful of all. Some men can outshine even the best of women. Don't you know that?"

She quizzed his thinking merely with a look.

"Undoubtedly true, my dear lady. How to explain? A woman may make herself temporarily beautiful by paint and powder, only to be plain before and after. For, it's a fact that a woman's face has fewer natural and interesting features than a man's, making a good many women look virtually identical to their neighbours. In fact, I would go as far as saying that too many beauties, all of similar appearance, can be downright boring. Yes, that is a fact, probably known only to men, who have a habit of keeping quiet on such matters. Now, on the other side, a man relies only on what God has gifted to him at birth, making a handsome man the most beautiful of all creatures twenty-four hours in the day. Am I not right? I remember saying much the same to Charlotte once, when her innocence had been lost beside the flames of a Midsummer Eve's bonfire."

She looked out to the garden, remembering Edmond as he had saddled. "Yes, I do believe you are right."

As the afternoon wore on, clouds began to gather in the sky, casting pockets of shade into the conservatory. Sally raised her head and looked upwards through the glass panels, shocked at the changing light and temperature. James pulled out his fob-watch.

"My word, Sally, I'm in for it now. We've been talking for hours. We must go our ways."

She rose politely, placing her plate on the tray and offering a slight smile as James helped her from her chair. They walked to the door and out into the open. Edmond was again to be seen across the extensive lawn, arguing with Fly.

She turned to James, her head bowed. "What am I to do?"

James felt shallow, having no immediate answer, only now realising that the long time they had spent together that day had compromised the woman and left her with the dilemma of her immediate needs. His mind told him to give her the fare for a private carriage back to Glastonbury or Cudwick, or wherever she wanted, and see her go forthwith, absolutely and unreservedly; his heart could not hear such words to be spoken.

"I have a furnished cottage near the school. It was occupied until a few days ago. You could stay there overnight if you wish. Make it your home for a day or two."

Sally stood in silence, looking into his eyes, which revealed everything. The moments allowed the heat of his offer to cool into the reality of what he had suggested, the full significance of his rash offer now dawning on him. Sally could read him like a book. She stepped forward and kissed him, although so lightly as could be dismissed as not being a kiss at all.

"Thank you, but I don't think your wife would approve."

"What will you do, then?" he asked too quickly, as if giving her no time to change her mind. She was taken aback.

"I'm not sure," said murmured, genuinely disturbed at her pending difficulty. If only she had not been so quick to play down his offer in a moment of politeness, she thought.

Each was transfixed by the consequences. She took a grip of the situation, desperate not to waste any more time.

"I'll find a way out of the hole," she said brightly. "I'm a big girl."

Again, she kissed him gently on the cheek. "Thank you for giving me a shoulder to cry on."

"Have I helped?" he asked softly.

"I think not, but thank you anyway. Please don't reproach yourself."

James watched her walk away. Charlotte, who had spied on them from a window ever since they left the conservatory, called to him from inside the house and he marched briskly in.

As Sally reached the gate, Fly unexpectedly appeared from behind a pillar. He begged to be heard. The dog was nowhere to be seen.

"Your pardon, if I scared you."

"You did."

He nodded in submission. "I carry a message for you from the young master."

"Edmond!" she exclaimed in complete surprise.

"Yes, miss. He says that if you need a place to stay for a few nights, that place can be a small house by the church. I have the key if you want to take it."

She looked towards the manor, but Edmond was nowhere to be seen.

"He sometimes uses it himself, whenever the fancy takes him. What he uses it for, I couldn't answer in politeness. Your reply is?"

Sally couldn't understand any of it. Why would Edmond offer to help a stranger, or even know that she needed it, or even care for that matter? It was all very odd.

"Did James Elvington speak to his son about this?"

"No. I got my orders direct from the young master before you left the conservatory. His instructions were quite specific."

"Has it anything to do with Charlotte Elvington?"

"The mistress? Why, no. As I said, it came from the young master and him alone. I don't suppose *she* would spare you much discomfort."

Understanding nothing, she held out her hand and a large iron key was dropped into her palm. She turned away.

"Oh, and I'm to say that you can expect a basket of food later. I'm under order to bring it myself. Everything else you need may be found in the house, including matches for the fire and candles in the wall box. The fire is always cleaned out and laid after Master Edmond has used it, ready for next time." She thanked him. "I'm further instructed to tell you not to return to the manor, or mention any of this to his parents. That is a condition. Do you agree to it?"

She said that she did.

"Then I bid you goodbye." He bowed and turned, taking only a few strides before adding: "Oh, and if you don't mind me saying, I meant you no harm with the dog. My life is not my own."

Sally, not created for ill-temper, refrained from acknowledging one way or the other, but merely took to her heels.

The small stone house nestled behind a little outcrop of trees to the east of the church, one of four built in a terrace by speculating tradesmen from the hamlet. The roof slates were thin, pitching down at a sharp angle to meet three rows of stone tiles at the base. The windows and doors were ill-fitting and of the poorest quality, and the brickwork showed signs of hurried assembly.

Sally opened the door, stepping straight into the living area and kitchen. There was little furniture, but what there was offered reasonable comfort and a quality that outmatched the surroundings. Even a little writing desk stood in one corner. Antimacassars protected the horsehair-stuffed soft furnishings and the wooden floor boards were hidden in places under various rugs of uncoordinated size and style. Any colour in the room came from a single oleograph, a chromolithograph of a farming scene printed to imitate an oil painting. Sally glanced hopelessly at the women gathered in the picture, their jollity in work depicting a romantic view of the countryside that only town-dwellers believed.

The picture hung above an open fire used for heating and cooking, although of impracticable small size for a house meant for a large working family. There had been sufficient space built into the room for a small range, but this had been omitted by the builders, unsure whether local tenants would be willing to pay additional rent for its use. An open fire had to suffice. Candles were held erect on small brass arms mounted to the wall, burnt down to their holders and in need of replacement. A wooden box hooked above ground level held several replacements. In all, it was pleasant enough, intended now as a bachelor's bolt-hole. She lit the fire.

While the fire drew flame, Sally climbed up the narrow stairs to the bedrooms. There were just two, both of equal size. The first was a yellow-coloured rectangular room, incongruously furnished with a double bed set into a polished wooden frame with four tall pillars, hung with damask curtains of a dark shade of blue. Beside it, a Bible rested on an occasional table. A mahogany wardrobe and a chest of drawers completed the scene, rather too large for the remaining space and clearly also borrowed from the big house. This would be hers, she thought, a little excited at the unexpected elegance.

The second bedroom was of very different style. Still holding the meagre furniture provided by the landlord, it had three single pine-framed beds slotted into the available space, made up to allow top-and-tail sleeping for up to six children. The only cupboard space was a rail behind a curtain. A liberal coating of dust and the general airless odour gave away the secret of never being occupied.

As the early evening passed, Sally began to wonder whether she had been forgotten. Hunger bit. She searched the cupboards and drawers for any scraps of food. There were none, the shelves being lined, clean and bare. Remembering her promise not to call at the manor, she settled back into a chair in a languid state, trying to read from the light of a candle.

She had noticed her reflection in the bedroom mirror and now, as she sat quietly and alone, she recalled a flushed look on her face. Was it because she had met James again, she wondered, distressed at the thought that the tiniest flicker can be fanned into a stronger flame if care isn't taken to prevent it. She didn't want to be hurt again, or cause hurt. Yet, stupidly, she had kissed him not once, but twice. It had to stop, and to this end she decided to write a short letter to him.

The letter turned out to be two full pages, much to her dismay, written in under ten minutes and without a pause to gather considered thought. Now finished and signed, she read it back to herself, realising that she had said far too much about the old days in her plea not to allow themselves to re-enact them. Yet, there was too much written to start again, and so it was decided that the communication had to stand as first drafted.

She returned to her reading, leaving the letter unaltered and open on the desk. Although she had promised herself to give the letter to Fly when, or if, he brought that basket of food, the thought of it not reaching its audience that evening gnawed constantly at her mind. As the clock struck nine, Sally found she could wait no longer to get it into James' hands, so setting into practice its firm but kindly-meant sentiments. Quickly decided, she jumped up with her heart pounding, grabbed the letter which she folded into two, and stepped outside.

Much to her surprise, the evening was becoming a little fierce, a fairly strong wind from the south fanning the warm breeze into a more stirring condition. It was that time when the first hints of the coming dusk greyed the sky. She looked up, believing that thunder could follow. Yet, something more was wrong.

Sally gazed at the distant manor and then at the adjoining field where a huge quantity of sawn timber had been stacked, open and unprotected, ready for delivery to customers throughout Wessex. The air, she thought, held the slightest ashy smell, indistinguishable in nature but foreign to the moment. She dismissed it and began her short walk, trying to decide where best to leave her letter.

As her paces quickened, another strangeness carried in the air, an almost imperceptible sound, at first a blur but gradually forming into music as she approached the small church hall, its doors flung open. She peered inside.

High up on a stack of straw bales sat a small band of two fiddlers, an accordion player and several others of assorted ages wrestling brass instruments, held in rhythm by a boy with a drum. A caller stood before them, frenzied from shouting instructions to several pairs of dancers, his face glowing red and his raised right arm soaked and dripping from the cider that constantly spilled from the tankard he grasped. Tables of half-eaten food took up one side of the remaining space, at its centre two large barrels of cider. Small puddles formed beneath the dripping taps.

"Are you coming in?"

Sally turned, shocking both of them.

"Good gracious, Mr Smith! What on earth are you doing here?"

"I could ask you the same. What a coincidence. I had absolutely no idea it was you. What a stroke of luck. Look, come on, we can talk later. Let's go in and have some fun before it ends." He took her arm and led her into the gas-lit hall. "Shall we dance? And, please, call me Hubert."

"Let's eat first," she said, looking along the tables at the cheese, hot sliced pork, pickles, pies and bread. "It's a feast to be sure."

As they approached the tables, she secretly folded the letter into a smaller parcel and slipped it furtively up her sleeve.

"What shall we have for the next dance?" shouted the caller, once the couples parted for the sides. "Do we have a request?"

"Something that makes me hold a lady's hand," replied a man in his late twenties, his face heavily weathered from outside work.

"Come, come Daniel. You need no such introduction to the ladies gathered. You've held most of them at one time or another."

"So he has," shouted another man, "and none be left that don't now avoid his sweaty palms."

"Nonetheless," called Daniel in merry delight, enjoying the attention, "I see someone who hasn't had the pleasure of me tapping feet."

He pointed to Sally, who only turned when she felt the stare of others, her mouth full of pie.

"Well I'll be. If I be not mistaken, aren't you me old teacher?" He came closer. "By heaven I do think you are. Remember me. I'm little Charlie, though not so little around the belly nowadays."

She swallowed quickly. "Charlie Richards?"

"I am that. Romeo, Romeo, where fort art that, you old bugger or something." Laughter burst from his face. "Remember, you wanted me to be Juliet in the school play, because I was all fair and pretty," he said, cupping his head in his hands and fluttering his eyelashes. "I was the fairest of them all, until Brilling put a stop to it, the pompous git!"

"The headmaster? Oh, yes, he could be difficult, but he was a good man for all his old-fashioned ways. Is he still at the school?"

"The old sod died years ago. We now have a woman in charge. Believe that if you can? My son, Will, is himself soon to play Romeo. They still use the books you bought us. And, what's more, a girl is playing Juliet! Fancy that . . . a girl!"

Sally smiled. "Things have progressed."

"And now a dance, I fancy."

"She is taken, my friend. She is promised to me." Hubert took her hand, squeezing it lightly in friendship and led her out to the centre of the floor, where other couples gathered in squares of eight.

"What about me tapping feet?" called Daniel after her.

"Clowns feet, more like," retorted a young woman through a generous smile. "Dance with me, Danny boy, and leave the lady to her red-headed beau."

"I saved you," whispered Hubert, as they formed one side of a square.

"Perhaps!" was her coy reply. "But you're a bit ahead of yourself."

"How so?"

"I'm promised to you, am I?"

"No! I didn't mean . . ."

She laughed. "I know, you silly thing. Let's dance."

Forty minutes and more passed before the band stopped playing, the tables were cleared and the couples began to leave. It was now quite dark, except for the residue glow from a fire that had raged outside the hall over which the suckling pig had been roasted, but was now a mass of red embers which twinkled as the wind passed over the charred remains. What little remained of the pig itself had been tossed into the embers, where the animals of the night would tear at the carcass and leave it bare once the fire had cooled.

"What's that in your hand?" asked Hubert, as he walked her back to her house.

"Oh, nothing."

"It *is* something. Come on, what is it?"

She reluctantly opened her fingers.

"It's a pork pie. You're holding a pork pie!"

"Yes, I know. I'm still hungry."

"Oh, you goose!"

"By the way, I didn't ask what the dance was for. I would expect merriment at harvest, but it's July. Was it someone's birthday or an anniversary, or something?"

"Yes, sort of. It was to commemorate St Margaret's Day. Judging by the number of pregnant women in attendance, it still holds some magic."

She stopped. "What does that mean?"

"The 20th of July is St Margaret's Day. You see, Margaret of Antioch, who probably never actually existed, is claimed to have been the daughter of a pagan priest, who abandoned her when she became a Christian. The story goes that she was tortured for her beliefs, never married and was even swallowed by a dragon. Anyhow, it's said that pregnant women who speak her name will suffer no pain in childbirth."

"That would make her extremely popular, I would think."

"Of course, that is until the remedy proves not to work, when I expect she would receive the odd curse of the tongue instead. Anyhow, it's likely to rain, so we had better get a move on. That's part of a superstition too."

"How so?"

"Margaret's flood, it's called. Although, now I think on it, rain is also supposed to represent Mary Magdalene washing her handkerchief. I think the two stories got themselves tangled somewhere along the line. Either way, it's an excuse for a knees-up at St Margaret's Church. Can I see you again, Miss Ayres?"

Back inside, with Hubert gone, Sally pulled the folded letter from her sleeve. It was a bit crumpled. She re-read her own words.

"Oh, what the heck!" She tore it into pieces and let the bits fall to the floor. "Tomorrow, I think, I'll retake what is mine from this place."

CHAPTER 17

A ring of steel

Against Hubert's prediction, it did not rain immediately. The evening remained warm, with a breath of wind that cooled nobody.

Having some acquaintance with the Elvingtons, Hubert had decided to ask if he could beg a bed at the manor, rather than ride back to Glastonbury. He was gladly received, even at this late hour, and his horse was taken away, fed and stabled.

"I've had the most unexpectedly wonderful evening," he said to the Elvingtons, who sat together in the drawing room. "You'll never guess who I met?"

They said they couldn't begin to speculate.

"Only Miss Sally Ayres, the woman I told you before that I talked to at the Browning's party. What do you make of that? Incredibly, she seems to quite like me."

"Where was this?" asked Charlotte, already smelling a rat and feeling irritated that another man of her acquaintance had fallen for her charm.

"Why, here of course, at the Margaret dance."

"What!" shouted Charlotte. "What!" She turned to James, her gritted teeth hollowing her jaw. "Was this your doing?"

"I know nothing about it," he replied in honesty. "Seriously, I thought she had gone from here."

"That just leaves you, Edmond. What do you know about it?"

The young man looked furtive, but strong. "Don't talk to me as if I'm a boy, Mother. I run this estate and I'm soon to be married. That makes me a man due for respect in anyone's book."

"Answer your mother, Edmond," said James, wanting to know why decisions about Sally had been made without his knowledge, while also seeing it as the perfect opportunity to deflect any suspicion from himself.

"Alright, but understand it's my decision to make. I could see she was lost, so I said she could use the terrace."

"That woman's in one of my houses?"

"No," replied Edmond, "she's in one of mine. I rent it. You are my father's wife and my mother, and I love you dearly, but understand that you own nothing.

"How dare you." She jumped to her feet. "How dare you." The door slammed behind her.

"That was incredibly harsh of you, Son. I suggest you go and apologise at once. Tell her you acted stupidly and meant none of it."

"I'll do no such thing. She makes me so angry at times, one moment treating me as if I'm the *sun* around which her *world* revolves, only then to make decisions that she has no right to make, as if I'm a nobody."

"That's women for you," interrupted Hubert through a pensive smile.

"And you would know, I suppose?" cut in James, secretly venting his anger at Hubert's attentions towards Sally, now that the sanctity of the polite evening had been broken.

"I only meant . . ."

"Shut up, Hubert!" Edmond rounded on his father. "I was already cross with her well before Hubert came." He turned to his guest. "Sorry, Hubert. You seem to have been caught up in family crossfire. Forgive us."

Hubert nodded, but sank deeply into his chair in submission, sipping from his whisky glass.

"Now listen, Father. I told Mother that when Lily and I rode out this afternoon we talked about wedding plans. Lily wants to be married in the Autumn, whereas I'm in no hurry. Mother scolded me and called me a spoiled boy. I held my temper, but now I won't put up with such insult again. No, I won't apologise to her, now or later."

As the men talked, Charlotte paced the hall, her temper at boiling point. All about her seemed to be unravelling. Fly entered from the kitchen, clutching a basket.

"What's that?" Charlotte asked in strong tone.

"It's food, Madam."

"I can see it's food, you idiot. What are you doing with it?"

"Taking it across the road, to the terrace."

"Across my dead body!" She grabbed it. "Who told you to take it there? My husband or Edmond?"

"Master Edmond, Madam. It should've gone ages ago, but I was polishing the silver and forgot."

"Here," she said, slamming it into his stomach, "take it back to the kitchen. If I hear you've taken anything to her, anything at all mind, I'll have you in prison quicker than your feet can touch the ground. Do we understand each other?"

He nodded, bowed and returned to the kitchen.

When the evening was over and Hubert had retired to his room, James poured another whisky for Edmond and took his own usual ginger cordial. They sat, each hardly knowing how to break the tense atmosphere.

"Did I really do wrong, offering a roof to that Ayres woman?"

"Of course not, Edmond. But, I would hope it was merely a generous act to a stranger in trouble."

"What else? Yet, she's hardly a complete stranger. I've seen her here and at the Browning home on a couple of occasions, and I assume she is the same woman we hoped to visit in hospital. Don't forget, Father, I know what happened to her off the African coast, and all because Mother hired an unseaworthy boat. That makes Miss Ayres our responsibility."

"To offer help is one thing, a few coins, perhaps. It's quite another thing to give her free use of the terrace. That seems too much. I don't want you involved with her. It could have repercussions you can't understand."

"Perhaps I should be told why Mother offered the sponsorship in the first place."

"I think, Edmond, that is private to her."

The next day, in London, a telegram reached the office of Russell Thackeray. Fairbourne had also returned that morning.

"Come and see this," he called to Fairbourne, who had only just sat at his desk for the first time in several days.

He read it with interest. "So, she's back in Westkings. I was so close."

"What should we do about it?"

"I would say, nothing, Sir."

"Nothing? I thought you were the one who was all fired up to carry on investigating."

"I didn't mean that we shouldn't keep an eye on her. I merely meant that we can leave that to Edmond Elvington. He may have the benefit of her trust, something *we* haven't managed. If he finds nothing to tell us, then I think the time has come to write a final report."

"Which would say what, Fairbourne?"

"That you cannot find a connection between Miss Ayres and any potential catastrophe indicated by the legend of the Predicted Nine."

"Is that what *I* think?"

"Most certainly, Sir."

"How wise. You see, Fairbourne, one day you may gain the ability to make such judgements. You must observe me and learn from it."

"I'll do that, Sir. As to the report, I'll start on it straight away. I can always change it a bit if young Elvington discovers anything new."

"Oh, before you go, Fairbourne, I take it you've heard what the Cabinet is proposing."

"No, Sir. I've been away from the office, as you know."

"It's another round in the battle between Gladstone and Her Majesty, Queen Victoria. You know she complains constantly that he addresses her as if she's a public meeting, not his monarch. But the real problem for the Government is that since John Brown died in March, Her Majesty has gone back into despair and mourning, just as she did for Prince Albert. We feel she is likely to shut herself away again at Windsor or Osborne House. The result of that would be catastrophic. It would bring the revolutionaries back out of the woodwork, sharpening their knives, calling for a republic if she becomes a recluse and removes all signs of the monarchy from the public eye."

"Do we have an answer?"

"A proposal, yes. A bit of overseas flag waving and commerce combined. Our strategic position in Singapore has been developing well and a British style of government has done marvels in New Zealand and Australia. But, between you and me, the Government is looking increasing likely to annex Upper Burma into becoming part of the Indian Empire. If we delay, we fear Burma might otherwise threaten British interests in the region. Worse still, the place could even eventually fall into French hands."

"I thought we'd already sorted out the Burma question?"

"So did the Government. It's been a great disappointment to find otherwise. You see, last century Burma had expansionist eyes on Siam. This worried the British in India at the time, as Siam had been left alone as the only Southeast Asian country never to have been the subject of *any* European power. Obviously, it couldn't be allowed to fall under Burmese influence either. The issue soured relations between our two nations. I don't need to remind you that since 1824 we've fought two wars against them, and a third may soon be on the cards. The King, a certain gentleman by the name of Thibaw, is thought to be pro-French. Indeed, rumour is rife that the

King might even try to confiscate the British Bombay-Burma Company and offer it to the French. That would almost certainly result in war."

"It sounds more of a case for the Royal Navy with its gunboats than the monarchy and diplomats."

"It would be, if there weren't wider considerations. The Government feels that the demise of the East India Company a decade ago projected all the wrong signals to the Dutch and Portuguese, who had always been affronted by our breaking their monopoly of the spice trade in the region. So, the Government wants to kill two birds with one stone, by getting Her Majesty to visit the region, along with several of our most prominent politicians and captains of industry, to show both our military strength and resolve in the region. Plus, it may benefit us to show what a bucket-load of cash can do for developing nations. The Government thinks it could even be possible to dip a toe into the areas around the Dutch East Indies, as the Dutch don't yet monopolise all the available territory. Tea is quite an export there, and tea is something we British are best at. Mostly, it's felt that we should do more to marginalise the Dutch, Spanish and Portuguese in Borneo, who take too much of the available trade. This could prove to be our greatest prize."

"And to this end, it's being proposed to put to Her Majesty in harm's way, as bait, so to speak. God forbid. I've never heard such complete treachery."

"You forget yourself, Fairbourne. No harm could ever come to Her Majesty, or anyone else on board for that matter. The Navy has put the ironclad battleship HMS *Alexandra* at the disposal of the expedition, plus escorts. This flotilla will remain in contact with fast support vessels in the Indian Ocean. Look at the details of the ship, Fairbourne. It's a monster!"

He passed the specification across. Fairbourne took and read it incredulously.

"The bloody ship has sails, for heaven sake. If we are to embark on this farce, why can't we have HMS *Ajax* or *Collingwood* that the newspapers are making so much fuss about? Now, they're truly modern. No sails, big guns in deck turrets and a speed of thirteen knots. Surely, if we are going to risk the head of state, we should provide the very best protection?"

"Do you honestly think I didn't ask the same questions of the Navy chiefs?"

"And they said . . .?"

"That I should concentrate on what I know best and leave naval affairs to them. They were quite firm about it. *Ajax*, apparently, was completed in March this year, but won't be commissioned for another two years. Even later for *Collingwood*. No, *Alexandra* it is. Look for yourself. It can reach over fifteen knots using its vertical compound engines, whatever they are, and six knots under sail. I suppose it must be an advantage to be able to resort to sail if the engines go wrong."

"Go wrong? Good grief!"

"What's more, it's heavier than *Ajax* will ever be, and carries two eleven-inch and ten ten-inch big guns, plus six smaller weapons. Admittedly, it carries its main guns below decks and will be the last ship of the Navy to do that, but that's of little issue to this mission. Despite its sails, I'm told *Alexandra* was only commissioned six years ago and is presently the flagship of the Mediterranean Fleet. Last year it was used during the bombardment of Alexandria, so we know the ship is perfectly sound. No, I feel we can have no valid objection, and nor should Her Majesty. Anyway, as I said, it will be escorted by other vessels to secure a ring of steel around the flotilla. Not a navy in the world would dare touch her, for fear of being Trafalgared!"

"It still looks an antique to me, whatever you and the Navy say."

"You go too far, Fairbourne. Do not question my integrity or loyalty to the Crown!"

Fairbourne shrank in his chair, allowing Thackeray to continue.

"The Queen, it is hoped, will set sail almost at once for the Indian Ocean, placing her on official national business while she privately mourns both Albert and Brown aboard this 9,500 ton symbol of British might. The first port of call will be a quick excursion into the Java Sea and Borneo for commerce."

"Has Her Majesty agreed?"

"I'm not privy to share with you any such information. What I can tell you is that she might be joined on board by Prince Edward and other members of the Royal Family. And, if she can bear it, Gladstone might also be recommended to go. Oh, and Lord Randolph Churchill will sail, partly I fear to get him out of the way because of his pro-Irish home rule views. He has a red-headed son of about nine who, he says, is always playing at soldiers and might also benefit from the education the trip could provide. Apparently, he's a dim-wit at school. He has an unusual name. Winston, I think."

CHAPTER 18

The night of fire

*I*t was the day after St Margaret's dance, another merry
moment in Westkings. It marked the beginning of
preparations for St Christopher's Day. In five day's time,
when the completed figure of the saint had been freshly
painted on wood and placed against the wall of the church,
opposite the south door, anyone seeing the image would
possibly be spared an untimely death, or so it was hoped. That
prospect was certainly reason enough to get in another barrel
of cider, or even two! Beneath would be written the words:

> *St Christopher's fair figure who shall view*
> *Faintness or feebleness that day shall rue*

Hubert had decided to stay for another twenty-four hours,
wined and dined by the Elvingtons. An impressive spread
was planned for an evening reception to celebrate their first
meeting with Lord and Lady Stevenson, Lily's parents from
Sherborne.

There had been a rumour circulating before the arrival of their guests that a relative of the Stevensons, by the name of Robert, was responsible for that year's best-selling children's story, *Treasure Island*. It was now out as a printed book, having caught everyone's imagination after serialisation in a children's magazine. The rumour proved untrue but, nevertheless, gave rise during the party to a lively discussion on the characters of Long John Silver and a certain naval gentleman by the name of Admiral Benbow. This caused great amusement among those who knew that, in the book, Benbow was merely the chosen name of a tavern.

"Nevertheless," replied Hubert against a tide of scoffing, "Benbow had been a real admiral once and a hero to boot. He had his legs and thighs smashed into splinters by chain-shot while fighting the French in 1701. The crew put him into a wooden frame on the quarter-deck, where he stayed until the French withdrew the next morning".

James could see the embarrassment he had caused by his playful disparagement and quickly changed the subject.

"And, so, Lady Stevenson, do you find the life of a politician's wife an interesting pursuit? I take it your husband sits in the House of Lords."

"Interesting, you ask? Why, no, it bores me to death, a languishing death at that. The House of Lords has two sorts of members, those meaning to do a great deal of good but without an ounce of ability to put forward a worthy argument, and those who act simply from self interest and can out-shout the rest."

"I trust your husband belongs to the former group, but is the proverbial exception to the rule by combining philanthropy with aptitude."

"You may think that. I don't care to perplex my mind by attempting to understand any of it. I realised a long time ago that philanthropy only attracts the interest of other do-gooders of lesser means than my husband, who, by gaining his ear and patronage, make themselves a thorough nuisance to both of us. They are single-minded creatures who are not dissimilar to blowflies."

"Blowflies, Madam?"

"Why, yes. They buzz around, annoying everyone in their way, and are impossible to get rid of. I, for my part, am happier with my lady friends, free of London and politics in general. Why do you ask? Are you political, James?"

"Only at parochial level. Nothing more taxing than that. I try to prevent the self-interest of land-owners or persons of elected or unelected position from treating everyone in the vicinity as part of their personal feudal kingdom."

"Sounds dreadfully, provincially political."

"It can be. I'm constantly amazed how a few decent men and women, when gathered together as a committee, can suddenly become totally irrational. I'm of the belief that local politics are for the benefit of all those who live locally, not to be used as a means by which well-intentioned laws made in London regarding the preservation of the countryside or even village greens can be manipulated to harm those who actually live in or around them. I constantly question motives in such discussions, trying to understand whether such obstructive committee members consider a patch of grass to be more important than a person's right of passage across it or their right to be left to live in peace.

"You want to converse about grass?"

"I do. Grass might be a rare commodity in London, but we have plenty to spare around here. Indeed, I try to stop people affected by such geographical trifles from being cruelly and unnecessary harangued by the harridans. My view is that locals should be left alone to enjoy their homes, away from harassment. I mean to say, how would you view this scenario? Our village has its own school, the one you must have passed on your way here. It was built seven years ago. Now, it sits beside the village green which, under the 1857 Inclosure Act and 1876 Commons Act, is a protected bit of dirt to ensure that it can be used by anyone wishing quiet exercise and recreation. All well and good. But, we have people who try to stop the children reaching the school, as they could cause *interruption to quiet enjoyment* when they cross *en masse*, or are dropped off by wagon. Can you believe that petty-minded nonsense? Those same harridans, actually of both sexes, say that tradesmen with their carts cannot cross the green either to make deliveries to the school or maintain it, as they could cause actual physical injury with the wheels, which the laws prohibits. Of course, without them crossing, the school becomes landlocked, but this does not affect the harridans' view one jot? Not a bit of it. Now, I ask you, who is right?"

"Tell me, if you must."

"Why, it's most certainly *not* the do-gooders. That's for sure. Such laws were never intended to restrict locals from going about their reasonable lives. They were meant to prevent such areas from being exploited for development or being used to graze horses and cattle and such like. It's all a complete stupidity, a manipulation of the law, and I feel it's my duty to expose such local political zeal.

"Quite a political speech, James."

"Was it? I'm so sorry. Was I boring, too?"

"A little tedious, maybe."

Fly entered the room, enquiring as to the time the carriage should be harnessed. He was told and left grumbling, knowing that he would be expected to remain on duty for some time to come.

"Why do you employ such an odious man as Augustus Fly?" asked Hubert quietly, gaining James's ear.

"He's Charlotte's lapdog. He's a blackmailer, an embezzler and a thief, taken in by my wife from the gutter where he belonged to do her bidding as a servant. I loathe the very sight of the man. I'm never quite sure whether Charlotte has a hold over him or he has a hold over her. A more noxious little slug I've yet to discover. He once worked for Schofield, our solicitor. Junior partner to worthless slug in a single, murky step. Now, that's quite an achievement by any measure."

"Can a slug *step*?" asked Hubert lightly.

He laughed. "It can be crushed underfoot and wiped off the bottom of your shoe, Hubert."

"What are you doing?" asked a maid in sharp tone, noticing Fly with his ear against the outside of the drawing room door.

"Mind your bloody business," he snapped back, shuffling away to the kitchen.

Edmond took Lily by the hand and led her to the window, its coloured panes no longer lit by the outside light, but reflecting a languid shine from the interior. The manicured lawn could still just be seen through the glass, all the way to the pillars.

Squinting through a section of soft yellow hue, Edmond strained to recognise a young woman walking across the grass and out towards the dormitory, where several of the women who worked on the estate lived in loft space above a kitchen and refectory. She was tiny and walked with a familiar gait, but further identification was impossible.

"What do you stare at, Edmond?" asked Lily, still holding his fingers.

"That woman. I don't recognise her. Did she come with you?"

"Of course not."

"Strange," he thought and turned back to the party.

As full darkness began to set in, the visitors began slow preparation to leave the manor, unhurried by the lateness of the hour. Their carriage had already been re-harnessed and driven to the front, where it awaited the Stevenson family. The evening air remained warm, scented by the gardens, but there was a menacing aspect in the sky. Hubert, feeling out of place during this family farewell, retired to his bedroom.

Looking skyward from outside the refectory was the new gamekeeper, Larkins, who had been forced from his own smallholding after the failure of his turnip crop two years earlier. A severe outbreak of turnip fly had put him into ruinous debt. Now removed from debt and his land, his responsibility was to others.

Larkins considered the weather likely to turn unpredictable and sinister. He looked across at a small enclosure, where sheep that had produced still-born offspring were kept under long-term observation. Alongside were the orphan lambs of dead ewes that had been given new coats, straight after birth, skinned from still-born lambs and put over them to fool their new surrogate mothers. Now much larger, the lambs had shed the coats, having been accepted as family long ago. Larkin noticed the sheep were huddled near the shelter of a hedge, all facing in one direction. It was a sign of things to come.

From her terrace near the church, Sally peered from the window, first drawn by the growing unrest in the sky, but now focussed on the lights of the manor house. She could see shadows moving behind the stained glass windows, but it was another light that caught her attention. She could just discern flickering against the outside wall, as yet small but traceable to the wood stacked in the adjoining field. It was on fire!

Grabbing a shawl, she fled from the terrace and out towards the manor. As she rounded the corner, through the pillars, she ran full-square into Larkins, who stood mesmerised by the impending conflagration.

"Don't just look at it, for heaven's sake," Sally shouted. "Raise the alarm."

He stirred, breaking his trance. "No, you tell them inside. I'll get the farmhands out of bed and the pails going." He ran one way, stopped, and ran the other. "Oh dear, oh dear."

Sally agreed and hastened to the door. She screamed violently, pulling the bell and slamming her palm against the panels.

"For pity's sake, answer someone!"

Edmond was the first to respond. "What the blazes is all the commotion?"

"Quick, the timber's on fire!"

He pushed past her and out into the drive, where he could see the flames fanned into a furnace by the breeze that blew through the cross-wise layers. The gaps created by the stack provided the fire with pockets of air and chimneys to carry the flames from top to bottom. He ran back inside. Sally made for the pile, where a chain of workers was already forming to pass pails of water scooped from a duck pond. A single boy of about fourteen stood alone on top of the wood.

"Sam, lad, get off there," commanded Larkins, placing a wooden ladder against one side that was furthest from the flames.

"I'm alright, Mr Larkins. I can see what I'm doing."

A sudden crackle led to a shower of sparks. A fierce new flame leapt skyward from the centre of the pile, bright against the lustreless night. The boy staggered backwards.

Glowing embers filled the air, becoming invisible as they slowly cooled and floated to the ground. Larkins pushed forward to grab the ladder and reposition it, catching a spark in his eye. He dropped the ladder and it fell backwards onto the grass. As he clutched his face in pain, Sally quickly ripped off a small section of material from her cotton skirt and plunged it into the pail she held, letting the rest of the water tip out as she ran to Larkins in panic.

"I'm blinded. Help me someone," he cried.

Sally pulled his head to her level and covered his eye with the wet cloth. "Hold it there if you can," she said, guiding him away from the embers and sitting him on a low wall.

"What's happening?" asked Larkins desperately. "Is Sam still alright? Where's Sam?"

Sally turned towards the fire. The water chain had stopped. Sam stood alone, beating his jacket against the flames with one hand and the other arm held across his face as protection against the heat.

"Get down," screamed Sally.

Sam looked around. "I can't get down!"

"How did you get up? Go the same way."

"I climbed up the side. It's too hot now. I need a ladder to get down!"

Sally looked across at the ladder lying on the grass. Satisfied that Larkins was safe, she fought the heat and tried to lift it, but it was too long and heavy.

"Leave this to me," exclaimed Edmond, now in his shirt sleeves, fresh on the scene after supervising the removal of the Stevenson's vacant carriage from the front. "Get back, right away from the flames. Tell the others the wood is lost and to stay completely clear. I've sent Fly for the fire brigade. We can't save the timber, but the house must be doused."

Edmond looked frantically but could see nowhere safe to rest the ladder. Knowing that time was precious, he took a deep breath and ran forward, crashing it against the top timbers that already smoked, ready to ignite. Sally raced to him, offering another large piece of her ripped skirt which had been doused in cold water. He grabbed it and wrapped it around his head.

"Get clear, Miss Ayres!" he bawled through the chaos," and began to climb.

Sally took a step back, but turned immediately and thrust her foot against the bottom rung, which shook as Edmond clambered upwards.

Edmond climbed quickly, stopping short of the top, where the heat scorched his face. "Sam, lad, I'm here. Follow my voice."

There was no response.

"Where is he?" he shouted. "Can anyone see the boy?"

The crackling drowned all response."

"Sam, for pity's sake, where are you?"

He tried to lift himself one step higher, but a new flame burst through a gap in the timber layers, licking around the uppermost rung.

Sally saw the danger and implored him to get down. "Edmond, please, I beg of you. The ladder's beginning to smoke. It's a lost cause."

Still with her foot steadying the ladder, Sally felt sudden pain. She instinctively jumped backwards, slapping her skirt with her bare hand where a glowing ember had settled on the fabric and burned through several layers, causing a ring of flame to spread outwards at alarming speed.

Above, Edmond was ignorant of Sally's plight, but had felt the ladder wobble as the support had disappeared. He froze until it steadied itself again, still screaming for the boy, realising that he had only seconds left.

"Give up!" shouted Sally at the top of her voice, no longer able to get near the ladder to hold it.

"No! I won't let it happen," he screamed heroically. His foot felt for a higher perch, but the rung splintered under pressure, causing his leg to break through and drop. Momentarily, he lost balance, desperately clutching to the sides of the ladder with his blistered hands, which took his full weight until his toes found something new and firm. "God help me. I won't leave the boy.

For mercy sake, Sam, come to me. Come to me! Where are you?" he cried in despair.

"I'm down here," followed a meek reply.

Glowing red from the heat, Edmond looked down through misty, smoke-sore eyes.

"Sir, please come down. I'll anchor the ladder."

At the bottom, a small figure stood holding a pail. Edmond's eyes were too watery to recognise anyone. He scrambled down. The moment both his feet touched the ground, water from the pail was unceremoniously thrown over him.

He staggered at the unexpected wet explosion hitting his face, but was grabbed from falling into the fire by Emmie's quick reactions and firm grip. Soaked and dripping, he was helped to the wall, where he caught his breath. James ran to him with a tankard of ale, pushing the girl away to get through.

"My God, I thought you were dead," stammered Edmond to the little boy standing directly in front of him. Sam grinned back, his face a sooty black and his hands burnt and grazed.

"I jumped. No good waiting to be rescued. Sorry I didn't give you any warning before I threw the water over you."

Edmond took the boy and gave him a hug.

"Why didn't you come down when you were told to?" thundered James. "Look what you've done to my son. You know what this disobedience means, don't you?"

"I'm for the boot?" replied Sam.

"By Jove, no!" said Edmond, breaking in quickly. "It means that you're a bloody hero, you scruffy little urchin. I'm more pleased to see you than a cart-full of wheat at harvest time. The timber might be lost, but who cares when you're safe. Get yourself off and get those hands cleaned and bandaged. Mrs

Redmarsh, though. No doing it yourself. And, tomorrow, you come to see me. I'll have a year's wages for you as a reward for your efforts tonight and the cost of a bunch of new clothes." He ruffled the boy's hair, which was matted with grease and ash. "Be proud of yourself, lad, as we're so very proud of you."

Sally, who had listened to all that had passed between man and boy, looked on with tears in her eyes.

"Let's get you indoors, Son," said James, gently helping him from the wall. As they entered the manor, Lily wrapped him in a blanket and the door closed, leaving Sally and the workers to find their own way home.

"Have I missed something?" asked Hubert from the stairs, wandering what all the noise was about.

"Not much," was Lord Stevenson's reply, a smirk on his face. He turned to Lily. "I most heartedly approve of your choice, my dear. Edmond is, indeed, the most worthy of young men and, may I say, as brave as anyone I have ever met." He kissed the top of her head. "I'm proud to welcome him into the family. Your wedding will be the grandest in all of Wessex."

Charlotte looked at her son, feeling greatly moved by the sentiment that the wedding would outshine all others in the county. The hero bit was of little value, though, she thought.

"Shame we haven't a few potatoes to roast in the fire," said Louise as they turned towards the dormitory. "It'll burn all night. You coming, Emmie?"

"You always think of your stomach," gibed Mary. "It's no wonder you're so fat."

"I'm not fat," she replied, "just a well built girl. Men like a bit of something to grab. Isn't that so, Emmie?"

Emmie didn't answer. The others left her to her own thoughts. Emmie had watched everything with intensity, particularly Edmond's heroics, and had been thrilled to hold him, albeit briefly. She was re-employed on the estate, by chance having the same bed in the dormitory that she had occupied before. There were now fewer girls using the loft room than previous years, their work on the land having been taken over in part by an ever increasing number and array of mechanical farm tools brought onto the land by Edmond, in a bid to exploit the most modern resources available. Some girls were still needed to milk and work the fields alongside the men, but other jobs had disappeared for ever.

Melancholic at having had to release Edmond too soon from her arms, and still transfixed on the manor where he had disappeared inside, a sudden clatter broke her mood as a horse-drawn fire appliance thundered down the drive and out over the grass. Uniformed men jumped off, quickly setting out their hoses and pumping for pressure. The little water carried by the appliance was quickly exhausted and the duck pond too was rapidly drained. As they searched in vain for a new source of water, a heavy downpour of rain began and they stood down.

Emmie stood in the rain, watching, her hair soaked and falling limply about her face. "What has changed for me?" she said out loud, knowing nobody could hear. "I think I still love you, Edmond," she whispered to the night.

CHAPTER 19

Aftermath

The morning light painted a pitiful sight. The timber stack looked half wasted, burned to ash and charcoal.

Edmond was still staring at the scene from his bedroom window. He had watched the sizzling destruction since the first noisy peal of thunder and lightning had dashed bright gashes across the sky, followed by a second, a third and more that forked in crackled stabs, amazed that smoke still rose from deep down inside the sodden pile. His bed remained unused, although he had managed an hour's sleep while resting on his arms at the window, until a sudden collapse of timber had roused him once more. What timber appeared at first sight to be untouched and saved, he knew on close inspection would be as consumed as the rest. The slightest touch would bring it all crashing down.

Edmond was mentally exhausted, hardly capable of gathering up all the impressions of the derelict scene. He relied on the income the timber and saw mill provided, and that problem alone was sufficient to fill his immediate thoughts. Although such a pile could be replaced, he would fail to meet orders already placed and deliveries promised, rendering his business unreliable and his cash flow starved.

From the vantage point, he now noticed through tired eyes two women standing below, who he felt sure had not been there only moments earlier. The features of one were unmistakably his mother's. The second, with her back to him, were indistinguishable, but she was crying. He strained to hear what passed between them.

"I hadn't realised it was you. Who told you that you could work here after all you did to us before?

Emmie looked askance, fiddling with the ribbon around her neck in nervous apprehension. "It was Sir, the Master. He took pity on me."

Charlotte said nothing, but the fast, rhythmical beating of her angry heart was apparent by her panting breath.

"Please, I beg you, let me keep my job," Emmie continued as a plea. "I was of great help last night and I mean to work hard. Look at my clothes. They're spoiled by the fire I fought."

Charlotte's gaze dropped. "They're in need of washing, I grant, but I see little evidence of fire damage."

"No," cried Emmie, "I remember now. I passed pails. The fire didn't touch me."

"Of course! I understand. It would be foolish to think you could remember in the morning things you had done the previous night. See if you can remember this, if I ask again. Who hired you?"

"On my honour, it was the Master."

"Are you sure, as you forget things so easily? Wasn't it my son?"

"It wasn't him, I promise. I haven't spoken to him properly, yet."

"Yet? You haven't *yet*."

"I only meant . . ."

"You have a bare-faced cheek. I'll give you that. My husband took you in last time and in return you eloped with a military man, stealing some our silver for good measure. And now you think we should open our arms in welcome once more? He is a fool to give you another chance."

"It wasn't my intention to break my engagement with Master Edmond. I fell for his friend after my hopes had been dashed by your son's desire to be with someone else. It was circumstance that forced me away, that and my broken heart. I knew nothing of the silver."

"I won't hear that! You and my son meant nothing to each other. Do you hear me? It's wildly absurd. I may accept that he spread his wings with you, but no claim can be made for more. I will not hear of it and you would be well advised never to raise the subject again, with anyone. Do I make myself clear?"

Emmie said that she did.

"You were sullied by Lieutenant Longborne Charles. It was your choice alone to elope with him. Being a gentleman, he may be excused. You are ruined."

"But it was Master Edmond who introduced us. I became the victim of his game."

"Game?"

"To throw me away, and make me feel as if it was all for my own benefit. I was very young and knew nothing about the world."

Charlotte held no pity. "What's that you fiddle with, girl?"

"It's a ribbon, nothing more."

"But it is. I see a ring dangling from it. Show it to me!"

Emmie untied the knot holding the ribbon around her neck and handed it to Charlotte's open hand.

She physically shook. "Where did you get this? Answer me at once. Where did you steal it?"

"I didn't steal it," she replied contemptuously, raising her voice to reinforce the truth. "It was a gift."

Charlotte closed her fingers around the ring, leaving the ribbon dangling from her palm. She closed her eyes, drawing energy from the object.

"It was given to me by a friend," Emmie added hurriedly. "She's dead now."

Charlotte's eyes flew open, her probing look aimed directly at the girl.

"What was the name of your benefactor?" she asked, bracing herself.

"Her name, Madam? Why, it was Christabel Mere."

The name pierced her deeply. "Christabel. Little Christabel. Can I believe it? Is this really hers?" she repeated in a whisper.

"No, Madam. It's mine."

"Be silent while I think!"

Emmie looked on in disbelief. "Can I be blamed for a gift?"

Charlotte lifted the ring to her mouth. "It's full circle."

"You mustn't think mistakenly of me, Madam. I'm innocent of any crime, other than that of loving the wrong man."

Charlotte collected herself, making a strong effort not to

cry. After a few deep breaths, she added: "You mustn't delude yourself that my son ever cared for you, or could in the future. He's engaged to a fine young woman of noble breeding and is utterly content in that wish. I have no reason for telling you this, other than to reinforce the point that it's true and final. Right now, I'm more concerned for the ring."

"My ring?"

"No, child, mine! It has been returned to me."

Emmie grabbed the ribbon which, worn through by age, snapped, leaving the ring firmly grasped in Charlotte's palm.

"Listen to me," said Charlotte in a mystifying and impressive tone, "it's the very ring I once gave to the father of a child. His name was Jack Mere. It was given out of care for the infant, to offer a small measure of protection against poverty by its value in gold. Discovering today that it was never sold is a miracle, and gives me some contentment in the thought that the baby must have been sufficiently well provided for to allow the ring to be kept. In that, I thank God."

"You mean to claim it as yours?" asked Emmie in despair.

"I mean to have it, as it *is* mine!"

From high above, Edmond closed the sash. He was bewildered by an argument he hadn't managed to overhear, beyond the words 'love' and 'Jack'. He wanted to understand more.

Charlotte stepped back into the manor, where Edmond stood waiting. She was surprised to see him.

"What's this? A deputation?" she said defensively.

"Of one, yes."

"I can't speak now. I need to see your father, urgently."

He moved to block her path. "No, Mother. Stop! Anything else can wait."

"It had better be good, Edmond. My business is of the utmost importance."

He said that it was. Hesitantly, she listened to his account of the past few minutes, when he admitted to have heard no speech as such, but was concerned by the body language.

"So, Edmond, you've been eavesdropping and decided that two and two make fifty-five."

"What part is wrong, then?"

"Almost everything. In future, eavesdrop well or not at all. For a start, it wasn't Miss Ayres out there, as you suggest. It was . . . oh, never mind who it was. It wasn't her, anyway, and that's all you need to know. Secondly, I'm free to express 'love' and not mean it in the way you imply, as an act of affection. I love roast beef, but I've never had the slightest wish to begin an affair with a sirloin steak!"

"But you said 'Jack'. I'm certain I heard that name mentioned. Don't deny it. I've heard it before, from older people in the hamlet, though I've always felt that I was never meant to hear them speak of him. He left Westkings with a wife and child before I was born, if I'm not mistaken. What are they to you?"

"Dead."

"Dead?"

"Yes."

"And now you fall apart after hearing the name again?"

"Fall apart!" she replied with indignation. "Do I look as if I care?"

He examined her expression, which had turned sour. "Maybe not."

"And Jack is a very common name. Don't forget that. Anyway, while I think of it, Edmond, have you seen Fly?"

"Not since last night. I assumed you had given him leave to rest in."

"Hardly! He's here to do my bidding, whatever I want and whenever I want it. Anyway, if I can be allowed to pass now, I'll look for your father."

Edmond stepped to one side.

"Oh! And if you find Fly, tell him I want to see him at once."

Later that same day, a charred body was discovered among the smouldering timber. It was only identifiable from a leather pouch embossed with the name *Schofield & Fly Solicitors* that lay discarded near the body but on the damp grass, and by the attention of a large dog which, it was assumed, sat pining for its master.

More than once in the past, Augustus Fly had repented his hasty actions. Now it had cost him his life. For years, Fly had kept the pouch hidden. It held the papers relating to the Elvingtons' dealings with Jack and Christabel Mere, which he had once promised to destroy. Instead, he had stolen them from under the very nose of his honest employer, their value for blackmail outweighing any sense of honour. Yet, after keeping them safe all that time, in a frenzied moment of fury the previous day he had finally burned them, not out of any sense of belated honour but to satisfy his immediate need for vengeance against the Elvingtons. The matches that had set the papers alight, stuffed within the timber stack, lay discarded in a shrub bed.

During the general panic and chaos over the fire he had started, Fly had found it a simple task to sneak away from 'Samain'. The horse he used had been a gelding stolen from the stables. For good measure, he had also taken a French ormolu and bronze mental clock that had sat on the Elvington mantel in the dining room for a quarter of a century, which fitted nicely into the pouch.

Yet, when only two miles or so from the estate, the miscreant had realized the foolishness of his actions. The clock had been a very poor trade-off for the documents, and it was all of his own making. In an instant he had turned about, returning quickly to the manor in the hope of retrieving at least some of the lost papers. But, on arrival, so many people had gathered at the scene, he had been forced to hide impatiently among the outlying trees until all efforts to save the timber had ended, leaving the way clear to dig among the ash.

Discarding the pouch and the clock it held, he had tried to kick smouldering planks to one side with the underside of his boot, making some inroad until several layers of now unsupported timber above his head collapsed. Fly had, indeed, been crushed.

CHAPTER 20

Kingsden wood

The circumstances being unusual and the remains macabre, it was not until late that afternoon that Fly's body was removed to a simple elm coffin. A policeman stepped up to it, took a piece of chalk from his pocket, and scratched Fly's name on the lid, after which it was taken to an awaiting spring wagon and covered by a frayed cloth.

Police had come from Glastonbury to investigate the scene and, now that they left, James gave the order for the timber pile to be set alight once more, using much oil, to fully raze it to the ground. The police had also found the clock in Fly's pouch, but saw no need to keep it as evidence. James couldn't touch it and asked that it too should be tossed into the pile and consumed in the fire. The dog, still sitting on the grass awaiting the return of its master, was leashed and taken away by a field-hand.

The shock of a death rocked the estate, causing all work to be halted temporarily, except milking and the production of associated dairy products. Only Charlotte appeared untouched by the tragedy, as if released from shackles.

Sally, who had raised the alarm and had been centre-stage to events that fateful night, needed the relief of open spaces to overcome an overwhelming feeling of mortality. In her mind, she imagined the flames and smoke consuming Fly's flesh and lungs, just as she remembered the sea consuming her whole body, out of reach of any help or hope.

And so, over the coming days of serene weather, Sally ranged further and further out on long country walks. They gradually calmed her thoughts and gave her the peace of mind needed to decide her future.

Hubert had called at Sally's house the day after the fire, hoping to arrange another outing together. She had not been in, and nor was she twice more that morning. As his stay in Westkings was ending, and in desperation, he had scribbled a note giving his address and asking her to contact him if she so wished. It was fondly written, well short of what may be called a love letter, but nevertheless a work of considerable effort. He had placed it under the heavy ring-shaped knocker on the front door, checking first that it was of sufficient weight to trap it. He had also tied to the door handle a small bouquet of flowers, freshly picked from the manor's garden. Satisfied, he left. Within an hour the letter had blown away.

Sally's favourite path took her over level ground that skirted Muncome Hill and Copel wood and past a derelict windmill, where the meandering River Geri could be crossed using rocks that lay just below the water's surface. With her skirt pulled above her ankles, she had searched with her toes for each stone, ensuring it was firmly fixed before taking the stride. It was a walk that Christabel had enjoyed once in the past, and one also familiar to Emmie and Edmond.

On more than one occasion during her rambles Sally had unexpectedly met Edmond, passing no more than a brief nod of acquaintance as their paths crossed. The perverseness of these chance meetings, where few others came, never occurred to her. It was, after all, his home ground.

One particularly bright day, when the sun speckled the ground as it tried to penetrate the high canopy trees and the air was filled with all the delights of Summer, Sally found herself meeting Edmond not once, but twice. As before, their first meeting had been acknowledged without words passing between them, but on the second, only half an hour later, the coincidence required comment.

Sally stopped at seeing him hurrying her way, although his stare was fixed firmly on the ground, where exposed tree roots made the going hazardous.

"Good morning again," she said in soft tone, a gentle smile making him feel welcomed into her private time.

He looked up with shock. "Oh, sorry, I didn't see you there. I keep catching my heel on these blasted roots." He looked at her dainty boots with tall heels. "How you can walk in those things, I can't begin to understand."

"It's the way of women. Pretty things take priority over function. Mind you, there are times when I'd gladly swap my shoes for a good pair of worker's boots."

"I'm so grateful for being male. Don't misunderstand me. I like pretty women, but I couldn't live with all that 'getting-ready' stuff. It seems so utterly pointless. Anyway, have you been anywhere nice, or met anyone on your travels?"

"Just out here, alone."

"Where are you going?"

She pointed homeward.

"I'll join you, then."

Without waiting for approval, he began the slow walk back, expecting her to join his side, which she did with good grace. The steps took away any of the awkwardness that comes from a standing conversation, as if the paces themselves were communal. It was in this fashion that several minutes passed before either engaged in further conversation.

"I'm grateful to you for the use of the house," she said presently. "It was an unexpected kindness."

"Think nothing of it. It was empty, after all. By the way, if you hear that my mother was less than pleased, take absolutely no notice. I run the place."

"Have I made trouble for you?"

"A bit, perhaps, but nothing I can't handle. No, I'm fully aware of what happened to you and it should be us doing all the apologising. What my mother was thinking of when hiring that ship is beyond my comprehension. Why she became involved with your expedition at all puzzles me. And, something else bothers me. Do you find my father odd?"

"Not at all," was her honest reply.

"I see. Only, I have become aware of an interest in you that perhaps goes beyond anything I would've expected from him, taking into account all the known circumstances. Little things, nothing in themselves, but when put together seem, well, curious."

Sally didn't like the direction of the conversation and changed the subject. "I hear you are to be married, Edmond?"

He agreed that this was, indeed, correct. "Please, I feel you should call me Master Elvington, and not by my Christian name," he added pleasantly and with dignity.

She apologised.

"How did you know?"

"Oh, it was a little something I overheard the girls talking about. The Elvington name and that of the Stevenson's being 'flung over the pulpit', I believe was their expression."

"Was it being said in a friendly way, or as disparagement? I only ask because some history has passed between me and the girls and they would know it."

She replied that she was unsure, but felt it was probably idle gossip spilling over from the dormitory, which didn't matter either way.

"Very well," he replied. "And you. What are your plans?"

"At the moment I don't have any."

"Are you not expected by someone or other, maybe to be somewhere or other, or to do something . . ?"

". . . or other?" She laughed. "No, I'm as idle as a clock without a pendulum. I'll need to work, that's for sure, and before too long. I have no independent means of support. This is one of the few times in my adult life that I've not been able to support myself. I thought my husband would keep me, but, as you seem to know, he died in the shipwreck. He did leave me a bit of money, though, but most of our things were lost at sea and were uninsured. I'm too old for anyone else to want me now. Marriage is generally a young person's pursuit."

He stopped to face her. "May I talk in a practical way?"

"Certainly, if you so wish. I'm most fond of practical talk, being a teacher. It's idle, dreary conversation I can't stand."

"By dreary people?"

"Yes, you're quite right. It's people who make talk dreary, not the subject. You're wise beyond your years, Master Edmond."

He smirked. "I think you may call me Edmond after all. How do I address you?"

In her mind she said the word 'mother'. "Oh, being much older, I think Miss Ayres may be proper. Your parents wouldn't want familiarity between us, of that I'm sure."

"Then, that's what I'll do. Miss Ayres, are you aware that there are certain people of my acquaintance who are concerned for you?"

"Hubert Smith?" she asked with considerable vigour.

"No. I didn't mean Hubert, though, talking of dull people, he has shown quite an attachment for you, as you probably already know.

"There are others?"

"Well! Maybe I've used the wrong words. I refer more properly to concern about your accident."

"Oh, no, not you too! Has the world gone mad? I was shipwrecked and saved. What more is wanted of me?"

"These certain people are convinced that there is more about you to understand."

"So I have been told, over and over again. But there isn't. Good heavens, people drown daily without such inquest."

"Drowned, yes, but you weren't. I am told you are in some mental anguish, and that concerns them."

"Edmond..!" Sally screeched bitterly, trembling, her face coloured a pale grey. She tried to say more, but her mouth would not form any words. She choked with anxiety, trying to draw breath through a windpipe now seemingly blocked except for the tiniest gap. She heaved to intake air.

Quickly, he took hold of her, gently rubbing her back in a calming massage. The air gradually returned to her lungs, her pulse slowing.

"Compose yourself, please. I was wrong to have mentioned it. I seem to have reintroduced into your mind a moment of your life that still terrifies you."

Sally regarded Edmond with perplexity. He felt the change of mood immediately. She pulled his hand free.

"I think the time has come for me to understand a thing or two," she said, still trying to get normal breath, ". . . about what's happening to me, and your connection to it."

"Meaning?" replied Edmond in resolute tone.

"Now I think of it, not once have we met by accident. I'm right, aren't I? Who sent you to look out for me?"

"Anything else?"

"Of course there's more. Explain how my tragedy affects you."

He searched for an answer.

"Has anyone explained to me what I'm supposed to have done? Not a bit of it. I just have to suffer this continual aggravation. If I've done something, knowingly or unknowingly, then perhaps you know and can tell me so that I may understand and rectify it. For a start, who are these 'certain people' you mention?"

"I can't tell you."

"Why not, if it concerns me? Can't anyone understand? I'm willing to co-operate. All I need to know is, co-operate over what?"

"You really don't know?"

"If I did, I'd hardly be in such a tizzy."

He thought for a few moments. "Look, I'm bound by a certain amount of secrecy. All I can say is that there are people of my acquaintance who think your accident has a meaning. I can't say much more, because I haven't been told what they expect of you. In truth, I don't understand any of it myself. I sometimes wonder if *I'm* not being spun a yarn. It's enough to say that it's from the highest office."

"Police?"

"Government."

"Oh, good grief!" she screamed, holding her head in her hands.

"My involvement? That's simple. I was approached to keep a watch on you while you were in Glastonbury. See what you got up to, where you went and who you spoke to."

"And?" asked Sally with a tear in her eye, feeling betrayed by the nearest person she had as family hereabouts.

"I told them you only did normal things any visitor would do."

"Thank you."

"However . . ."

"There's more?"

"I'll be completely honest with you. I let you use the terrace so that I could continue to keep you in my sights."

"No! So it wasn't through kindness, but for spying on me?"

"I suppose so, but not entirely."

"I was right all along. We keep meeting because you're watching me?"

"Yes."

"And now?"

"It's over. I can see you have no motives and I shall send a message to that effect this very day."

Below the dormitory, where Mary and Louise had joined other girls wearing their Sunday best clothes in preparation for the walk to church, Emmie came rushing in from milking. She threw down her wooden yoke, relieved to be among friends. Grabbing Mary, she dragged her to one side.

"You'll never guess what I've just heard from an inside maid?"

Mary replied that she couldn't.

"That Catherine Charles woman. You know, the sister of Lieutenant Longborne Charles of the Surrey Dragoons I ran off with. She's coming here, to 'Samain'."

"Good gracious. How do you know?"

"The maid was asked to despatch a letter to her. It wasn't properly sealed, so she read it."

"Are you going to confront her?"

"You don't understand. The maid told me that she thinks Longborne must have heard of Edmond's forthcoming marriage and wants to be in on it, perhaps even to be best man. As he stole things from the manor, he probably wants to send his sister ahead to see if he's still welcomed."

"How could he be?"

"I don't know. Forgive and forget, perhaps, or push more blame onto me. Perhaps he's in need of money and wants to tap into Edmond's good nature. Catherine was a particular favourite of the master, so Longborne probably feels she might be able to persuade the family that it was all a big mistake and not his fault at all."

"How could she do that?"

"By blaming me again, as I just said, like last time.

"Why? I thought they knew the truth?"

"I don't know. Listening to one side of a story always gives the wrong impression. Things like that just happen. I'm me and they're posh. I'm really worried, because I've done something else really stupid too."

"What?"

Emmie went to one of the pails that was still attached to the yoke, now lying on the floor. She removed a parcel wrapped in a shawl and handed it to Mary.

"A clock?"

"Of course it's a clock, dummy! I saw it being tossed onto the ruined timber the other day, just before they set it alight. Nobody was looking, so I took it. I hid it in the cow shed."

"Why?"

"Oh, come on. Isn't it obvious? Look at it. It must be worth a few shillings of anyone's money."

"So you stole it!"

"But, did I? That's the point. It was thrown away and I retrieved it. Is that stealing?"

"Did you ask permission to have it?"

"No."

"Then it's stealing. Does anyone else know you have it?"

"I expect so. I've been showing it about a bit."

* * *

It was true that Catherine had contacted James, announcing that she had greatly missed his company, that she thought of him often with all the fondness of a daughter, and that she would like to make an unscheduled visit. It was, she said, her dearest wish to see the estate in its full Summer beauty, and an unexpected gap in her otherwise busy social calendar made the present month preferable to any other. She had ended her message by saying that she hoped it would be possible for the Elvington carriage to be sent to collect her.

In sending the letter as confidential to James, she had contrived to circumnavigate both Edmond and Charlotte, hoping that once an invitation was returned by James, the others would be unable to block her progress. The plan was well considered.

James had indeed replied, but in less cordial terms than she had hoped. He had said that she could indeed come for a short stay, but that the invitation applied only to her and not that 'brother of hers'. He would send the carriage on the written date.

Wearing a broad grin, Longborne viewed the reply handed to him by Catherine, unashamed of his reputation among the Elvingtons and unafraid that he would feel any embarrassment if Catherine could work her charm and get him, too, into the manor. The plan had passed its first hurdle.

CHAPTER 21

The day of reckoning

After Edmond had finally left her side, and because of all that had happened on the walk to Kingsden wood, Sally had chosen to turn about and head south, making for unknown territory which added several miles to the outing. Her feet were now tired. It was, therefore, solace to her heart when the terrace house came back into view, its small frontage and little windows being as friendly as a warm blanket after a cold bath. She was lighter in spirit and wanted nothing more than a nice cup of tea.

She had half expected to find a letter pushed under the door, giving her notice to leave. After all, she had fulfilled Edmond's uses and he had no further reason to let her stay on. Thankfully, there was none. She walked over to the bouquet she had discovered attached to the door a few days previously, now neatly arranged in a pottery vase. Picking out a single bloom, she lifted it to her nose with mixed emotions. She had assumed it had come from Edmond as a house-warming gift, but now thought it was much more likely to have been a present from James. What did that mean, she wondered?

Once back inside the manor's walls, Edmond had indeed scribed a letter, but not to Sally. It was addressed to Russell Thackeray, stating in no uncertain terms that Miss Sally Ayres was clearly the subject of much malign and that he was quitting the task of shadowing her. He warned against asking anyone else to follow her, making it entirely clear that not only was she unworthy of such attention, but that if it continued he would blow the whistle. A stronger message he had never written to anyone. The letter, received by Thackeray in London some days later, was received with more than a little smugness.

"You see, Fairbourne, I was right all along. Read this communication."

He took it and scanned the lines. "Are we to take the word of a boy, Sir?"

"Yes, Fairbourne. He was man enough to do your bidding and shadow her. Now he's man enough to decide it's a pointless exercise. It's over, with her at least. Tell me, how are *you* doing with writing *my* report? I must be seen as intellectual. Am I collating the paragraphs well?"

"You have a knack for writing, Sir. Yes, your understanding of all matters is second to none and the sentences will reflect it."

"And when shall I finish it, Fairbourne?"

"If *I* work all the hours there are, in a few days I think."

"A few days? I'm exhausted at the very thought."

"You could always write some of it yourself, Sir, if you're worried about the time."

Thackeray did not reply, but removed his coat from the

stand. "Turn off the gas when you leave, Fairbourne. I'm off to the club."

Finally, the day arrived for Catherine's visit to 'Samain'. The carriage had been sent hours before and only then had James told Charlotte of his invitation.

"You've done what!" bawled Charlotte, throwing her glass into the fire in outrage.

"I knew you would react that way. That's way I didn't tell you before it was too late to alter the arrangements. And, you should know, I put out the old glasses in case you threw one, so no harm done there, either. Anyway, I like her and I could do with a bit of cheering after all that business with Fly."

"Did it not occur to you that the house isn't ready for a guest, welcomed or otherwise?"

He looked around the drawing room. "Looks fine to me."

She stormed to the door. "Men!"

Outside, Edmond dismounted after returning from a long ride to see Lily in Sherborne. He called for a groom, but nobody responded. Walking the beast in a wide circle, he tied the reins to a large decorative urn, where the horse could nibble at the lush grass on a steep bank. As he turned for the manor, a call came from the direction of the dormitory. Emmie came rushing over.

"By heck, it's you!" was his surprised response, given no time to feel embarrassment or annoyance. "What on earth are you doing here?"

"I've been here for some days, Sir. You must've noticed it was me who helped you away from the fire."

"Be damned if I did. Who hired you?"

"Your father, Sir. He took pity on me. Did you really not know?"

"Nothing. Still, as long as we understand ourselves and leave the past in the past where it belongs, it won't be a problem. Is that all you wanted, to introduce yourself?"

"Begging your pardon Sir, but no, Sir. May I speak to you in confidence?"

He said that she could, but it would have to be out in the open, not inside where onlookers could misconstrue the situation.

"Very well." She looked about her. There was nobody. "I don't quite know how to say this, Sir. I've tried to think how to approach the subject, but there's no easy way other than being direct."

He stared, waiting for more.

"It's about my ring."

Edmond flared into sudden temper. "Your ring? The ring I gave to you as a token years ago and you so freely lost in Kingsden woods? The ring Christabel found for you among the undergrowth and handed back? That ring? You *do* raise old times and past affection."

"Please, Sir, I don't. It's not the engagement ring at all."

"Not?"

"No, quite another. I was given this one by Christabel Mere."

In a flash his mind conjured Christabel's beautiful face, a face which had taken his breath away and caused his youthful heart to burst. He had loved her so much, dropping Emmie in her favour as yesterday's news. He had fought for her affection against an older suitor from Cerne Abbas and won, or so he had hoped, although she had still purposefully avoided him for reasons he had not understood. Then, they had met one fateful day as he was leaving the estate on horseback. She seemed to care that he was going, and for his part he had said enough to indicate his own feelings without laying himself open to the embarrassment of rejection. But, such play with words and the touching of pulsing hands had come to nothing and he had ridden out of her life before they had finally declared themselves.

How he had been saddened by news of her death, and the thought of what might have been. But such grief had been temporary and to all appearances he had plunged head-long and willingly into a new world of social events Charlotte had organised at the manor to revive the Elvington name in public esteem.

"Are you alright, Sir?"

"Oh, yes, quite alright," he said, coming around from his thoughts. "It was hearing that name. I was just thinking . . . Oh, never mind."

"I know what you mean, Sir. I still get a lump in my throat when I think of her. Never a more generous person ever walked the earth. You loved her, I think."

"And so did you, Emmie. Perhaps Chrissie came into my life a few years too early. But now such things are best forgotten."

"I can't forget her, and I would wager neither will you."

"That's for me to know. Now, returning to the matter in hand. Christabel's ring. What about it?"

"She gave it to me the day we parted company for the final

time. I've kept it safe ever since. It means the world to me."

"And?"

"And . . . I haven't got it any longer, because your mother took it away."

"Pardon?" exclaimed Edmond in shock.

"She took it, the morning after the fire."

"So it was you she was talking to, under my window. I thought it was Sally Ayres."

"It was me, alright. She asked where I got it from and I told her. I took it off to show her and she kept it. I want it back."

"And you shall have it," said Edmond looking towards the manor. "What's this new nonsense about?"

"Can I go, Edmond?"

"Yes, you should. Leave it with me. I'll get to the bottom of it. Oh, and please don't call me Edmond. Stick to Sir or Master Edmond, but not plain Edmond. Understood?"

"Yes, Sir, but you could never be 'plain' to me." She ran off, leaving Edmond bewildered.

Inside the manor, all was confusion and panic. Dusty rugs from the drawing room, dining room and bedrooms were being hastily lifted, ready to be beaten. Freshly washed and starched antimacassars replaced the old on the back and arms of the sofa chairs, and counterpanes were readied for when the beds could be made-up after the rugs were put back.

Furniture began to gleam as glass, and the best plate and silver were being carried up from below stairs to decorate the table and sideboard, that is until James pointed out the error of leaving silver out to tempt Catherine, whereupon it was taken back to the appropriate cupboard and placed under lock and key. Clean collars and cuffs were spread ready for the staff once the chores were ended, and a stiff collar of radiant white was taken to the Master's bedroom, although James had protested against the need to be so formal and refused to wear anything other than his usual hunting attire upon her arrival.

Edmond dodged the maids polishing the highly carved banisters and picture frames and made directly for Charlotte's voice of command, which took him to stairs leading to the kitchen. Here, the cook rummaged through the larder to see if it contained the ingredients in sufficient quantity needed to make the meal asked of her. Charlotte sat on a long bench to one side of an oaken table, beneath a pine dresser groaning under the weight of copper pots and pans, jelly moulds, dish covers, blue pattern chinaware and much more. A portrait of Queen Victoria perched on top, next to another of Crown Prince Frederick of the German Empire and his handicapped son, Willy.

"Mother," Edmond called softly, trying to draw her attention away from the kitchen and beckoning her to the sanctity of the stairs. He called a second time, again without response. Annoyed at being deliberately ignored, he descended the final two steps, making himself fully obvious to the cook.

"Go away, Edmond," scoffed Charlotte, proving that she had heard his pleas. "I'm in no mood for men of any shape and size."

Edmond stood firm, making it clear that he intended to have his way.

With a giant sigh of frustration, Charlotte rose, shuffling indignantly along the bench. "If it's a trifle, you'll catch it."

"The only trifle in this room is the one Cook's preparing. As for me, for the sake of gaining relief to my worries, I care nothing how much I add to yours. If you want the servants to hear our business, just say the word. Otherwise, do as I ask."

Edmond turned for the stairs, followed begrudgingly by Charlotte.

"What is so urgent that you make an exhibition of yourself? And, make it good."

"Oh, it is. I won't disappoint. What I want is an explanation."

"Explanation?"

"Just so. Tell me, why did you take Emmeline Sturry's ring?"

Charlotte froze. "Who told you I did?"

"She did and I believe her. Well? I'm waiting."

Feeling more than a little awkward and somewhat faint, she turned to sit on a stair, where she sat for some while, anxiously considering what to do or say. Her usual brusque nature had forsaken her. She had undergone a material change that robbed her of her normally fluent tongue.

"I'm still waiting, Mother!"

More seconds passed.

"Well?"

Charlotte retained the look of someone in shock, caught between concern to cover an existing lie and a strange but definite light-headed feeling that fate had presented the chance to lift a burden that had gnawed at her soul for far too long. Thus decided, she raised her head and said in an abnormal tone that was as harsh as her features: "Maybe, as your father has already shocked me today by what he's done,

I ought to shock him by revealing *our* little secret. It's time you knew, anyway."

Now it was Edmond's time to feel anxiety. "Is it serious? You look serious!"

"About as much as can be imagined."

"But you said *little secret*."

"I lied!"

"Then tell me quickly, for I begin to tremble."

"Life has taught me, Edmond, that pain cannot be avoided, trouble sidestepped, or responsibility shirked. Even within families, the love a mother has for her child is not sufficient to shield that child from harm caused by the very person who most wants to protect it. Does that make sense?"

"I assume 'it' being me, in this case?"

She thought only of Christabel. "Yes, you," was her dishonest reply.

"And the harming mother is you?"

"Both of us, actually. Your father and myself. We are both complicit."

"Oh, dear. It's going to be bad, isn't it?"

"The worst, and more so."

Charlotte, now with considerable clarity of thought, told Edmond of the unbelievable circumstances that had led to her conceiving a child, the father of that child being a field worker on the estate by the name of Jack. She explained how James had given her the choice, either to give the baby away or to leave him and the estate forever, and that she had chosen to stay with her husband.

"You see, Edmond, that baby, so cruelly given away, was

no other than someone you later met. She was Christabel Mere."

Edmond was numb with shock. "Christabel? That can't be right, it just can't be."

"It is so."

"Are you saying in your sick little mind that Christabel was your own daughter and that you let me have a relationship with my own sister?"

"Certainly not!"

"Then tell me how can it be any different?"

"You need to know something else, equally appalling. I can hardly find the courage to tell you, but be told you must now that I've started. To reveal all that I must is every bit as hard as the ultimatum given to me by your father over my baby's future twenty years ago." She steeled herself, finally letting the words go. "You, my dearest and most beloved son, were born to another woman. James is your father, but I'm not your natural mother, although in every other way we are as one and I remain your mother in all but the act of giving birth."

"Oh, my Lord! Good God! You're not my mother?"

She took him in both hands. "I'm so very sorry. You had to be told now or never."

"Hell, *never* would've been kinder. Ten minutes ago I had a family. Now I'm half an orphan, and you're a stranger to me."

"Nobody could be more remorseful than me. You were born of another woman, yes, but your natural father is my husband, James. In my fear of being rejected, I agreed to raise you as mine, having lost my own child. And, I'm so glad I did, for you are as real to me as any child to his natural mother."

"I can't get my head around all this! Am I being told that you were Christabel's mother and not mine, and Father is my parent but not Christabel's? Is that what you say?"

"Only in blood, Edmond. In all other respects I'm still your mother."

"So, Christabel, who I loved as a woman and not as a sibling, was, in fact, my sister all along?"

"Half sister, Edmond, she was only a half sister. But, and most critically, there were no blood ties between you two whatsoever. Neither of you children had the same parents. That's why it would never have been incestuous."

"I had a sister. My God! But . . . but, Christabel died. My sister died of . . . neglect. You let my sister, your daughter, die a pauper."

"I did, and I shall end my days in utter shame. I'm tormented by the very thought. Yet, I hardly knew her because of your father's attitude when she was born."

"You dare blame Father for this? It's his fault, is that what you are saying?"

"No, I didn't mean . . ."

"I can't think. It's all too unreal. You've exploded my family, my world. All those years of my youth I had two parents. Now, suddenly, I have only one parent and a dead sister. I need room to consider everything."

He jumped up, not looking back at Charlotte, who watched him go with new fear in her heart. She called after him.

"Edmond, you're not a boy any more. You should be able to cope. You're not a child. Edmond. Edmond! These things happen in the best families. Edmond!"

Determined to leave, he nonetheless pulled up by the door

leading to the hall, turning back to shout: "Am I without a mother? Is she dead, my *real* mother, I mean?"

Charlotte gave no reply, which he took to mean that she was.

Edmond ran from the hall and out into the garden, his mind in turmoil. Charlotte gave him space but strode briskly to the drawing room, where she could watch Edmond through the coloured panes.

From an outside direction, James pounded heavy footed into the drawing room.

"I've just seen Edmond. He brushed straight past me without apology. What's going on?"

Charlotte, cowering, explained everything.

"You idiot! You bloody little fool. You . . ." He raised his hand to her, but could not strike, even in anger. She looked up through red eyes, asking for no pity. It was a replay of that time before Christabel was born. With gritted teeth, he swiped at the pipe-rack on the mantel, sending the lot flying across the room. Charlotte knelt to pick up the pieces.

"Leave them, woman. Bloody leave them where they fall. You're not my servant."

She raised her head, tears now streaming down her cheeks. "Am I still your wife?"

"You are, damn it," he replied gruffly. "I wouldn't choose you as a mistress."

She smiled, but it was misplaced. "Your best pipe," she said in gentle tone, holding the pieces.

"Sod the pipe, woman, and the rest of them." He quitted the room, deliberately crushing in his path everything on the floor.

* * *

James caught up with Edmond sitting on a wall. He looked tranquil enough, perched with his legs hanging off the ground, his head bowed. He played with a stick, dragging its tip through the grass. He looked up as he heard James approaching, but immediately returned his gaze to the ground. James sat beside him, at first saying nothing to relieve the awkwardness.

"So, now you know!"

Edmond let the stick drop.

"It's all such a mess, Son."

Edmond turned slightly towards his father, but didn't look at him. "Is this nightmare really true? Is it, all of it, I mean?"

"I don't know precisely what your mother has said, but I can make an educated guess. I doubt she has told you any inaccuracies."

"She's not my mother. She's merely Charlotte, your wife. She's nothing more to me anymore."

James shook his head. "That's not true, Edmond. She's the one who brought you up, bathed you when you were sick, taught you to ride, played with you, and made you the man you are. That's what good women do. One day, perhaps, men will be more involved in the upbringing of their children. But, as things are now, you must acknowledge that she alone made you the wonderful man you have turned out to be. Can you understand that and find it in your heart to forgive her all past mistakes, and me for that matter? I'm not free of guilt."

"Any governess can do what she did."

"No, my boy, only a mother, because only she can add angel dust to nurturing. It's in the twinkle of her eye, the gentle velvet of her voice. It's the pain she feels when scolding, and the wish that she could take upon herself all the aches and pains that distress a child. It's called unconditional love!"

"So tell me, where was that unconditional love for my sister? She enjoyed none of it."

"I robbed her of that, the day I forced the servants to put baby Christabel into that blighter Jack Mere's wagon. Just think how Charlotte, your mother, must've hurt, a terrible wound that lingered for months or even years in her breast, unable to be adequately expressed to another living soul. Her humanity dried with the milk she carried for nurturing her baby. It made a gentle woman hard. And when, seventeen years later, a beautiful young woman came here to 'Samain', proud and healthy, and is discovered to be that lost child, how was she to react? Charlotte's allegiance was to you, the boy she had raised as her own. Charlotte was by then another woman, not so thoughtful and not so nice, but still made of flesh and blood. You should know, Edmond, that we finally resolved to tell Christabel of her lineage, and to this end we caught up with her in our carriage as she left the district. We asked her to rejoin our family."

"And she said?"

"It was a most distressing episode, almost as agonizing as seventeen years before. I believe Charlotte wanted to hear her voice again, for the first time with the understanding of their true relationship, yet she feared the outcome, the look in her estranged daughter's eyes."

"What did she say, I asked? Not how you two felt. I don't care about that."

"She rejected your mother's plea in its entirety. She

wouldn't accept any extenuating circumstances. Most of all, she wouldn't believe that her mother was any other person than Verity Bates, the simple field worker who had joined her in Mere's wagon. You see, Jack Mere and Verity had been her parents in all important ways and she loved them dearly. They were both dead by then, but all their affection had been poured into Christabel and she wanted no other parents, blood or otherwise. You see, Edmond, Verity wasn't her natural mother, but she was her *only* mother all the same. The comparison to your situation is real and you must take comfort from it."

"I suppose I could try, for Christabel's sake," said Edmond, wiping his eyes. "You know, Father, it now seems so wrong, but I openly confess that I loved Christabel and wanted her so much."

"I know that, Son. Please, never think it was wrong. You weren't of the same blood. You were merely strangers who met in perfect love in an imperfect world, at an imperfect time."

"And the ring, Father, Christabel's ring?"

"What ring?"

"The one Mother stole from Emmie."

"I'm confused, Edmond. Start again."

"Mother took a ring from that milkmaid, Emmeline Sturry. It used to belong to Christabel."

James looked all amazement. "Then, Son, it is hers, Mother's I mean. I think she slipped several little objects into Jack Mere's hand as he left with the baby, one of my boxes among them. If the ring had belonged to Christabel and was precious in more than sentimental value, then it was almost certainly something given by your mother to benefit the baby girl the day she was taken from Westkings."

"Emmie wants it back. I told her she could have it."

"I'll speak to your mother. I can promise nothing." With that, he rose and headed back to the manor, leaving Edmond with his dark thoughts.

"Father!" called Edmond as an afterthought, catching James just before he disappeared inside. "Who exactly *was* my mother? My natural mother, I mean."

James thought he had got away without having to answer that difficult question. A pensive look came over his already grave features. He walked back to where Edmond remained sat, not wanting to raise his voice. He believed the quietness of Edmond's tone meant that he had not been condemned as the worst of men.

"Are you sure you want to know? Is it that important?"

"Of course it is."

"And, it cannot wait for tomorrow?"

"Now, Father. I want to know who."

"As I said, your mother is my wife. The person who gave you life, and nothing more, was somebody you already know. It was Sally Ayres."

"What!" exclaimed Edmond, quickly turning in the direction of the little terrace house. "Surely not her?"

"I can add nothing else. I can offer you no comfort from the revelation, other than my gravest apology for all that your mother and I have heaped upon you."

"Which mother are you talking about now, because I no longer know to whom you refer?"

"Charlotte, of course."

"Oh, her!"

"Believe me, Edmond, beneath all this scandal remains two good women. In different ways, each is your mother."

"Oh, no! I now see I've been really stupid."

"How so?" James asked.

"I obviously didn't know who she really was, Sally Ayres I mean. And in that ignorance I've worked against her."

"What nonsense."

"It's far from nonsense. It's true, if you care to hear me out."

James was astonished by his firmness.

"You wouldn't know this, but there are people, high-ranking people at that, who think she's a mental case and a risk to others. So, I offered to watch her movements. It was Schofield who introduced me to them. As he's someone I've always trusted, I agreed."

"Without asking me first? Damn it, Edmond, I could've put you straight."

"I wasn't allowed to approach you. I did ask if I could."

"So you spied on her anyway?" He was astonished by the turn of events. "Alright, let's not get ahead of ourselves. Tell me every small detail. I want to know who these people are and what they think she's done. But, most importantly, you must stop spying on her immediately. I will vouch that she's a most agreeable person, incapable of wrong doing and perfectly sane."

"Oh, it *has* ended, believe me. She's innocent of fault."

"Good. We are agreed." He suddenly thought of Charlotte and what she must be feeling, waiting alone and probably hysterical. She would be frantic to know the outcome of the revelations. Hearing Edmond's confessions was no trifle, but there were matters more urgently pressing.

"I need to know everything, Edmond, but can it wait until later? Right now I must see how your mother is standing up to all that has happened. Charlotte I mean. It's been a terrible day, but more so for her. She has the most to lose. And, while felicitous to me, I'm also inflicting Catherine Charles on her, who she detests. Today of all days. Goodness, what terrible timing! I must go to her. Meantime, be strong, my boy. Men have to show character and strength."

CHAPTER 22

The arched roof

With the Elvington family in disarray, Catherine arrived. James, Charlotte and Edmond stood outside to greet her, forced into unified congeniality that belied their true feelings. Having to be pleasant to one another for the sake of family dignity was not easy, yet the smiles the farce engendered softened the hurt a little until it was possible to guarantee that nobody was likely to break the absurdity of the situation.

Catherine stepped from the carriage, playing the part of a much-welcomed guest, but knowing deep down that only James was likely to be pleased to see her. For the others, she knew she was as wanted as a rat in a corn store.

Careful to give exactly the right first impression, neither too poor to be unfashionable nor too rich to put off any small financial gestures that might come her way, she wore an understated dress of striped blue silk. Her tiny waist moved with elegant vivacity, giving her the s-shaped figure of a woman barely into her twenties, yet, actually, several years older. Her face was porcelain white and her hands an ivory imitation, with manicured blush nails and rings on every finger. In the city she was fashionably languid and extravagant, but in a small hamlet she was out of her pond and unhappy. Of course, this was not so much a visit to friends as a campaign to win favour, and so it was her intention to show no such indignation.

"My dear James, I can't tell you how excited I am to be here. It's a place I dream of, in a country setting that has my heart in its hills and my soul in its vales. In short, I commune with nature."

James kissed her outstretched hand, whereupon she offered the same to Charlotte, who shook it, pressing Catherine's fingers slightly harder than would be expected. Catherine winced a little, but bore the same smile as she passed to Edmond.

"My goodness, you're even more handsome than before. You greeting me here is prodigiously civil. If only I was a few years younger. But, there we have it, a problem that my trim waist cannot endure alone, although you may still look at it if you wish, Edmond, while your mother remembers when she had one similar." She returned to James. "Lead me to my room, my dear James, so that I may refresh myself. I'm fatigued from the journey and must look a fright. You really should get a new carriage, James, for this one is out of date and hard in ride. Edmond can bring the bags. All five are mine, but the box has little gifts for you all from Longborne. He is so thoughtful over such things. Some might say manners are but a trifle. I believe his to be sincere."

James led her inside, leaving Edmond and Charlotte aghast.

"Now, you will be careful with the box, won't you Edmond," said Catherine from the door. "The contents are delicate and offered with the fondest love by Longborne."

Edmond snatched the box from the rack, holding it by the string which held the lid. He let it dangle unceremoniously. Its weight was unexpected. The bags were left for the servants.

Sitting on the edge of their beds in the dormitory that evening, the girls gathered to discuss the latest visitor to 'Samain'. She was causing quite a stir among the maids and servants, by virtue of the dramatic events surrounding her last stay.

Emmie obliged the amusement by giving a full but highly coloured account of what had happened, including when she and Longborne had eloped to Dorchester. Throughout the story, Mary and Louise burst out in constant little giggles, as if holding back on a secret known only to them.

"Didn't you care that you weren't married?" asked Louise, eating an apple in great bites and winking to Mary. "Sharing a room with him, a man, alone?"

"Forget the room," added Mary, "it's the bed we want to know about!"

Emmie's face took on a blushed expression, but she loved every minute of her fame.

"Well of course I cared. He promised me we would be married before he returned to the regiment and I believed him. He said we needed to get some money together first, but, when he was given twenty pounds by a friend, he took it and ran. That's the last I ever saw of him. He left me with nothing, not even the means to pay for our rented room. I ended up in a factory, sleeping under a turning machine."

"At least you weren't left pregnant," added Louise, biting on the core.

"I was spared that," replied Emmie, her head bowed in embarrassment.

"What's it like?" enquired Louise, shifting nearer to Emmie to keep her voice low. "You know, *doing it!*"

Emmie looked up and smiled wickedly, having had an experience unknown to the rest. "To be honest, it's quite nice but it doesn't last long."

"He was a bit quick in the gallop?" mocked Louise.

"It starts all romantic like, with rampant expectations that make your heart pound and your skin sweat. The shame of it is that it doesn't stop there, as sweet as sugar. Actually . . .," she began, closing towards Mary, "it all ends up in a frightful mess, hardly worth the trouble, with him changing in mood from sugar to vinegar as quickly as a hawk catches a sparrow. Romance goes out the window the second his fingers do up his fly buttons."

"What's rampant," cried Louise, now holding a bun, "the size of his mood or the size of his thingummy?"

They laughed.

"Seriously, though," enquired Mary, in apprehensive tone, "will you confront Miss Catherine now she's here, or ask where *he* is?"

Emmie gave the reply two seconds thought, instead of the usual one. "It would do me no good. Best leave that sleeping dog lie."

"But what if she could? What if she has Longborne's ear?"

"Then I would cut if off." She turned at Louise's snigger, offering a sly grin. "I mean his ear, not his . . . dangly, you slut!"

A creak on the stairs brought Mrs Redmarsh into the room, flushed and panting from the exertion of the climb. "Did you tell her?"

Mary replied that they hadn't.

"Why, little sausage, you have a letter."

"Me?" said Emmie in total shock.

"Of course, my little goose. A proper one at that, folded and everything!"

She opened it with relish, staring at words she couldn't properly read.

"Give it here, my little dewdrop. You never was a scholar."

"Is it from my parents?"

"I'm thinking so. Let me see. It starts '*To my dearest Emmeline*'. That's a nice start, bain't it be."

"Go on, please."

"Very well, my impatient little buttercup. It goes on: '*Be not surprised to receive this letter and for my humbling myself before you*'. Humbling myself it says, now that's nice too. Then it says: '*The foolishness at leaving you in Dorchester can never be forgiven, even by your generous heart*'. Generous heart, that's good!"

"Mrs Redmarsh," interrupted Mary, "is it your intention to stop at every sentence and tell us how good or nice it is? Please, save the platitudes for later."

"Platitudes? What are they, my dear?"

"Animals with flat beaks, I think," put in Emmie.

"Is that so, my little cowcumber. Why did you ask me to save those, Mary dear?"

"I give up!" exclaimed Mary. "Just read the rest, would you?"

"Alright, alright, my little snap turtle. "It says: '*It is my fondest wish, as your once betrothed Longborne, to return to Westkings in the single hope that you have returned there also*'. Well, that's . . ."

". . . nice?"

"No, Mary, my little vulture, I was going to say 'despicable' after all that man did. I hadn't realised it was from him. Tear it up, Emmie. I'll not read another line."

"Is there much more?"

Mary took the letter from Mrs Redmarsh's hand. "There is. I'll read it, if you like."

"Don't you go listening to anything he says, my little plum fairy. He'll only cause you more harm. Mark my words, forget about it and him." With that advice given, Mrs Redmarsh left for downstairs.

"Do you want to know what else it says?"

"Of course she do," put in Louise, anxious to hear for herself.

"Do you?"

"Should I, Mary?"

"It's up to you. It can't hurt, in my estimation. Not knowing could be worse than knowing. Mind you, I'm with Mrs Redmarsh about not regarding anything he says as having any worth. But, it might say something you should know, or guard against. What do you think?"

"Alright."

"Now," said Mary, looking down the lines, "where did we get to, my little floppy thingummy. Oh, yes, here we are. It goes on: '*To make this possible, I trust you will join my sister in speaking well of me. For the sake of all that we ever meant to each other, and may do so again, tell the young master that it was you who took the goods from the manor when we left and not me. It is a sacrifice worth making for love. Then, when I am invited back into the bosom of the Elvington home, I can explain that it was me all along and that you were innocent. I will make up their loss by treasures I brought back from Southern Africa, gold and diamonds that were in the hills for the taking. All will then be forgiven and we can be together as was meant. I trust you to do this small thing for me. Fondest love. Your Longborne, a wounded soldier from Africa'.*"

"Oh dear," cried Emmie. "He's wounded."

"There's more. At the bottom of the page he adds: '*In preparation for my return to 'Samain', I could do with a little help. Have you any money I could temporarily borrow, or perhaps you could lay your hands on a little something from the house? Being recently back in England, I haven't a bank to draw on. It will be repaid with love and interest. Kiss, kiss, kiss'.*"

Mary's hand dropped to the bed. "The very cheek of the man. What a bastard."

"What do you mean? He's a hero, wounded in action fighting the natives. He just needs a little help and all will be fine."

"For goodness sake, Emmie, you can't be serious! He probably isn't wounded. In fact, I doubt if he ever got nearer to Southern Africa than Portsmouth. He certainly didn't come back rich with gold and diamonds, or he wouldn't be asking you for money. He's the same scoundrel he always was."

"But he explains all that. He has riches, but I suppose

they can't be spent until they're exchanged for real money."

"She might be right!"

"No she's not, Louise. Are you deaf, blind and stupid? He hasn't a farthing to his name. You mark my words. Not a penny piece. He's using you again. Can't you see it?"

"I still love him."

"No you bloody don't. Only yesterday you told me you still loved Edmond. You just don't like to work for a living and so you see him as a way out, you lazy little sod. If you even attempt to see him, or contact that sister of his, I'll break your head with a pail. I'll guarantee no brains will spill out. Anyway, he didn't send this. It must have come via Miss Catherine. Let's ask Mrs Redmarsh."

Downstairs, Mrs Redmarsh was struggling with a sack of potatoes, ready to be peeled for the evening meal.

"Are you still going on about that letter? I want no part of it. Wish I hadn't given it to you."

"Yes, but, who gave it to you, to give to me?"

"Sam. He gave it me. Where *he* got it, I don't rightly know and care even less. He took the carriage bags into the house, so I suppose he was slipped it then."

"You see," said Mary. "It's all a trick to get him here."

"Maybe," replied Emmie, pushing the letter deep into her pocket. "I could find out."

"How?"

"By sending him my clock. I don't want it, but it would make him show his cards."

"Risky, I would say, but it's not my head for the chopping block if it all goes horribly wrong."

* * *

Back at the manor, an early supper had been taken and all four had retired to the drawing room, where oil lamps offered a subdued elegance and a tranquil atmosphere, and a small fire brought worldly comfort. James and Edmond joined in having port and cigars.

"I thought you were a pipe man, James?" asked Catherine, wafting the smoke away from her face.

James stubbed out his cigar, although only partly consumed. Edmond carried on smoking as before.

"By and by, is that little trollop Emmeline someone or other still here? You must get rid of her if we are to expect Longborne to visit."

"Reason enough to let her stay," whispered Edmond to his father.

"Did you say something, James? I missed it."

"If you must eavesdrop, Catherine, I merely said that we have a milkmaid named Emmeline and she pleases us much. We have forgiven her for all her wrong-doing."

Catherine was secretly pleased to hear that Longborne's letter would have reached its intended victim. "But not Longborne? You continue to blame just him?"

"Certainly, and I wish you not to mention him again in our company."

"But I must. You accuse my brother falsely. I'm his twin. We are as one. He's no more false than I am. Anyway, he's recently back from Southern Africa, where he was wounded fighting the Boers. He has returned a rich man and wishes to make substantial amends for past . . . indiscretions."

"Stealing my things, that sort of indiscretion?"

"No, James, to repay any losses incurred from the things

that milkmaid took. He has no charge to answer, but merely wishes to share his new fortune with anyone who might think well of him."

"He intends to keep it all, then?" laughed Edmond.

"He's rich?" enquired Charlotte with renewed interest, snubbing Edmond.

"As creases. And to show his good fortune and high regard, he sends gifts to you all. Call for my box, Edmond dear."

The box, the size for a hat and round in shape, was duly brought in and left on a table.

"Now, let's look inside. Isn't this marvellous? Just like Christmas!" She took the first gift, wrapped in paper and labelled 'James'. "Here we are. This is for you. You know my brother found gold and diamonds. Isn't that simply marvellous?"

James was surprised by its weight, causing him to smile with anticipation.

The package was unwrapped. James stared at the content.

"What do you have, James?" enquired Charlotte greedily, lifting herself from her seat to get a better view.

"It's . . . a stone, a painted stone."

"Gold coloured, perhaps?"

"No, just an ordinary round grey stone with a painting of a fox and hound, or so it says beneath."

"Isn't it just wonderful?" remarked Catherine, grinning for all to see. "He painted it himself while huddled from enemy gunfire under the protection of the garrisons' arched roof, while waiting for the Boers to attack again in the Sudan."

"Where?" asked Edmond.

"Where what, dear?"

"Where was he painting under this arched roof of artistic inspiration? I thought you said the Sudan."

"And so I did. Did I say something wrong?"

"Probably not," said James. "Only, the Sudan is thousands of miles north of the Boers' homeland."

"Oh," cried Catherine. "It's still Africa, isn't it? Yes, I'm sure it is. Africa is Africa."

"No, Catherine, Africa isn't Africa at all. No more than Sudan is in the south with the Boers. It's like saying England is Russia."

"Longborne told me to say he was at Majuba Hill."

"Unlikely," added James. "That military action took place over two years ago. It was widely covered in the newspapers. We lost three hundred brave lads to enemy sharpshooters. Even the commander, Sir George Colley, was shot through the forehead by a Boer marksman."

"I told you poor Longborne had been wounded."

"Yes, but not in the right place," grinned Edmond, thinking Longborne had shot himself in the foot. "Anyway, a wound doesn't take two years to heal. It's all fabrication, isn't it Catherine?"

"And for you, Charlotte," said Catherine hastily, to retrieve the situation, "Longborne has this, given with his greatest love and admiration."

"It's a duck . . . painted on a stone."

"Edmond," said Catherine depressingly, now wilting at the handover, "Longborne has this for you, to remind you of your long and lasting friendship."

"Oh, great joy!" he exclaimed. "It's a stone. I have a fish on mine!"

They all laughed, except for Catherine, who ran from the room in tears. "Be unkind if you will, all of you. Make fun of him." She slammed the door.

"Well, what a performance," said Edmond, smirking at his mother.

"Stones. She gave us stones and thought we would like them. My duck looks strangely like a two-legged dog."

"For sure, he's no artist," added James. "I have a dog chasing what looks remarkably like a ferret. Still, I must say, I do like Catherine. She's certainly spirited. Imagine how we would feel if we had to give our hosts a pile of painted stones out of obedience to a sibling."

"Extremely embarrassed, I would say."

They made merry on more port, poured by Charlotte, who took her own glass. "After such a terrible day, I think she has succeeded in lifting our spirits. We toast ourselves, the Elvingtons!"

"The Elvingtons!"

"And I will add one more. To my friend Catherine, who you all despise and I still treasure for her sheer nerve. I wonder what tomorrow will bring?"

"If she decides to stay after tonight's embarrassment."

"Oh," said James, "I think she'll get over it. We haven't heard the last of her, or that reprobate brother of hers. Not by a long chalk."

CHAPTER 23

Turn and turnabout

Throughout the following day, the Elvingtons waited patiently for Catherine to leave her room. The revelry of the previous night waned in their thoughts as the hours passed, turning to concern for the woman as lunch was served and only three persons appeared at the table. A tray of cold meats was sent up to her room, which still lay untouched in the corridor until three o'clock that afternoon, when suddenly it was taken and the remains placed back outside an hour later. Charlotte took this news as a sign that all was well.

At six o'clock a maid was sent up to Catherine's room to announce that dinner would be served at seven. Catherine opened only the merest crack in the door to receive the news, but it was sufficient for the maid to see that she had already applied her make-up with the aid of candles placed either side of the dressing table glass, to improve upon the limited natural light, and had a sumptuous dress laid out on the bed.

Before the gong was sounded, Catherine had already walked down to the dinning room, where James alone stood waiting. At seeing her regal elegance, he placed a finger under the stiff white collar that chafed his neck, feeling that it was a discomfort he had to endure for appearance sake.

The table had been laid out for a marvellous feast, looking almost festive, as if it was Christmas and every little effort had to imply an expected spirit of revelry. A large vase of cut flowers decorated the sideboard and another stood at the centre of the table. And, although it was Summer, a fire glowed heartily. By its side perched a small pan on a trivet, holding mulled wine, offering a heady bouquet of cinnamon throughout the room. Upon seeing Catherine, James took the silver ladle that hung from the rim of the pan and poured a glass for his guest, which she took with silent civility.

Despite all these efforts and more, when Charlotte and Edmond entered together there remained an atmosphere wanting in celebration. Unlike James, Charlotte expected no pleasure from the evening, but held the strongest curiosity as to how exactly Catherine intended to extricate herself from yesterday's farce. Charlotte and Edmond also received glasses of warmed red wine in silence. Thus, as the brew was sipped, all four stood in absolute silence in a small but awkward circle.

"I think . . ." began James.

"Yes?" said Charlotte expectantly.

"Oh, nothing," he replied.

"Only . . ."

"Yes?" she asked again.

"Sorry, the thought's disappeared from my head."

"Oh, this is absolutely absurd," announced Edmond, becoming irritated by the behaviour of his seniors.

There was a knock at the front door, followed by a second, this time answered by a maid.

"Is anyone expecting somebody?" enquired Charlotte, suspicious of Catherine. She wanted to point her question directly at the guest, believing her capable of inviting Longborne to the manor behind their backs, but she was equally concerned not to provoke further discord if her thoughts were unfounded.

James and Catherine said they were not. Charlotte looked at Edmond, suddenly breaking out into a smile.

"It's you, isn't it? You've invited Lily as a surprise. How lovely!"

Edmond, smiling, left the room, only to re-enter with a woman slightly underdressed for the occasion.

"My God, what's this!" cried Charlotte.

"You were right, Mother. I did invite a guest, in fact two guests. The other is yet to come. Catherine Charles, may I introduce my mother, Miss Sally Ayres."

For once, Catherine was entirely speechless, her mouth hanging open.

"Father and Mother you already know, Mother."

James glowed red, not through fury but acute mortification. He was frozen to the spot.

"Shall I pour my mother a glass of mull, Mother, or will you Father?"

"I don't understand," said Catherine in unusually timid tone.

"Why ever not? It's a simple triangle. Perhaps Father can explain better than I."

All eyes turned on James.

"I . . . I . . ."

"Come, come, Father. You can do better than that." He turned to Catherine. "You see, what we have here is a little machination. Don't you just love intrigue?"

Still Catherine stared ignorance, void of any comment.

"James, do something," implored Charlotte, now visibly shaking from the thought that Edmond was standing next to Sally, rather than herself.

"I . . . I . . ." he offered.

"Pull yourself together. I can't bear it."

"I . . . I . . . I thought you and I had an arrangement, Miss Ayres, to let bygones be bygones," he spluttered feverishly.

"Is that it? Is that all you have to say?" bawled Charlotte.

"Umm! What do you expect me to say? I'm lost for words." He withered at her incredulous look. "What I meant to ask you, Miss Ayres, is," he murmured, "doesn't a good woman keep her promises?"

"Only when it isn't disadvantageous to her," Edmond replied in her defence, with quick and meaningful wit. "Isn't that right, Miss Ayres, sorry, Mother?"

"Quite right."

"What do you want of us?" asked Charlotte with faltering bitterness.

"Actually, nothing at all," was Sally's honest reply.

"I don't understand!"

"If you believe I came here for personal gain, you are quite wrong and I resent the implication. I think you, James, know me better than that. In fact, for the present company, you have known me far too well! Anyhow," she continued, "Edmond came to see me this morning and told me everything that happened yesterday. At first I felt sorry for you and your husband, who I shall now call James because of our known close acquaintance."

"I doubt that," threw in Charlotte, gaining some of her old tone.

"Frankly, my dear, I don't give a tinker's cuss what you think. I alone know what I felt. Any incredulity you hold for me is a mere drop for what I've felt for you over the years and the state of your so-called marriage. The only thing that I ever wanted was my son, yet I denied myself even this in the belief that he was better off in a family with property. Yet, as poor Christabel was testament to, such a family as yours is built upon wrongful deeds, mistrust and, above all, false loyalties. I now believe Edmond would have lost nothing and gained much if I had accepted James' alternative offer of support for Edmond after he was born."

"Balderdash! You gave him up in a trice," exclaimed Charlotte. Then, turning to James, she added: "Did you pay her off?"

"Actually I did offer."

"There you are!"

"Let me finish, Char. I was about to say that I did offer her silence money, but she wouldn't accept anything at all and said she needed none. Not a silver sixpence."

"Unlike you," interrupted Sally. "You put your home comforts before your own child. And then, given by heavenly grace a second chance to help her, to bring her back into the bosom of your family and offer shelter and sufficient to a struggling girl who had nothing more than what she stood up in, you once again threw her away because it was 'inconvenient' to your life."

"It's not true," howled Charlotte, "I still loved her. I went after her. I did!"

"Funny, isn't it, how we have changed positions. Since this morning I have become a hopeful woman, and you a calamitous one. I can hold my head high and say for God to hear and judge me that I abandoned Edmond for entirely philanthropic reasons, while you acted only out of self-interest. If Edmond so decides, today will be your judgement day!"

"Is this so, Edmond?" asked Charlotte, her eyes glistening.

"I have that choice, it's true. It's mine alone to make. Since this morning I have known Miss Ayres in a different light. We have talked and readied a plan."

"Oh, sweet Jesus, you are to abandon me!" she cried, her head cupped in her hands. James stepped forward and took her in his arms, her head nestling against his chest.

"Listen to your son, Char. I don't believe he's finished."

"But I am to him! He said so."

"No, he didn't. Just listen to him, my dear."

She looked up at James, who returned a gentle nod of comfort.

"You knew about this?" she asked.

"I spoke to Edmond early this afternoon, before he rode off. He wanted to talk to me and I decided to listen for once with a totally open mind. He's not a boy any longer. He wanted my advice, but I let him make up his own mind instead. It's for the best. He's a fine young man and I trust his judgement, whatever it is to be."

She turned to Edmond, still pressing against James. "I am

alone left out of this conspiracy. I fear for my sanity and my family. Does nobody care for me?"

"Shush, Char. Just listen. That's all he wants you to do," whispered James.

"Say the words, Edmond, as you said to me. Get this travesty over with," suggested Sally eagerly.

"Maybe, Catherine, someone will explain more to you later. But, for the present, you can only be a passive onlooker. Please forgive me if I ignore you for a moment. You should stay in the room, though."

She agreed to move away and sat alone at the table.

"Mother, Father, Mother, for nearly twenty years I've been in blissful ignorance of all that once passed between you three. Tragically, my sister lived out her short life without knowing me as her brother. Yet, happily, we did know each other for a short time as close friends. No, more than that, we loved each other, and in that I hold great comfort. At the tragic end of her life, she must've known that she was loved, by me and that other man from Cerne Abbas. What she felt for her real mother, my father's wife, I cannot say. That's for you to search out within your hearts, remembering in sorrow all that was uttered on that last day you meet. If you parted well, then be comforted. If not, then I would not wish you harm by reviving such memories. It is now dust to the past. All that we really need to know is that Christabel is happy once more, in God's brightest sky, above the sodden ground that made Wessex so very special to her. As to my future and my mothers', I am decided."

"Oh! Hold me James," whimpered Charlotte. "I think I lose a second child."

Edmond stepped to Sally, holding her hands with outstretched arms.

"You, who I only knew as a wronged stranger until yesterday, I recognise as my mother at my birth. You are already dear to my heart and I hope our relationship will blossom like the wild petals in the field, myriad in colour and enduring." He let go and turned to Charlotte, taking her trembling fingers. "As for you, I cannot feel wronged by you for pouring your love my way. You will always be the mother who nurtured me, as Father so rightly reminded me yesterday. You too have my heart, for love isn't divided by the number of recipients, because it multiplies without end. Father, of course, is my father, who I respect despite his obvious flaw amongst pretty ladies. So, my decision is . . ."

At the moment of highest drama, a further knock came at the door.

"Ah," said Edmond, "just in time."

To everyone's surprise, Hubert entered, holding a huge bouquet of roses.

"Now, before I finish, Hubert has something he wishes to say. Come on, don't be shy."

Hubert stumbled forward, fiddling with his tie and flattening his uncontrollable hair with licked fingers. "Oh, yes, right! Well, when Edmond rode over to my home this afternoon, having acquired my address from Ella Browning, I was thrown into immediate turmoil. That I freely admit. For, not being of any great importance, small in stature and with a mop of ginger hair, I could hardly believe the message he brought. I could have hugged and kissed him on the spot. In fact, now I think of it, I probably did!" He smirked at

Edmond. "I forgive him his smell of sweat from much hard riding! Such a cupid never did exist before. I thanked him again and again until it was time for him to leave and for me to scrub and polish myself for the task ahead. And, my dear friends, here I am."

"Yes," said Catherine from the table, "but why *are* you here?"

He looked at the face he didn't know. "I have come to dinner!"

"Is that all?" asked James, somewhat amazed at the eloquence for nothing more than roast lamb. "I'll send for two more place settings. Anyone else coming, Edmond?"

"Of course it's not all," offered Edmond. "Come on, Hubert. Don't bottle out now!"

He cleared his throat, washed down with a gulp of wine from Edmond's own glass. "Have I thanked you, Edmond, for all you have done?"

"Yes, prodigiously."

"Right. And for inviting me to dinner?"

"You'll have to thank me for my right boot up your bottom if you don't get on with it!"

"Ah! Right! Well! In that case, I would like to ask, and I understand if the answer is 'no', for I can see no good reason why it should be otherwise, but, well, Miss Ayres, Sally, would you accept these roses."

"Why, there're wonderful," said Sally, stepping across to kiss him on the cheek. "So unexpected."

"And..?" commanded Edmond.

"And . . . well . . ." he braced himself. "I have no right, but I have the very great honour of asking you to be my . . . wife. Will you marry me?"

"Oh, Hubert," Sally cried, flinging her arms around his neck. "Of course I will."

"You accept?"

"More than that. I insist upon it!"

"But my hair, it's so 'ginger'?"

"And I'm so much older than you. Who cares?" She hugged him again. "Anyway, I like unusual hair. My own father had a huge beard, which I much admired. I was reminded of it in St John's Church in Glastonbury. The image in a stained glass window had a face just like his. I could hardly take my eyes off it."

"Well, that turned out alright, I think you'll agree," added Edmond, a smug look on his face. "Hubert says he wants his fiancée to choose a new house for them in Glastonbury, if she is agreeable."

"Glastonbury!" choked James, thinking of another relationship from the past, still secret to all but Sally.

"I think not," said Sally, winking in James' direction. "Why not Sherborne or Taunton?"

"Sherborne. Yes, my Lily could help you look. Indeed, we could consider a double wedding!"

"Thank you, Edmond, but no," said Sally. "This will be our day, not to be spoiled by Hubert's red hair against your brown and my wrinkles against Lily's fair skin." They all laughed, for the moment called for it, except for one person. Charlotte kissed the couple before gently and covertly pulling on Edmond's sleeve.

"What of us? Are you going off with your new mother or . . ."

". . . staying here with you? Is that what you were about to say? Of course I'm staying, that is until my wedding. As the Chinese might say, you are my Number One Mother and Miss Ayres is my Number Two."

"Two suits me exceedingly well," remarked Sally, still hanging from Hubert's shoulders. I am all amazement."

"And One suits me," said Charlotte, at last carrying a smile so wide that her mouth looked likely to tear. "It suits me just fine."

"There," said James, "it's all worked out nice, hasn't it! Oh, and I have something for you, Sally, for I will call you that in front of my family." He handed her a small parcel. "This is yours, I think."

She took it with momentary suspicion. "My shoes, the ones I broke at Cudwick. You've had them repaired."

"Now, can we eat?" suggested James through his smile.

Suddenly the room became festival, just as James had planned.

"No more secrets," he said. "Is that agreed?"

They all answered positively, except for one.

"I didn't see your lips move, Catherine. Are you not in agreement?"

"How can I? You know why I came, but I can't say the words."

"Then I will," said James. "Longborne wanted your help to get him here and, after all, he is your brother."

"I didn't fool you a bit, did I?"

"I'm not the fool you take me for, Catherine."

"I'm sorry, not just to you but everyone."

"Look," said James in his most agreeable tone, "you might as well know that Longborne will never set foot in our home.

Not now, not tomorrow, not ever. You, on the other hand, give me so much satisfaction and acute pleasure from your strutting about like a peahen that you will be welcomed to come back at any time . . . so long as it's not too soon," he chuckled.

"I'll go tomorrow, but with a heavy heart for leaving the friends I think of as family, the manor I think of as part my own, and the countryside that holds such beauty that . . ."

"Leave it out!" cried Edmond. "We've heard it all before. Just go, tomorrow, please!"

"Very well. If it wasn't as dark as pitch, I would leave now."

James put his hand on hers. "Don't concern yourself, dear Catherine, I already have a purse ready for you. You may share some of the coins with that good for nothing brother of yours if you wish."

She cheered instantly. "I think . . . not!"

CHAPTER 24

God save the Queen

Against all advice, Emmie sent the clock retrieved from the timber fire to Longborne. It arrived after Catherine had returned home with all the news. Still, he thought, he had gained something out of it all and duly took the timepiece to be pawned. Emmie, as might be expected, received no thanks and no further declarations of love. Her future remained open.

Charlotte kept Christabel's ring, the only small physical reminder of her daughter's life. She explained to Emmie the reason for wanting it and softened the blow by giving her a jewelled ring as a replacement. Emmie had, at first, resisted the exchange, but, having remembered that she still kept Christabel's shawl, was content.

In London, Thackeray and Fairbourne were also satisfied, having finally delivered their findings to the Prime Minister. It was a lengthy document, full of facts and figures regarding the Romans at the time of Christ and then the Romans in Britain, Joseph of Arimathea, the cavalry warrior known as Arthur, the Crusades, Glastonbury and much more, none of which had offered a definitive answer to the original question, that being the meaning of the Predicted Nine weeping maidens.

Many of the conclusions were erroneous, as the only link between all the events that could be discovered had been various unsuccessful quests to find the chalice of The Last Supper, The Holy Grail, searches covering millennia and continuing unresolved to that very day. Notable academics such as Dutchman, David Burgerhout, remained strong in their personal conviction of the existence of the cup of Jesus.

Thackeray and Fairbourne now considered much of what they had so painstakingly found to be completely irrelevant, concluding in the final paragraph, under the heading *Summary*, that any 'threat' to England could only be, in fact, one aimed at Christianity itself, and in particular those so-called progressive European minds or the radical and zealous leaders of some foreign religions who would benefit from diminishing the faith and suppressing the pride of the British people. After all, such an attack on Christianity would affect every aspect of British life, from schooling to Sundays, from the Christian Church itself to the Monarchy, and all that enriched British life in between. Onward Christian Soldiers would have no meaning, making a mockery of British attempts to civilise the world and bring democracy to the darkest places, where tyranny kept the population hungry of food and away from the grace of God.

***

Following the tragedy of *SS Daphne* in Scotland on 3rd July, a coaster which had rolled over during its launch into the

Clyde and quickly sank, killing 124 workers on board, concerns had been voiced among members of the Royal Household as to the safety of modern ships. This was now particularly poignant as supplies were then being loaded on to *HMS Alexandra*, which awaited them at Portsmouth. But, they had been assured by Gladstone and an Admiral that *Alexandra* was an entirely safe ship of already distinguished service. Indeed, Gladstone, who was no great sailor, was not in the least worried and was looking forward to the opportunity of building bridges with Her Majesty during their long sea voyage south.

Some considerable time later, and on the other side of the world, David Burgerhout and his daughter climbed joyfully onto a small charter steamer being used to carry passengers on sightseeing voyages around islands in the Java Sea. He had been true to his word and had decided to visit his investments in the Dutch East Indies before doubling back to Europe and the Mediterranean to continue researching the cup of Jesus. The Lance of Antioch was safely in a British bank vault and he alone held the key.

For Burgerhout, now that his business affairs were settled, the day's sea journey was to be purely pleasure. The small ship was loading a mixed party of men, women and children, all bound for the Selat Sunda, a narrow strait between the main islands of Java and Sumatra.

Burgerhout settled onto a hard wooden bench to read a newspaper, while Helen walked the deck. His newspaper, dated 20th August, was already six days out of date, yet it was the nearest he could expect for current European news.

He read with interest the progress of Queen Victoria and her entourage on their journey into the Indian Ocean, somewhat concerned about renewed British interest in the region.

Helen stopped by railings to read a brief handbill given to her when the tickets were purchased. It stated that sea voyages to see the volcano had become extremely popular since 20th May, when one of the volcanic cones on the island of Rakata had suddenly exploded into action, sending ash clouds six miles up into the sky and causing a tremendous rumble that was heard one hundred miles away in Jakarta. It claimed that by the end of the month the volcano had resumed silence, allowing visitors the unique once-in-a-lifetime opportunity to be taken safely to Rakata, not only to see an active volcano but to walk on the island itself. It went on to say that on 19th June the eruptions had resumed, increasing the popularity of the place to hardy visitors, making early booking a necessity. Not since 1680 had it so erupted, and the chance to see the place was not to be missed.

As the ship steamed its way into open water, a sudden loud crack was heard, followed by another, then one more, each of greater ferocity than the previous. Many of the passengers became alarmed as the steamer pounded the unexpectedly turbulent waves, made worse still when suddenly the Captain ordered a turnabout manoeuvre, making the steamer roll dramatically and slip sideways into forming hollows. As the ship reached safety, the passengers watched with horror as a black cloud of ash burst skyward.

"Father, what's happening?"

Burgerbout took his daughter's hand, gripping it tightly as

the ship bumped into the side of the wooden quay which projected out from the beach.

"The island's going to explode again. I'm sure of it. Quickly, we must be prepared. Get off this boat, fast."

"But, Father, we can't be in any danger. It's miles away."

"I'm not so sure, Helen. That cloud must be fifteen or more miles high. It's a very ominous sign of something larger to come." He suddenly froze. "My goodness, look at the tide."

The sea drew back as if sucked away, leaving fish gasping and marooned on the sand. Small boys raced out, picking up the fish in woven baskets as they jumped for air. Small boats tipped over onto their sides.

"What does it mean, Father?"

"I don't know. It's beyond anything I've ever seen before."

Just as suddenly, the eruptions ended and the sea returned, reclaiming the beaches in a rapid and unstoppable foaming crest. The sight was of such immense surprise that nobody turned away for minutes that became stunned hours, waiting to see if anything more was to happen.

By early evening the Captain gave the order to ready the ship for sea again, and that passengers should make haste to get on board. He had freight to deliver and would take the opportunity to crowd in the expectant but, so far, disappointed passengers. There would be just enough light to get to the island before turning about for a moonlight return.

Burgerhout was stunned by the announcement. Pushing his way through the clambering passengers, he jumped back on board and grabbed the Captain's arm.

"What madness is this?" he demanded, furrows deep in his face.

"We're going back, of course. I've a ship-load of passengers wanting to see a volcano. Eruptions have stopped, so the decision is out of my hands. We have a job of work."

"This is utter foolishness, complete madness of the worse magnitude."

"Make ready to cast off," he shouted, taking no notice. He turned to Burgerhout, removing the man's hand that gripped his arm. "You'd better get off if you don't want to come. It's your choice, but I can't refund you for the ticket if you choose not to join us."

"I don't care about that. Don't you see, you can't be sure there won't be any further explosions."

"Look," he said in a knowing tone, "I've seen this all before. Believe me, it's exactly what happened in May and then June. Loud bangs, followed by clouds of ash and then silence. It's perfectly safe to sail, I can assure you. Now, are you coming, or not?"

"Give me a minute." Burgerbout hurried off the deck and onto the quay, where Helen awaited anxiously.

"The Captain says it's safe."

"Do you believe him?"

"Probably not. However . . ."

"However? Don't tell me you're thinking we should get back on board?"

"No, not *we*. Look, I'm an old man of learning and I really would hate to miss the opportunity to see such a sight. I may never return here. Who can tell? Others have made the trip over the past weeks and all have returned without incident. I'm inclined to take my chance. I might be the only person on board who could write a proper report on what's out there. It might save lives in the long term. Don't forget, this is also where we have our business, where our wealth originates. It's vital to our future. Nobody properly understands such phenomenon. I could be of the greatest help to mankind, and make an international name for myself to boot."

"I'm afraid to go!"

"Good, because you're not." He kissed her. "I must hurry. I'll see you when I get back in a few hours." He smiled, turned and left, just catching the gangplank before it was hauled on board.

Helen watched him go, yelling: "Don't take any unnecessary chances, Father. Remember, I want a child to hold as my own before I die and he or she will need a grandfather to play with."

The ship shuddered as its propeller turned, causing the water to boil at the stern. Burgerhout was momentarily out of sight, but then came running to the rail, holding his hands to his mouth to amplify his anxious voice.

"My goodness, Helen, I've just realised. Get to the authorities at once and tell them to warn the British that the area is becoming dangerously volcanic. Wave to me with both hands if you've heard what I said."

Helen lifted both arms and waved.

"Goodbye," he shouted. "And be quick with that message. Goodbye, Darling!"

As the steamer took to open sea, the waves once again became violent. The word went around not to panic, as it would settle as they eventually approached the strait.

But it did not. The sea began to churn cruelly, tossing the

steamer into a series of highs and hollows until even the Captain began to fear for his charges. Hatches were ordered closed and everything loose on deck had to be stored away or lashed. Passengers were ordered to the cabin below deck and the doors fastened. Time became lost to the moment, dragging for those below deck in their anxiety to understand what was happening, but full of fury and motion above, where the sailors worked frantically to secure the ship.

Still the waves increased, the air now becoming dark and sinister as ash fell. The Captain ordered the ash to be scooped from the deck and tossed overboard, its accumulated weight beginning to seriously destabilise the vessel.

From the bridge, the Captain summoned his officers to consider the options. Peering at the threatening sky, he gave the order to steam ahead at all possible speed, intending to make for the relative safety of the open sea on the far side of the strait. It was a risky decision, but turning the ship in such worsening conditions could prove calamitous. It would mean steaming through the night, although the blackened sky had already started to shade out the daylight and bring on an early dusk. He ordered a bearing to be taken relative to Rakata, but the compass was affected by the magnetically-charged ash that continued to rain down.

Hour after hour, the steamer rolled its way through the seas. Still the ash fell. Frightened passengers were now ordered into the very bowels of the ship, their combined weight intended to act as human ballast. Dilemma turned to crisis, and crisis to impending catastrophe, but still the bow split the waves on its slow passage forward.

By sunrise, the sky remained as black as night. A lighthouse keeper on a rocky outcrop kept the high beam flashing, while his wife and child huddled below among stone walls of seemingly impenetrable thickness.

Ever onward, flashes of electrical charge now danced on the steamer's furled rigging, appearing to the crew as evil spirits of the underworld. Then, as the worse seemed to be over, thunder crashed through the air of such magnitude that it deafened the crew and caused their ears to bleed. Millions of tons of fresh magna that had risen from the bowels of the earth blasted skyward from Rakata, up to a height of fifty miles, some rocks swelling into pumice by the gas contained within, others blowing themselves apart to form more powdered ash. Pressure waves from the shattering explosion circled the entire Earth.

A final great crack pierced the air as the entire island detonated, shattering the volcano until the rock-face fell into the immense subterranean chambers made empty by the discharged magma. Pumice rocks plunged into the sea, forming floating islands large enough to disable a ship. Once again the coastal seas drew breath, malevolently sucking the water away from the beaches as far as the eye could see. The Captain peered ahead, terrified at a wall of water forming on the horizon, travelling at great speed.

He ordered the ship to be turned into the gigantic wave and the sea anchor dropped. If the little steamer could be held upright as the wave hit, their souls had a small chance of being saved. In the bottom of the hull, the precious cargo of humanity expected at any moment to be sent to their deaths.

Then the wave hit, carrying the steamer up its near vertical face. Against all that was reasonable, the tsunami was ridden, but the wave continued to grow as it sped at unbelievable velocity towards the coasts, reaching a height of 120 feet. Others followed of lesser magnitude.

For the next two days the sun remained hidden behind the blackout, and dust circled and re-circled the Earth. The explosion had been heard in Australia, over 2,200 miles away across the Indian Ocean.

From the deck *HMS Alexandra*, on the day following the final eruption, Queen Victoria looked out on a spectacular red sunset, having heard the explosions from a long distance and felt the sea tremor beneath her feet. Gladstone was below deck, feeling sea sick.

Thanks to the wonders of the Victorian age and the industry of the free peoples of the world, telegraph messages had been sent across continents via land and underwater cables for the first time in living history, giving grave warning and then details of the greatest explosion the world had ever known. Modern science had alerted the British in time to have the great warship diverted to safer waters.

The volcano of Krakatoa, on the island of Rakata in the Selat Strait, had blown itself apart, changing the world's climate and giving grave warning of God's power over man.

Among the 36,000 lives lost to the tsunami in Java and Sumatra was one belonging to a young Dutch woman who had raised the alarm and returned to anxiously await news of her father. When eventually the steamer appeared, it was to devastation beyond description.

Burgerhout was a broken man, vowing to remain in the

region to assist in its reconstruction in the memory of his beloved and brave daughter. He was as good as his word.

In London, news of Queen Victoria's safe keeping was greeted with the greatest joy and celebration.

"So," said Lord Salisbury, having summoned Thackeray into the hallowed walls of the Peer's Library, "you missed it!"

"If you mean my report didn't predict the unpredictable, then, yes, I missed it as you say."

He got up and walked over to a mullion window, offering lofty views over the indomitable River Thames. "God saved The Queen." He turned, caressing his substantial beard until his fingers dropped from the end. "Man to man, Thackeray, what do make of this Predicted Ninth stuff? Did you honestly believe any of it? I mean to say, it's all a bit of a coincidence, but surely nothing to do with the supernatural."

"How can I answer that? Legend predicted that Arthur would rise to save Britain from impending national catastrophe. One way could be through the Nine Arthurian weeping maidens. After all, if it hadn't been for Miss Ayres and that stuff she said about surviving a drowning, we wouldn't have searched for a meaning that eventually involved David Burgerhout. And, without Burgerhout and his daughter, The Queen would have sailed headlong into disaster. The country would have been plunged into crisis, losing not only the monarchy but so many heads of government. Even little Winston Churchill would have perished, and heaven knows what the future has in store for him. I suppose, in the final analysis, it will be for the historians to sort out."

"But Burgerhout would've been in the Dutch East Indies anyway! The right place at the right time."

"I doubt it. I'm sure he was there as the result of my visit to his home, with Fairbourne, triggering him to up-sticks and leave. Without us questioning him, he might have remained in England several months' too long, or even years."

"You may be right, but as a man of reason I'm troubled by that. It isn't good for a nation with a superstitious past to revel in goblins and ghouls. Look, this Miss Ayres woman, even you suggest she might not have been the 'ninth'. You cite in the report several reasons for this conclusion, including doubt about the 1443 case and because Ayres was found not to be a virgin, a *maiden*."

"What are you telling me?"

"What I am suggesting, and I put it no stronger than that, is for this damned report of yours to be filed away."

"In a bottom drawer?"

"In the bottom of the deepest vault! The deed's done. Her Majesty is safe. It's the nation that matters now."

"But Her Majesty ought to know at the very least."

"To what purpose? To confront her Government and Opposition as to why we put her in harm's way? I think not. No, for all concerned, I believe the report should be buried, never to be entered into the annals of history, at least, not in our lifetime."

"As if it never happened?"

"Exactly."

"In the dark box, perhaps?"

"Why not?"

* * *

In the last moments before the tsunami struck, Helen had fled the beach for higher ground, carrying a small boy separated from his mother. The speed of the wave was unbelievable. She had turned in the final seconds to watch the wall of water bear down, taller than the Tower of London. She knew she would drown.

Instinctively, she had darted into a building, knowing it held no safety. The child's face was turned to her breast, his tiny head cupped in her hand, shielding him from terror and comforting him with gentle words during his last moments of life.

The giant wave had struck with a terrible and crushing force, ripping up trees and destroying the front and rear walls of all buildings in its path. Whole boats were lifted, dumped hundreds of yards inland, where the land had temporarily turned into sea bed.

Swirling in the deep sea, Helen had watched frantically as the child sank beside her. She tried to reach him, but her breath was exhausted. Her body gave up the struggle, her mind insensate.

In her final moments of semi-consciousness, as she drowned, Helen saw a woman gliding towards her, lifting the boy in her outstretched arms, her tears untouched by the water that engulfed them all. The weeping woman folded Helen's limp arms around the child and, together, they perished.

Helen, a virgin, had held a child in her arms before she died. She was, indeed, the Predicted Ninth.

BUY NOW

The highly acclaimed Book 1 in the Wessex Trilogy
The Angel of Wessex
ISBN 978-1-874337-08-9
First published in 2003/4 as ISBN 1-874337-08-X
and first reprinted in 2005.

The West Country in the late Victorian era is seen through the life of Christabel Mere, a girl born into splendour but sent away as a baby to be raised in the poverty of the Wessex farming countryside.

She knew nothing of the circumstances of her birth and cared even less for wealth, but it was a time when women had to live by society's strict codes. To join the fight against a government wanting to introduce new laws that further discriminated against women seemed a cause worthy of support. But this innocent act would, itself, reintroduce her to her true ancestry and threaten to destroy not only her happy childhood memories but the Elvingtons, one of the greatest families in all Wessex.

'A beautifully written, gentle and moving read, with an unexpected twist'

Jacket Price £6-99
Postal Price £5-99 including postage and packing
Cheques made payable to 'Michael Taylor offer'
F4M Publishing, Farringdon House, Nr Langport TA10 9HT, England

Essential Maroc

High-quality and high-finish wood and other crafts beautifully handmade in Morocco and imported for retail and wholesale

HOW TO VIEW AND ORDER

Visit the Essential Maroc Website or order by telephone, e-mail or postal services.

Visit the Essential Maroc stand at major Country Events in the South, South-East and South-West of England During exhibitions, telephone 079 04 035 350

Visit the wholesale facilities in Somerset and Surrey

RETAIL & WHOLESALE

with new products regularly added

Essential Maroc, a sponsor of the Avalon Ninth